D0989016

GREATER LOVE

Greater
Love

LUCY WADHAM

faber and faber

First published in 2007
by Faber and Faber Limited
3 Queen Square London wc1n 3au

Typeset by Faber and Faber

Printed in England by Mackays of Chatham

A CIP record for this book
is available from the British Library

ISBN 978–0–571–23489–9

2 4 6 8 10 9 7 5 3 1

'This is my commandment,
That ye love one another, as I have loved you.
Greater love hath no man than this, that a man lay down
 his life for his friends.
These things I command you, that ye love one another.'

(The Gospel According to St John. Chapter 15, verses 12 to 17)

I OFTEN WONDER IF IT IS POSSIBLE to miss something you never had. When I look at the child asleep in my arms I know that it is. We're encoded for love. Each cell of us strains towards it, from the first breath. A smile on the lips of a sleeping baby should make every last receptor within us vibrate. I bring my own love with me, it says. Don't be afraid.

I am afraid. I'm afraid of the person inside me, the person I once was. My old self haunts me so that I sometimes look down at my own sleeping baby and feel a shock of fear for him.

Forgiveness, I'm told, is the key to a new beginning.

'Try and forgive her,' my husband Christopher says. 'And then you can get on with your life.'

I sit on the far side of the world, on the very edge of Satan's empire, with this new child in my arms, and I know that, even in death, my mother has none of my forgiveness.

I only have to imagine her funeral to remember how far she is from my absolution. I see myself standing with the rest of the village at her grave's edge. I look across the hole in the ground at Katarina, the midwife of my mother's sorrow, standing opposite me and at the widower Sylvino, slack with misery beside her. Katarina is in her element here, straight as a pin among us all, while Father Antonio intones the dirge in his plaintive Latin and my dazed, red-eyed sisters throw clods of earth on the coffin of this woman who bore them and then just seemed to bow out.

I picture my sister Barbara, handing me the aspergillum to sprinkle my mother's coffin with holy water and send her on her way to paradise. But there is no paradise for my brother Jose, no paradise for her only son, just an eternity of pain, and all at once anger, my old companion, makes me dash the aspergillum against the varnished coffin.

It is late afternoon and we're sitting on the deck overlooking the lagoon, enjoying the silence while our three-year-old daughter sleeps. Christopher knows what is preoccupying me.

'You don't have to go,' he says quietly.

'You said I was supposed to forgive her.'

He looks up from the document on his lap. It's the Audubon recovery plan for the California population of the marbled murrelet.

'Will going to the funeral help you to forgive her?' he asked.

'I don't know.'

He looks at me, waiting patiently for an answer. When none comes, he goes back to his reading.

Here, in his presence, I can live with myself. Far from his gaze I'd be lost, all over again.

I look down at my baby and this time the self that feels worthy of this love enfolds the child, holding it as every child should be held, in a total embrace.

I AM A TWIN. I ALWAYS WILL BE.

The terrifying reality of twinship, even dizygotic or non-identical twins like me and Jose, is that you are not born alone. And so, in the deep recesses of your psyche you do not believe that you will die alone. As long as the other lives, your own heart, you think, will keep beating. Because of the circumstances of our birth, Jose and I, even more perhaps than most twins, were held in thrall to this myth.

I should begin before our birth, with our conception. Our mother never told us this story. All through our childhood it was left about in shards for us to pick up. I would turn these pieces over, first with fear and later with curiosity as I began to understand that what some people take for evil can be good in disguise.

I know it happened on a hot day. That summer, the summer of 1980, fish were boiled alive in the muddy *rio* and floated, milky-eyed, to the surface. The oldest olive tree died, a tree said to have given shade to the Romans as they marched through on their way back from the coast, dropping their oyster shells as they went. It was the day before the festival of Santa Barbara, the patron saint of the village and of thunder and lightning. Our mother was taking her father's lunch to him in the valley where he worked as foreman in the lead mine. She had just turned fifteen.

It usually took her forty-five minutes to walk down to the mine and an hour and a half to climb back up. As the only girl in a family of seven boys, she had been required to leave school at eleven to look after the house. Her own mother worked with the other women, cleaning and sifting the lead and minerals in the river. Our mother was said to have been happy on that August afternoon as she sauntered along the shaded path, with her father's lunch wrapped in a clean cloth in a basket. I heard that she often sang in those days and that her voice was clear and lovely.

It happened on the journey home, on the last bend. The chalk road is blinding in summer at that time of day and after the steep climb your pulse bangs in your head. Our mother would have puzzled at the memory, so recent, of herself making the climb with no effort; running up the path, as quick and agile as any boy. Now she walked like a woman, tugged at by the earth.

He was watching her from the chestnut tree that hangs over the bend in the road. It was said that he had been waiting for her in the tree for days. He was from Perdrilha, the village that faces ours on the other side of the valley, a village of thieves and bandits, people always said. Perdrilha was inaccessible even in our lifetime, except by mule. They built a road in 1992 but this has made no difference. People still think it's forsaken. They have no patron saint.

I have never met our father. There are no photos of him, except for the one that I stole from a file in the basement of the Bragança courtrooms, and that one has faded. All you can see now is a blanched, featureless face, with dark ellipses for eyes and dots for nostrils. What's left of his mouth looks like a bird in flight. People often told Jose, usually out of spite, that he looked just like him.

That day our father would have been watching our mother Cassilda Cortez, the foreman's lovely daughter, walking towards him along the white path. He would have watched this beautiful girl, with her beautiful black hair swinging in a heavy plait at her back, with her beautiful golden skin and her beautiful white teeth and her beautiful collarbones and her beautiful arms and wrists and neck and her beautiful tits coming towards him, dappled, all of her, as she passed beneath him, by the shadows of the chestnut leaves. And our father jumped down from his hiding place in the tree and blocked her path, gazing down at her from his great height, so the story goes, with his idiot's eyes: pale green and heavy-lidded like my brother's. He did not speak to her because he was born mute. This, like many things, was a lie. Our father didn't talk much in his short life, but he was no mute.

Cassilda didn't cry out. She looked for an escape and then darted into the chestnut grove. She ran, her feet sinking into the soft, newly churned earth, towards a tank at the far end of the grove where old Dino, the owner, kept rainwater for his trees. She heard the sure feet of the idiot boy close behind her. No one knows why she headed for the tank. Perhaps she guessed that our father couldn't swim – few people could in those days and the tank was deep – but he grabbed her as she was climbing up the ladder. Here she must have fought him because when they caught him his neck and cheeks were covered in scratches. He pinned her to the ground in the oblong shade of the tank – I have often stood and stared at that bed of shadow – and he raped her.

❦

In the early months of my last pregnancy I had a dream. In this dream, I experienced our mother's rape. I was Cassilda, lying on the soft earth with my father's face above me. I was his victim.

The next morning I told the dream to Christopher.

'I feel as if I know what she felt,' I said.

Christopher looked across the pillow at me.

'What did she feel?'

'Resistance and . . .'

'And?'

It wasn't easy for me to explain. Christopher was raised in California by a couple of hippies. His father was a tree surgeon who believed in ley lines and his mother was a masseuse who had run away from her bourgeois French Catholic background and embraced all the shining dogma of the New Age.

I'm from an archaic village in southern Europe, enfolded in an inaccessible valley, where the rules have hardly changed since the Middle Ages.

In the dream, I told him, I saw my father's face at the point of ejaculation. At that moment I could see his return to himself and with it, a look of recognition as he gazed at me, or the young Cassilda, lying beneath him. I knew then what our mother had seen in his gaze that afternoon. It was a strange, puzzling thing, one that she had never seen before and although she did not know it yet, something that she would look for all her life and never find.

'So what was this thing your mother felt?'

'A kind of surrender,' I said.

'To rape?'

I shook my head.

'To what then? Love?'

'She didn't even know him,' I said, leaning over him and kissing him. I wanted to end the conversation because I knew that I was still unable to make sense of the story I'd been told. How could I possibly see into the dark spaces between my mother's memory and her imagination? There was no fact, only fable: the stuff that places like Coelhoso are made of.

⁜

When my father had gone, Cassilda Cortez rose to her feet, crawled up the ladder and dropped down into the deep, icy water of the tank. Beneath the green surface with its diagonal shafts of sunlight, she must have felt safe. This would be her last moment of peace before the ugly birds of consequence flew up.

Years later, when I took my brother to the tank and told him the story, he didn't believe it. He dipped his hand into the freezing-cold water and shook his head. Our mother could not have withstood that temperature. She hated the cold.

'Perhaps we were conceived while she was in there,' I said.

8

We both looked back towards the village and imagined our mother walking home, her torn and muddy dress dripping on the hot path. She still hadn't shed a tear. When she entered the village and the dirt road gave way to cobbles, her body and mind must have been numb from the cold water.

If it hadn't been for Katarina, our mother might have kept the rape a secret. She could have done away with us quietly in a bath of mustard with her own mother standing guard at the door. She could have carried on being the prize of Coelhoso, the beautiful daughter of Armindo Agosto Martin Cortez, a man of high principles. But Katarina saw her go by. As Cassilda passed between the church and the ruined barn where the rutting dogs would congregate, Katarina saw her. She saw her torn and muddy dress and she saw the blood.

At the time, Katarina could not identify exactly what it was that she was seeing. But a habit of clairvoyance had revealed a gift for smelling disaster. She knew in the moment that our mother passed between the two buildings that her life was there, in the shadow of the lovely girl's misfortune. She darted across the room and out into the street, following Cassilda unseen, so that when our mother stumbled at the foot of the stone staircase that led up to her father's front door, Katarina was there to catch her. Cassilda must have looked into the dark, shiny pebbles of those eyes and seen her gaoler. She did not struggle. She let Katarina take her up the steps and into the house. That was the moment when our mother let guilt into her life and she has hugged it close ever since.

I often picture them sitting side by side on the porch in silence, Katarina with her crochet and our mother, her hands idle as always. Their need for each other was a bizarre thing: Katarina the virgin and Cassilda the whore.

After Katarina brought the raped girl up the steps to her father's house and after her father Armindo Agosto, had finished beating his breast and smashing up the furniture, he set his mind to the business of finding a husband who would be willing to take his daughter in and possibly his bastard grandchild. Armindo had three candidates in mind: the least favoured of whom was the man who would become our step-father.

Sylvino Ribiero wasn't a bad man, just a stupid one; one of those stupid men who could have gone either way, to kindness or cruelty. Sadly, Sylvino's own father was a tyrant and so the boy took his revenge, at first on animals, then on the weak and vulnerable. Our mother told me that in the early days of their marriage he was still catching water snakes by their tails and dashing their brains out on rocks, still pulling the whiskers out of kittens and cutting the ears off dogs. Over the years, our mother got used to his ways. Sylvino would still, on occasion, show his childish side. He would grab our mother's dog, tickle its genitals until it reached an erotic frenzy, then hurl it at Katarina's bitch. He would shake with silent, toothless laughter as the bitch fought and squealed and snarled. Our mother would look up at the din, smile indulgently and then go back to shelling peas.

By the age of thirty-five, Cassilda was old. She had lost almost all of her teeth and much of her hair, which clung to her scalp in wisps dyed an untrue black by Katarina. She was too heavy for her frame and her bones would snap like twigs when she rode on our stepfather's tractor, and so, while Katarina sat beside her husband on the tractor, Cassilda would have to travel behind them on a mattress strapped to a mule. Going anywhere by bus or by car was out of the question, as the unnatural motion would make all three of them throw up.

The last time I saw Katarina she had hardly aged. The angular face, with its deep-set eyes, shone like leather from the sun, but she had few lines and all her teeth, and her hair and bones were still strong. Katarina hadn't known much pain in her life. She never knew childbirth or even penetration. Instead she had been handmaiden to our mother's pain. She tended to Cassilda whenever Sylvino gave her a beating and she delivered all six of our mother's children, including my brother and me and one stillborn boy.

I'm the one who paid for the tractor. I paid for the big square house they now live in, for the brown ceramic tiles on the façade, for the electric blinds, the lock-up garage, the washing machine, the fridge/freezer, the barbecue and the microwave. All the suffering has vanished into that house. Our stepfather has boarded it up with his wondrous tools. He has double-glazed, sealed, waterproofed and insulated all the suffering with fibreglass wool and polyurethane varnish, with MDF and Acrylic One-Coat and polyurethane foam. People come by and marvel at his house. He takes them on a tour, stamping on the solid floors, rapping on the well-heeled walls; from the basement, with his pristine tools, all the way up to the rat-poisoned attic.

Though our mother was prematurely aged, her beauty sometimes used to break through, usually when she laughed. You could see a flash of it in her mischievous golden eyes. As time went on, the two of them would laugh together more and more. It became a wonder to me, knowing how much she had once hated the man she married, to see them sitting at the table together, giggling and poking at each other like children. Our stepfather seemed to have forgotten his grievance: that his wife had been sullied goods, magnanimously relinquished to him by his stuck-up father-in-law.

I remember them laughing about their neighbour's wife. Ever since her *boceta* had caught fire in a thunderstorm, they'd called her Flaming Fanny. Our stepfather would weep with laughter every time he told that story.

It was during the worst thunderstorm in living memory. The whole village had put statues of Santa Barbara in their windows in an attempt to appease her and ward off her fury. The neighbour's wife was alone in the house. Everybody knew you didn't use the phone in a storm. Well, old Fannyflames was stark naked when the phone rang. (Our mother always loved it when our stepfather said 'old Fannyflames', but she wanted to save her laughter for the end when they could let it out together.) The neighbour's wife insisted that she was about to put on her nightdress but it was our stepfather's guess that she was about to have a go. A *go*, he repeated, winking at our mother and suddenly all the pettiness and cruelty between them were forgotten: they were two ribald soldiers in the trenches together – comrades. Our mother suddenly seemed lucky and free.

The neighbour's wife picked up the phone and held it to her ear and said, 'Hello?' (Our stepfather put on a woman's high-pitched voice for this and our mother wanted to pee, she thought it was so funny.) 'Hello? Who is this?' And it was obviously the devil because the lightning struck: BOOM! And the flames leapt along the telephone wire into her lap and all of a sudden her fanny was a bed of flames and she was danc-ing round the room. '*Boceta fosforescente!*,' Sylvino wept. '*Boceta fosforescente.*'

Katarina was too chaste to laugh. She sat there blinking patiently at the couple as they rocked back and forth in their chairs. Our younger sisters, Marisa and Isabella, smiled shyly, looking from their laps to each other, unsure of the full mean-ing of the story. There were only six of us round the table that night. I was back from Paris for the first and last time. Barbara was spending the summer in the Algarve with her new hus-band and their baby boy, Kevin, named after a character from their favourite American soap, and Jose was up in his cave in the hills. Seeing our mother laugh and weep and clutch her belly, I felt the sting of rage. To see the woman who used to hit me in the head with her wooden clog when she was angry, behaving like some dizzy child.

Christopher doesn't know hatred. In our first year together I would watch him sleep and envy him his peace. A life free of hatred was hard for me to imagine and even harder, as it turned out, to live. The habit of resentment was so deeply ingrained in me that, for a time, I felt lost without it. Hatred had always been an alloy of love to me, a kind of emotional equation: I hated my mother and I loved my brother; I loved my brother because I hated my mother.

I often take the creased, faded picture of our rapist father from my wallet and look at what is left of his face. I have no photograph of my twin and so this elliptical image of Fausto has become a template for them both. I sit and stare at the image as if the clue to my brother's life and my own might be found in those blank spaces.

I think of our freakish gestation: two separate ova fertilized by two separate spermatozoa. Everything is accident and necessity, its sluggish twin.

⳹

Jose was born a full five minutes after me. Katarina was our mother's midwife and she had pulled me out and cut my cord and swaddled me before she realised that there was another baby in there. Our mother was still in pain but she was too weak to push a second time and so Katarina went in with both hands. For those few minutes my brother must have been short of oxygen because when Katarina dragged him out, she thought he was dead. His beautiful face was grey, his closed eyes like fresh scars. Our mother had passed out and Katarina decided to swaddle the dead thing up with me. She bound us close together, chest to chest. She always said that his heart had started beating at the sound of mine.

It was Katarina, the vicious clairvoyant, who saved my brother. Without her he would have passed straight through this world to the next. Instead he was dragged into life behind me and he did the best he could to live it out in my shadow.

Our father's name was Fausto Mendez. After he raped our mother, he ran. I know this from his police statement because they quoted his phrase: *I ran and ran and ran.* He ran from the chestnut grove all the way back to his village, usually a two-and-a-half-hour journey at a walk.

When they caught him he was curled up in a ball on the floor of somebody's barn. I know why. Fausto suffered from terrible headaches. According to the minutes of his trial, he lay inert in his cell and never spoke unless it was to beg them to turn off his light. This was used as an example of his lack of remorse for his crime. All he could do, they said, was moan about the light in his cell. It would have been because of a headache. Jose inherited them. The pain would make his eyes stream. He described them to me as sheets of light burning through his brain. I could picture our father lying on the cement bed of his cell, tears rolling out of the corners of his eyes.

Neither our mother nor our father could read or write. Had they been able to write to each other, we would have had some trace of the strange love that grew up between them while he was in prison. As it is, all we had were neighbours' hearsay and our mother's own whimsical testimony. In the years before she began to torment Jose and before she and I began to fight, she would talk about our father. She would sit on our bed and brush and plait my hair and tell me stories about Fausto, her beloved, her hero. The stories were not for Jose but he heard them anyway as he lay beside me in our bed, pretending to be asleep.

My brother and I heard these stories and treasured every detail of them. We learned that Fausto had loved her hair, that when she visited him in prison he had buried his face in it. From the way she talked about him, you would have thought that their love had lasted for years, not months.

In fact my mother went to visit my father in prison only three times. Each visit was recorded in the prison log. I don't know how she managed to escape from Katarina and her father. Bragança is a long way from our village by mule and no one had a car in those days. She was under heavy surveillance, so her absence could not have gone unnoticed. She must have been punished when she got home.

Cassilda's first visit to Fausto was in December, a little less than four months after his arrest. My brother and I would have been sprouting genitals in her womb. The visit was registered at eleven a.m., so she must have left the village before dawn. Perhaps she hitched a lift. But who would have agreed to take a whore to visit her lover in prison? There is only one person I can think of and that is Mad Polo.

Mad Polo is perfectly sane. He was just the only man of his generation who managed to get out of the village and see something of the world. Polo had been a naturally intelligent child. He had caught the attention of the village priest, who made him his altar boy and taught him to read and write. When he was eighteen he joined the Foreign Legion and went to Africa, where he caught syphilis from a prostitute in Djibouti. He came home and settled in Porto, where he participated in the revolution of '74. When he returned to the village, beaming with joy and hope, a carnation poking from the barrel of his rifle, nobody welcomed him as a hero. Instead of being admired, he was shunned. General Salazar is still referred to in the village as 'The Father' and perhaps it's a mercy that Polo, with his little pebble glasses and his rolling tobacco, his stack of pornographic magazines and his blasphemous opinions, is just called mad.

I think it must have been Polo who took our mother to Bragança. She would have ridden on his horse Leila (named perhaps after the Djibouti whore). Leila was a magnificent grey mare with enormous fringed hooves, strong as a plough horse, with a long flowing mane. He had bought her from a gipsy in Faro and ridden her all the way back to the village, the full length of the country. Leila was his pride and joy. He very wisely loaned her each year to the village for the festival of Santa Barbara, to pull the float. Had she not been so useful to the village, she would certainly have had an accident; envy being the driving force of Coelhoso. Every year, while Leila was parading through the streets, Polo stayed indoors, his TV on full volume to block out what he called 'the ugly din of their superstition'. Polo doesn't believe in God or in Santa Barbara and since superstition is what binds the villagers together, Polo is doomed to isolation. As the years go by, his loneliness has made him bitter and cantankerous and so Mad Polo has grown into his name.

He would have been quite different back in the winter of 1980. Still a young man and not yet bitter, he must have been a little smitten by the lovesick Cassilda as he lifted her onto the front of his horse. She might not even have needed to ask. He would quite naturally have wanted to help a romantic outcast like himself. And so they would have taken the path through the olive groves until they were out of sight of the village and then the main Tras-os-Montes road to Bragança.

The prison that held our father was an eighteenth-century fortress. His cell was on the second floor. On her first visit, our mother told him that she loved him and that even if they made her marry the pig Sylvino, Fausto would always have her heart. She planned to retract the statement she had given to the police and request his release. On her second visit, a week later, she arrived at ten-thirty a.m. The prison officer on duty mentioned, during the trial, that her hair was down on that visit. It was cited as proof of her unhinged state. Fausto and Cassilda didn't waste time: they made a plan. He would build them a house from a ruin that had belonged to his grandfather on the other side of Perdrilha and when it was ready, she would run away and join him. For some reason she did not tell him that she was pregnant.

As we grew older, our mother stopped talking about our father and it became hard to imagine that she had ever referred to him as her One True Love. She had her comfortable house, a man who would never leave her and a best friend who wait-ed on her hand and foot. She had no use for love any more.

When our father came to trial Cassilda was six months pregnant. It was the last time he saw her. I imagine Fausto gaz-ing across the courtroom at his betrothed, standing luminous with love between Sylvino and Katarina. He would not have noticed the pregnancy as she was hardly eating at the time but, as Katarina would say, 'living on love and cold water'.

As they had planned, and to the horror of her family, Cassilda retracted her statement and Fausto was released. The judge ignored the prosecutor's argument that even if Cassilda had changed her mind about the rapist, a rape had still taken place. He ruled that if the young woman decides that there had been no rape, then there was no rape.

Fausto went to the ruin in the hills and began work. While he was repairing the stone walls, building the roof, laying the floors, Cassilda sat in her room in her father's house, her belly growing and her breasts ballooning. Her room was above the stable and she would sometimes go down and press her cheek against the soft flank of her father's mule and cry.

Katarina was never far away. As chaperone, she attended Sylvino's daily visits, watching him stagger blindly back and forth between lust and repulsion. She even stood by on the several occasions when Sylvino tried to force himself on our mother. Cassilda would lie perfectly still, her eyes blank, refusing to give him the satisfaction of a struggle. While Sylvino was on top of her, she would keep her mind fixed on the little house in the hills and she would shut out his grunts with the thought of the whispering grass and imagine the sound of Fausto's hammer echoing against the cliffs.

In the end it was Katarina who found the single thread that would unravel our mother's passion. The more Sylvino ranted and raved and the more brutish he became, the more sublime our mother was in her obsession. Katarina watched Cassilda looking at herself in the mirror, saw the martyrdom make her more beautiful by the day and saw the chink that was our mother's narcissism. She took Sylvino aside and convinced him to stay away from his fiancée, just for the last few months of her confinement, then she went to Father Antonio, the new priest, and told him Cassilda's story.

There were many tales in the village of Santa Barbara intervening in favour of lovesick women. A favourite was the story of the patron saint appearing in our very own village to a girl called Fatima, whose father had cut off all her beautiful hair as a punishment for refusing the man he had chosen for her. The next morning the girl woke up in her bed with her magnificent hair undulating from her head, across the pillow and along the floor. In the face of the miracle, the father dropped to his knees and let her marry the man she loved.

One year after his arrival, Father Antonio had still to find a place in the villagers' hearts. His predecessor had won the women over with such stories as Fatima's, which had made them the protagonists of God's drama on earth. After he died falling from a ladder they walked about crying into their handkerchiefs. Father Antonio, the dour replacement from Braga, made the women feel resentful and morose with his patriarchal leanings. Here, Katarina convinced him, was his chance. He could sweep away the heresies and the self-love that had been encouraged in the women by his vainglorious predecessor. Bring Cassilda, the whore, to repentance, bring her back to God and the women would fear and love him.

For the last three months of her pregnancy Father Antonio visited our mother for two hours every afternoon. Katarina spread the word and the matter of Cassilda's salvation became one which concerned every woman in the village. In the late afternoons they would gather beneath Cassilda's window and speculate on the advancement of her redemption. Some must secretly have longed for her to resist the priest and fly with her bastard child to her lover in the hills. But no one admitted to it. They all murmured prayers for her repentance.

Inside the dark house the priest set about trying to convince Cassilda that her lover was marked by the Devil. He argued that she would find no greater glory on this earth than by giving him up and legitimising the poor bastard growing in her womb. When he had gone, Katarina would finish the priest's work by whispering to her about the shouts of joy that would go up in the village as she stepped out onto her father's veranda with the news that she was marrying Sylvino Ribiero. She even told Cassilda that on her wedding day she would be carried through the village on a float, just like the statue of Santa Barbara.

In the end, Cassilda did not have her float. Instead, she shuffled to church on swollen feet. By the time of her marriage to

Sylvino, she was overrun by hysterical symptoms. Her hair was falling out and her hands and feet were swollen and covered in eczema. At the wedding people began to guess at twins.

Sylvino Ribiero was not displeased with the way things had turned out. The new Cassilda was less trouble without her looks and he was commended in the village for his kindness in taking her in. For the first time in his life, he could hold his head high and drink with his father-in-law as an equal. He began to wish only for his own father's death, so that the memory of his ignominious childhood might die with him.

When Fausto hanged himself from the rafters of that freshly built house, he did not know that Cassilda was about to give birth to his children. I wonder, would he have stayed alive if he had known? Would our lives have been different?

I often imagine Fausto during those three months before he killed himself. He must have been delirious with hope and happiness, waiting for Cassilda up there in the hills. When his beloved didn't appear I imagine his joy imploding. I imagine him withdrawing into his mind as Jose would have done. Nothing would have brought him down to our village to fetch her. He was an outcast, like his future son would be, and proud and stubborn, like his future daughter.

He would have gone on working and hoping until the news of Cassilda's marriage to Sylvino finally reached him. No one knows who told him. There was no evidence that he had any friends. But in that place nothing stayed secret for long. They found him in March, two months before we were born. He had tied a rope around his neck and jumped from the roof beam. He had my brother's agility. It took the men a whole morning to work out how to get him down. In the end they sent a child up there with a knife to cut the rope.

By the time the news of her lover's death had reached her, Cassilda had retreated into a state of catatonic self-absorption. She lay in bed all day, waited on by Katarina and henceforth offered up her womb for the careless manufacture of Sylvino's children.

In the end, Katarina would set upon and destroy the myth of our father as a romantic hero. Until the summer of our tenth year Jose and I believed that Fausto had died up there in the ruin on the hills, of a broken heart. By the time she told me the true story of our origins, my hatred of my mother was so firmly in place that there was no room for any other object. Our mother's defilement, her shameful confinement and her matrimonial martyrdom left me cold. All my compassion went to Fausto, the loyal and thwarted lover.

Katarina must have waited until she thought I was old enough to grasp the full meaning of that terrible word 'rape'.

She was sitting on the veranda doing her crochet.

'You know, I pity your father,' she said.

I stopped watching the swallows swooping in and out of the narrow holes in the neighbour's barn and looked at her.

'Do you know why, Aisha?'

'Why?' I asked sulkily.

'Because his soul is burning in Hell.'

'No, it's not.'

'Yes, it is.'

'Why?'

'Because he took his own life and that's a mortal sin.'

'What's a mortal sin?'

'It is a sin for which you are punished for all eternity.'

I stared at her ugly face.

'I don't believe you.'

She shrugged and went back to her crochet.

'He died of a broken heart,' I murmured.

'No, he didn't. He hanged himself for shame.'

'He died of love. Mother says so.'

'He went to prison,' she said patiently, setting down her crochet.

'I know that. He went to prison because he wanted to marry Mother and Grandfather Armindo wouldn't let him.'

Katarina shook her head slowly.

'No one goes to prison for that. He was sent to prison

because he raped her like a *dog*!'

I watched her twisted mouth vomit that last word, such an ugly word in Portuguese: *caen*. This, not rape, was the word I settled on.

After that, a blind went down in my head, protecting my father's memory. Try as she might, Katarina never succeeded in destroying my love for this father I never had. I clung to it like a rag to barbed wire.

'Everyone knows,' she told me. 'Ask anyone,' she added, taking up her crochet. 'Ask Sonia.'

Sonia was my friend. Like most people in the village, she had been told the story of the rape and the suicide. At my request, she took me to the place in Dino's grove where it had happened. I remember looking at her long, dark hair as she told me and liking the way little sweaty curls at her hairline stuck to her forehead. She spoke in a matter-of-fact way, pointing out the exact spot where it had happened, and I remember looking at the heavy clods of earth and thinking that it must have been an uncomfortable place to lie.

'Do you hate me?' I asked her.

'Why would I hate you? It's not your fault that you weren't made in the normal way.'

'What is the normal way?'

'On Christmas Eve,' she said happily. 'In front of the fire.'

◈

When Katarina put the newly revived baby boy to our mother's breast, he was too weak to suckle. Katarina says that as soon as she set eyes on my brother, our mother recoiled. His frailty must have felt like an accusation and she never fed him. Katarina had to give him goat's milk from a bottle. I can't look at my own child suckling at my breast without thinking of Jose as a baby.

I fed my first child for almost two years and I'll suckle this baby until he too pushes me away. Making amends.

'You can't live with ghosts, Aisha,' Christopher's wonderful, crazy mother told me. It was last September and we were sitting on her deck, looking out over the lagoon. My daughter was sitting on her lap, sucking her thumb, dozing. 'You have to ask them to leave now,' she said.

My daughter sat up and paid attention.

'What ghosts, Grandma?'

Natasha, whose real name, as I discovered recently, is Marie-Hélène, answered both of us.

'Ghosts from the past. She has to ask them politely,' she said in her purring French accent. 'Ask ghosts politely and they always leave.'

For all her hippy-dippy nonsense, she is still a great believer in the value of politeness.

Christopher laughed when I told him. He has a big laugh. Amber has it too. A big, Californian laugh: wide mouth, head thrown back, guffaw.

'She's right,' he said. 'You'll never have any peace until you do.'

⚜

When Jose didn't scream at the christening and let out the Devil, everyone crossed themselves and prepared for the worst. When he turned out to be mute, it only confirmed their suspicion that he had been sent by God to punish Cassilda.

I was pretty as a child. At first, our mother saw me as the embodiment of her best self. When I was very young she tried to separate me from my brother, mostly by neglecting him and pampering me. She would spend hours plaiting my hair. She would get Katarina to make clothes to her design and she would keep me away, not only from Jose but from the other children. She said that she did not want me to get dirty, but it was moral contamination that she feared. She didn't sing to me, or hug me, or show me any affection beyond the business

22

of tending to my appearance but in those days I adored her. I thought she had a beautiful smile and I remember loving the way she smelt.

I can't remember when I began to defend my brother (I think we were about four) and I don't know which came first, the estrangement from our mother or the fusion with him, but the two were certainly linked. I will never forget the ugliness of her face in anger whenever I protected him. The rage that poured out of her at such moments disturbed even Sylvino. He would look up from sharpening his pocket knife and beg her to calm down, reminding her that I was only a child. But my mother would spit and scream and pull my hair.

'Tell me where he is!' she would shriek. 'Tell me where he's hiding!'

I would clamp my lips together and close my eyes, waiting for the blow. My obstinacy must have reminded her of her own resistance in the months of her confinement, but unlike her, I never gave in. She would threaten, then cajole, then hit me. Then she would drag me, kicking and screaming, along the floor and lock me in the muddy hut with the black pig.

Jose and Fausto: I wish they had known each other. Like our father, Jose was unusually tall. He had Fausto's eyes, his headaches and his irresistible smile.

It was always a puzzle to me that our mother was not beguiled by her only son's smile. While we were growing up, it became a thing that I looked forward to. It was like some natural phenomenon: a rainbow or a sunset. Perhaps that smile of his augured what my brother's spiritual mentor, the Sunni Sheikh of Blanville, would one day identify as his special gift. I don't know. All I know is that when he smiled, a miracle of pure, unrestrained joy shone from his face.

Only once did she appear to notice it. I remember the day. I was in the bathroom in the old house, the one our mother had inherited from her father. Our mother kept the meat in a bath of cold water. I remember looking down at the skinned sheep's head she was saving for soup. Its gory face peered up at me through a veil of milky skin and I made myself stare back at it, knowing that it would give me nightmares if I didn't. Then Jose ran in, jumping up and down with excitement, gesturing for me to follow him. Out on the veranda he pointed to a young swallow that had fallen from its nest. It was flapping in forlorn circles on the ground. Our mother put down her broom, picked the bird up and put it into her bra. My brother followed her around as she went about her business, the injured bird wedged between her breasts. She finished sweeping the veranda, then watered the geraniums while I sat on the stone steps and pulled ticks from the dog's ears. At last there was a fluttering at her chest. She reached in and pulled out the little bird, held it out to my brother for a moment, then raised it up, opened her hand and watched it fly off. Jose looked up at her and gave her a smile of infinite gratitude. For a moment, she seemed taken in by it.

'He has his father's smile,' she said. 'You don't have it. Just as well. A girl with a smile like that would only bring trouble on herself.'

Jose's beauty as a child did not endear him to people. It only set him further apart. His green eyes were haunting and spoke of gipsy heritage. As his twin, I suppose my infatuation with his physique had a narcissistic ingredient. In the warm weather I loved to lie with him by the *rio* and rest my head on his smooth, skinny torso, which smelled of the sun and river and sweat. He wore his christening medallion on a long chain around his neck and I would run the gold disc back and forth over the chain and ask him to give it to me because I had lost mine. But our uncle Jose Manuel had told him that it was bad luck to take it off, that the Saint Christopher on the back would protect him on all his journeys, however long and however short.

Let me think back to the early days, before our separation, to the long summers when my brother was always beside me. For many years life was a blur to him. As I have said, he moved in my shadow, eluding first our mother's hatred, then the scorn of the villagers. For me, things were sharp early on. I saw our mother for who she was: an ignorant girl who had lost her lover and then her looks and was filled with bitterness. I saw Katarina, the handmaiden of doom, watching the poison of her envy work its magic. For as long as I can remember I stood between my brother and these women, protecting him from their unfathomable spite.

As we grew up, our mother developed what Katarina was to call 'bad nerves'. Given that she was usually pregnant, miscarrying, giving birth or breast-feeding she must have been in a state of constant hormonal disarray. Whatever ailed her drove her to bed most afternoons. Katarina's self-appointed duty was to look after the house for our mother and to keep her five children away, in particular her only son, the living proof of her sin.

When our stepfather Sylvino came home from the fields everything was in order. Our mother was up, washed and dressed, the house was clean and his supper was on the table. Katarina was the candle-bearer of their marriage, shielding our stepfather from all his wife's shortcomings.

In those days I would take my brother by the hand and lead him out of the dark house that smelled of fermenting olives and rotting salami. We would go out of the village and up into the hills. At five, he was already strong and agile and fearless. There was, I remember, even at that age, something remarkable about the relationship between his feet and the ground, as though he were physically incapable of disequalibrium. In fact, the sight of him, at all ages, simply walking up a hill made me feel proud. At six, he could use a catapult and set traps for birds. He could dive from the high rock behind the lead mine and I would stand on the bank and watch his little body – back arched and arms and legs akimbo – flying through the air. As I watched him resurface, my hand clapped over my mouth, I felt thrilled and afraid. He tried to teach me fearlessness but he was too susceptible to my anxiety. I remember standing beside him on that rock, looking down into the brown water of the *rio*, my heart pounding and my knees knocking together. He held my hand, patiently waiting for me to feel ready. We stood there for most of the afternoon, my hand in his. Occasionally I would lean over the edge, poised to jump, and then I would pull back, the anger and frustration growing with the realization that I was not like him. At last, I snatched my hand away and ran and hid from him in one of the disused mineshafts.

It was dark in there and full of ice-cold draughts. My hair was still wet from the river and I sat in one of the many galleries, overlooking a huge piece of rusting machinery that looked like the skeleton of a dinosaur. I sat with my teeth chattering, listening to Jose's search. He ran up and down the labyrinth, slapping on the walls; his distress all the more frantic for the strange, repressed sounds of the habitual mute. As I sat there I was filled with the exhilarating fear that Jose could die: the mines were dangerous, full of holes; grown men had disappeared into them.

That night I had a fever and slipped into delirium. I caught pneumonia and was ill for several months. Now I know that such a reaction must have been psychosomatic: a trick to mask those fratricidal fantasies.

After that I regularly pretended to die. There is a plant that grows on the hills around Coelhoso and everyone knows that the smallest drop of its milky sap is poisonous. Once I pretended to swallow some. Jose was up ahead. I dropped to my knees and made a rasping noise, clutching my throat. Then I fell back onto the stony path. I closed my eyes and practised being dead. Jose ran to me and knelt down beside me. I kept perfectly still, making sure that not even my eyelids fluttered. He did not have the presence of mind to do what he would have done for a trapped bird, to feel the pulse in its neck. He might have tickled me and I would have sprung to life but instead he started to cry. I opened my eyes and looked up at him. Instead of rebuking me, he buried his face in his hands.

Jose's nightmares began soon after that. He would wake in

the middle of the night, his eyes wide with fear. Sometimes he would grab me in his sleep and make my heart race. I began to sing to him to get him back to sleep. As I sang he would watch my face, fighting the return to sleep, but he would soon lose and I would see his eyes half-close, the irises roll up and his face turn pale and calm. He was my baby then, and I lay down beside him and moved him close to me so that I could fall asleep with his breath on my face.

When we turned five and Jose still wouldn't speak, Katarina and our mother began to try to force him. As far as I was concerned he didn't need to speak. He spoke to me with gestures, or with his eyes. I always knew what he wanted to say. But our mother cared what people thought. In the village Jose was coming to be recognized as a half-wit. The other children taunted him when they could get near him, which was not often – I made sure of that.

Our mother was convinced that Jose's muteness was her punishment for Fausto and so, with Katarina's help, she set about trying to make him talk. The more the two women tried to drag sounds from him, the more he withdrew into his silence. They made endless offerings to Santa Barbara in the hope of his cure, believing that this would be the sign that our mother had been forgiven.

One day a young doctor came from Bragança to examine him. I watched from the kitchen door as Jose sat on a stool and let the man poke around in his throat with a tiny light. He looked in Jose's ears and rattled objects on either side of his head to make him turn round. Then he put his hand on my brother's neck and asked him to hum. My brother just stared at the doctor until the young man became uneasy and turned to my mother.

'Does he understand?'

My mother stepped forward, raising her hand to slap Jose, but the doctor stopped her. He asked her again if Jose could understand him.

'Of course he can understand. He's stubborn as a mule.'

27

The young doctor turned back to Jose and spoke to him in a gentle voice.

'Can you hum for me?'

Jose looked at me and so I began to hum. We hummed the song, 'Borboleta', to the doctor and he smiled and nodded, all the time moving his fingers on Jose's throat.

When he had finished he announced, with great satisfaction, that Jose had perfect hearing and that his vocal cords were intact.

'So?' my mother snapped. 'He can speak.'

The doctor shrugged.

'If he wanted to, he could. As far as I can tell, there is no organic reason for his muteness.'

If that poor young doctor only knew what curse he had visited on my brother by his cheery diagnosis. From that day on, our mother and Katarina set upon him and his ordeal began.

In our mother's bedroom, the same bedroom where she had pined for her lover in the early months of her pregnancy, there was a green painted chair. I remember looking through the keyhole and seeing my brother tied to that chair. I could see the back of his head and hear our mother shouting at him in her terrifying voice.

'What is your name? I asked you your name!'

And he would moan, making a painful, guttural noise that sounded like the word 'Lea!'

'That's not your name!' our mother shrieked. Then she slapped him in the face.

I would bang my fists on that door and scream until I was hoarse.

As soon as we turned six we went to the village school. On the first day my brother would not let go of my hand. He was afraid of the other children. When the teacher prised him from my grip and pushed him into a chair, he sat with his face buried in his arms. At break time he covered his ears with his hands to block out the din of the other children. He wanted to go to the toilet and so I went with him. I waited for him outside one of ten cubicles, each with a tiny toilet with no seat and no door. I turned my back on him and looked in the mirror. Although she had tugged impatiently at my scalp that morning in the making of it, I liked the plait Katarina had laced with a narrow red ribbon. At that moment the door opened and the head teacher Senhor Maltez burst in. I turned round in time to see him grab Jose by the ear. Jose had missed the bowl and had crapped on the floor. Maltez was tugging Jose's head towards his shit, so I flew at him and bit him on the hand to make him let go. Jose ran out and Maltez cuffed me and then rushed after him. But Jose had disappeared through a gap in the hedge. That day I spent without him. It felt like the longest day of our lives.

Jose never returned to school after that. He spent his days in the hills.

A few days before Christmas, a social worker came from Bragança to talk to our mother. The village women gathered round the social worker's car, speculating wildly on what was going on inside. He told our mother that the government would not tolerate truancy. This was 'The European Union', he said. School was not optional. If she did not make Jose go to school, he would be taken into care. Our mother was torn between her fear of the disgrace of having a child taken by the authorities and the temptation to be rid of her son. She went to Father Antonio. For the priest, our godless government was the enemy. There was no question of losing a child, even a half-witted one, to The State. The priest talked to Maltez. I don't know what he told him, but from that day on Maltez called my brother's name after mine at assembly every morning: *Ribeiro Aisha! Ribiero Jose!* I called out 'present' both times and Maltez put a tick by my name and his.

Jose waited for me every day after school and I would wave goodbye to my friends and follow him into the hills. He would carry my satchel for me as we climbed. In the summer term of my first year at school I learnt to read. The first book I owned I had been awarded by Maltez for consistently high marks. It had my name printed in careful italic lettering inside the front cover. The book was *The House of a Hundred Joys*. It was a magical title for something so dull, a reading manual for six to eight-year-olds with short extracts from fables and fairy tales, but I devoured it. Jose made us a platform on the branch of a cork tree not far from the house that our father had built for our mother. Every day after school we climbed the tree and I would teach him what I had learnt. I remember him learning the alphabet, shaping his mouth loosely around each letter, which he carved into the bark of that tree with his knife.

Every evening when the light had gone, we would return home together, always holding hands as we approached the house. When we were nine our mother decided that it was time for us to sleep in separate rooms. She put Jose in the tiny room above the mule which she had used to hang the meat in. It never lost the bloodstains on the wooden floor or the slight-ly sickly smell. The first night we were apart I could hear Jose crying through the wall. His tears, as always, drove mine away and I sat up with my palms on the wall, trying to soothe him.

In the end he grew to like that little room. It had a tiny win-dow, the size of a bible, with a view of the hills. The mule below kept it warm. Our mother never went into that room, so it became our retreat.

Jose learnt to keep out of our mother's way. He rarely ate with the family, except on Sundays, at Katarina's insistence. She, unlike our mother, never despaired of civilizing him. At these meals, our mother would simply behave as if he were not there and over the years I really think he disappeared for her.

Until he turned thirteen. Perhaps his likeness to Fausto sud-denly became apparent. He was turning into a tall, lean, hand-some youth, like his father.

One Sunday evening in June, we came home to find our mother in one of her dangerous moods. We knew from experi-ence that a certain kind of silence in the house was either the prelude to one of her rages or its aftermath. Sylvino was on the terrace, cleaning his rifle, and we sat with him to keep out of her way. When it was time for supper, Katarina called us in. The seven of us, including little Barbara and Maria, sat around the table in silence watching our mother serve the soup. I held out my bowl, avoiding her gaze. Sylvino sat at the head, between his two women, dipping his bread in the broth and slurping noisily.

We had had a good day that day, reading by the *rio*, and Jose was happy, but when his laughter spilled out of him, I knew he was in danger. I shot him a warning glance but it was too late. Barbara and Maria were looking at their father, sucking the soup from his spoon and laughing too. To my horror, our mother was not looking at the girls but at Jose, and I saw murder in her eyes. Sylvino stopped, held his spoon suspended in front of his mouth and glanced back and forth between the boy and his mother.

'Silence, Jose,' he said.

But Jose could never just stop laughing once he had started. I knew that. There was terror in the air as we all watched our mother. I thought he was out of her reach, but her hand shot out across the table and gripped his throat, throttling the laughter. In the commotion of the little girls crying and Katarina coaxing and Sylvino barking orders, Jose's face turned red. He could easily have prised her hand from his throat, but he didn't. He let her squeeze, staring at her with the bulging eyes of his hanging father.

No one saw Sylvino leave the table. When the shot came, it sent my mother into the air, almost as if the bullet had hit her. We looked at Sylvino brandishing the smoking rifle above his head. No one noticed my brother slip out of the room.

We were thirteen when he ran away from home. He had already found his cave in the hills and he was already skilled at hunting. For me the village was divided after that between the good and the evil, between those who felt for Jose, who gave him their old clothes, made stews for him on feast days, remembered him on cold nights, and those who didn't. I was the arbiter of good and evil. I dealt out punishment and reward, stealing from the vegetable gardens of the wicked and running errands for the good.

'Too much power for one little girl,' Christopher once said.

It suited everyone when Jose left. With her son no longer in her sight to remind her of her sins, or perhaps even of the life she might have lived, Cassilda calmed down. She was able to take on the housework, freeing Katarina to work in the fields with Sylvino. I was happy because I had my twin entirely to myself. No one knew where his cave was. I kept it secret from everyone, including our little sisters, Barbara and Maria, whose memory of their brother faded with each passing year.

I would bring him things to decorate his cave, presents that I had made or found. He kept his possessions on a shelf that he had dug out of the rock: pretty stones we had found down at the mines, Roman oyster shells, a sewing kit from Pan Am, a broken tugboat made of varnished matchsticks, a coloured ID photo of our cousin Cidalia, who died at six from a bee sting in her throat.

My teacher in secondary school was a woman called Teresa Montero. It was she who nurtured my ambition, sheltered me from envy and mediocrity and offered an escape from the violence of life in my mother's house by keeping up a steady supply of books. Teresa's father was a Spanish exile who had been tortured by Franco's police in Zagora and escaped. He had hidden in the hills on the Portuguese border, hoping to escape to France when the search for him had died down. But Teresa's mother, a girl from Coelhoso, had found him and fed him and they had fallen in love. They were married, not in the village chapel but in Bragança town hall, and so the villagers had turned their backs on them. When Teresa's mother had died giving birth to her, there was no one there to help him and he had brought up his little girl in defiant solitude. He had taught her everything he knew: English, French, mathematics and a heavy dose of Marxist-Leninist ideology. Teresa grew up an outcast, cut off from the rest by her father's foreignness and her education. If it hadn't been for her father I'm sure she would have left the village and gone to Paris, but she stayed to look after him and ended up marrying a kind man called Luis and running the school and making a library and bringing my dreams to life.

Everything I knew I learned from Teresa and her library. Over five years I borrowed all her books one by one and read them with my brother in the hills. First the novels translated into Portuguese (Jose had favourites, which he made me read several times, such as *Twenty Thousand Leagues under the Sea* and *David Copperfield*), and then Shakespeare. The library only had four of his plays, all in Portuguese: *Hamlet*, *Othello*, *Julius Caesar* and *Romeo and Juliet*. We read them over and over again the summer we turned fourteen. Jose learned all of *Hamlet* by heart and would irritate me by mouthing the words while I was reading.

'Stop it, Jose, or I won't read.'

And he would clamp his lips together.

We even struggled through Teresa's five English books, starting with *English for Beginners*, which had a line drawing of a London bus on the cover. We learned phrases like 'my tailor is rich' and 'the butter is on the table'.

Once Teresa took Jose and me to Bragança and we saw an Angolan man selling sunglasses on the pavement. Jose could not stop staring at him. He knew perfectly well that he wasn't Othello, but was happy just standing there, drinking the man in with his eyes. I tried to move Jose on because the man was getting offended and abusive, but he wouldn't budge. It was only when the man stood up and threatened to hit him that Jose was roused from his trance.

My brother and I would often go up to the house that Fausto had built for our mother. Even when we found out how he had died, the place was still a sanctuary for us. Over the years it had become a ruin again and a lilac tree began to grow up through the roof. It sat on a gentle slope overlooking Perdrilha, our father's village. Every summer we would lie in the long, dry grass, watching the lizards flick in and out of its walls, and imagine Fausto working there alone, listening to the same wind in the poplars, his head full of love. That is the story that we both clung to. Perhaps because it was the only story that made any sense to us.

It was here, during our eighteenth summer, that I told my brother I was leaving. Ever since I was eleven Teresa had talked to me about Paris. Under the dictator Salazar, the first busload of workers had left Coelhoso in the dead of night and crossed the border into Spain. For some reason, which no one remembered, those people had chosen Paris, and since then no one had ever sought their fortunes anywhere else. The Paris emigrants helped the new arrivals from Coelhoso settle in. The women got jobs working as *concierges* in the grand buildings of the sixteenth *arrondissement*, while the men worked as builders, electricians and, if they were lucky, mechanics. I decided to follow these people, but I would not use their network of support. I would strike out on my own. As Teresa had taught me to believe, my life would be different.

Every summer the emigrants would return to the village, their big Mercedes weighed down with microwaves, washing machines, video recorders – gifts for their families from the modern world. They would spend the summer building big houses for their retirement on the outskirts of the village, with big windows and sliding patio doors. Many of them remain unfinished: ugly concrete palaces with two-car garages. Soon every family in the village had a relative in Paris, but still people couldn't help themselves; they watched the emigrants return every summer with envy and mistrust. They came home with the children they had made in France and there was no doubt that, although the girls looked the same as their sisters from the village, there was something sluttish about them.

'I'm going to Paris, Jose,' I told him. 'As soon as I have enough money, I'm going.'

He lay there, inside the ruined walls of our father's house, petrified, as though the earth had just cracked open beneath him. I put my arms around him and promised that we'd soon be together.

'I'll come and get you when I'm settled. You'll live with me in a big city with parks and cathedrals.'

That summer I got a job as a secretary in the Bragança law courts. I was enrolled at the University to study literature and was due to begin in October, but I didn't go. Instead I told Cassilda and Sylvino that I preferred to work. They were delighted that I had come to my senses. Cassilda had fought Teresa's influence all through secondary school, convinced that it was the reading that was making me so wilful.

'What you're doing to her is madness!' our mother shouted, knocking her temple with her knuckles. 'She'll never come to anything! She's clever. She could work in a bank! You're making her sick in the head with *stories*!'

After our mother had snatched Teresa's illustrated copy of *The Arabian Nights* from my hands and torn it in half, my teacher had stopped letting me take books home and she was careful not to speak French to me within my mother's earshot.

The job in the law courts paid well. I went to Bragança every day on the bus and came home to the village at night. At the end of each week, I gave Cassilda and Sylvino half my salary and hid the rest in my bedroom. The following September, I stole our father's mugshot from his file in the basement of the courtrooms, bought a one-way ticket and boarded the coach to Paris.

A T THE TIME, I SHUT MY MIND OFF from the suffering I had caused my brother by abandoning him. When I left, he painted hundreds of eyes on the roof of his cave. Then he lay down beneath them and began to starve himself.

I don't know where he went in his mind that winter, or why he pulled back from death that time, but I know that he was never the same again. Those months broke him and nothing would mend him, but I didn't know it then.

Teresa, the only person apart from me that Jose trusted, didn't see him all winter. He had stopped appearing, like some wild thing, when she was out walking by the mines. She would sometimes take books for him and a meat casserole and leave them beside the entrance to the main shaft. But that winter he took neither.

One day I would discover what I had done to my brother, but at the time I was out discovering the world, supposedly in order to share it with him.

❧

When my coach arrived in Paris in the autumn of our nineteenth year, I couldn't believe my eyes. The broad streets, wet from recent rain, shone luminous silver under a slate-grey sky. I couldn't sit still and kept leaning over my neighbour to see the churches and statues and fountains as they flew past. He was a boy my age from Bragança who was also coming to Paris for the first time. His head lolled as he drifted in and out of sleep. At last he sighed and stood up and let me take his seat. I sat with my nose pressed against the glass. As we crossed over the Seine at Concorde I looked at the glazed

39

dome of the Grand Palais set ablaze by the setting sun and I smiled and told myself that I would bring Jose here as soon as I had the money to pay for his bus ticket.

The coach stopped at Trocadéro and I crossed the square to the Museum of Mankind and stood on the Esplanade and looked across the grand vista to the Eiffel Tower, lit up behind a veil of mist. I sat for hours on the steps until darkness fell and my hands and feet were numb with cold. Then I bought a postcard of the Eiffel Tower for Jose and began to walk about in search of a cheap hotel.

In the end I found a place near the Jardins du Ranelagh called L'Hôtel des Acacias. It was covered with ivy and smelt of damp and cat piss, and it was run by an old woman called Odile Moulin. Above the reception desk hung a photograph of Odile's dead husband winning a bicycle race, and a number of his cycling cups and medals were displayed on a shelf dedicated to his memory. He had died of a heart attack going up the Mont Sainte-Victoire. Bizarrely, Odile also displayed a postcard of Cézanne's vision of that deadly hill next to the photo of her husband. There was also a picture of her mother and father taken on the beach at Algiers.

Odile was lonely. She had a neurotic parrot called Kiki and a weeping, farting ginger cat called Fanta. I moved into her smallest, cheapest room on the top floor and when I was still there after two weeks, she began to invite me to join her for dinner. We would sit in front of the TV with the sound turned down and she would tell me her life story. Thanks to Odile's incessant chatter my French progressed rapidly. Her father was a North African Jew who came from a wealthy family of horse traders from Oran and her mother was a Catholic girl from Brittany. In 1960 they came to France to escape the Algerian war of independence. Odile's father bought the hotel and then went into decline. His wife ran the hotel and brought up their only daughter while he sat in the local PMU betting away all their money on horses. He died at fifty while he was watching TV in the armchair that sits in the entrance. Odile has put a yucca on it so that no one can sit there. She seemed to begrudge neither her father nor her dead husband Thierry their antipathy to work.

'Some men simply aren't meant for it,' she said. She nodded at the blurred figure of Thierry crossing some finishing line. 'Will you look at that man? What charm!'

I was lucky to have walked into that woman's stinking hotel. She was very kind to me. She found me a cleaning job at the Museum of Mankind around the corner. I loved it there: the great silent rooms, the dust motes turning in the yellow light from the long windows, the smell of floor polish. Every morning at six o'clock I would clean the museum for three hours before it opened. I had a mop and bucket and a trolley full of cleaning fluids. Once a week, I would wax and polish the parquet floors with a heavy, old-fashioned machine. I would slide along behind the machine, through the shafts of sunlight. I was free because in those days my conscience was clear: I was doing all this so that my brother and I could be together again.

After the museum, I would help Odile at the hotel. I cleaned the rooms and made the beds while she made breakfast for the guests. She was strict about breakfast, which went from eight until ten and not a minute longer. There were many adulterous couples that would come to her hotel for the night and she didn't like them lazing in bed. I felt sorry for them, having to face each other so early in the morning. They sat in the gloom of that dining room, with its ivy wallpaper. You could tell that they were not there for that kind of intimacy. The men looked depressed and the women looked haunted.

Every weekday evening I went to a French class at the *mairie*. Thanks to Teresa I was well ahead of the others, and the teacher, Madame Ziou, started to give me novels to read. I read Gide and Flaubert and Maupassant and Sartre. In my class there was an epileptic boy from Kiev who liked to sit next to me. His face would always fall when the seat beside me was taken, so he began to make sure he was right behind me when

Madame Ziou unlocked the door. His name was Ivan and he had been a jockey back home in the Ukraine. He believed it was Chernobyl that had given him the epilepsy. He had his first fit just after he won his first race. He told me how he had fallen from his horse when he was pacing the paddock, his silver cup raised above his head.

'There I was, surrounded by everyone in the business, lying on the ground, my eyes rolling and my mouth foaming. That was the beginning and the end of my career,' he said. 'My trainer threw me out like an old sock. Then they put me in hospital and experimented on me. They opened up my head,' he said, drawing a line around his skull. 'And put electrodes on my brain and watched the patterns on a screen. They gave me so many drugs that I couldn't walk and I got fat. Look at me. I used to be like this.' And he held up his little finger.

French was hard for Ivan so he spoke to me in English. I would try and help him with his French homework. One afternoon when we were sitting on a bench in the Jardins du Ranelagh and I was trying to explain the past participle to him, Ivan lunged at me, sliding his fat tongue into my mouth. I pushed him off and slapped his face. He looked at me for a moment then went back to his grammar book. Shortly after that, he stopped coming to class.

I loved French, and Odile enjoyed teaching me the most obscure words she could think of. I would try to build sentences around the archaic words she chose, like *engoncé*, trussed up, or *languir*, to languish.

'*Je languis d'ennui*,' I said. 'I languish with boredom.'

'Good. Now use it with the word "love".'

'*Je languis d'amour.*'

'No! *Je* me *languis d'amour*. With love it becomes reflexive!' Odile said triumphantly.

One morning, as we were stripping a bed, she looked at me, a pile of dirty sheets rolled up in her arms, and said:

'You're just the kind of daughter I would have wanted.'

I shook the fresh sheet out over the bed. The habit of mistrust prevented me from enjoying the compliment.

'I don't think so,' I said.

'Oh yes you are,' she insisted, smoothing out the creases in the bottom sheet. 'When I was thirty-six,' she went on, 'I had a check-up. The doctor was a dreadful man. He looked like a pig. He had orange hairs on the back of his hands. Open the window, will you, Aisha?' I opened the window, letting the smell of cat piss waft in from the gravel yard below. 'He told me I'd been carrying a sexually transmitted disease. When he said *sexually transmitted disease* he seemed almost pleased. I knew who the disease came from. A boyfriend I had before Thierry called Maurice Plouvin, who sold women's shoes. That's how he wooed you. Through the feet. It took me years to get away from him. After I found out that I couldn't have children, I cried for months. I lost eight kilos from the grief. It was like a pregnancy in reverse. Thierry was sweet. He never held it against me. That's why I always did what I could for his cycling career.'

In the afternoons Odile took me sightseeing. We went on a *bâteau-mouche*, up the Eiffel Tower and to Sacré Coeur. When the warm weather came we made picnics. Odile always packed *rillettes*, her favourite pâté and strawberries. She had a pass for the gardens of Bagatelle and every Sunday we walked in the rose garden. Sometimes I would find myself on the verge of telling her about my life. Her compassion seemed boundless. I wanted to return her affection but I never could. So I told her nothing, giving her no sign that I too would have chosen her for a mother.

❦

One morning Odile brought me a letter from Teresa in which she begged me to tell her where Jose's cave was. She said that she was worried, that he had not been collecting the food she had been putting out for him. After a sleepless night I telephoned Teresa. I remember standing in the phone box in the

43

Jardins du Ranelagh watching a pair of children in the sandpit. They were fighting over a bucket.

'Shall I come back?' I asked her.

'No, no. Stay there, Aisha. Please.'

I knew this would be her answer. Teresa would never give up the vicarious joy of my escape from Coelhoso.

'I'll tell you if he needs you,' she said. 'I promise.'

As I told her how to get to Jose's cave, I watched the boy and girl in the sandpit, still locked in their struggle for the bucket. After I had hung up, I walked out of the call box and marched up to them. I snatched the bucket, ignoring their open mouths, and hurled it as far as I could, watching it land in the branches of a horse chestnut. Then I walked away from the shouts of the indignant adults surging forward, and the cries of the two children in their care.

As I walked back to Odile's, I turned my mind away from betrayal. I had told Teresa where to find Jose's cave because he was in danger. At the time I didn't know about concepts like the desire for omnipotence. I had not identified that terrible need in me to control all aspects of his life.

❧

I met Professor Pierre Magnand two weeks later. It was a Saturday in July and I was sitting on a bench in the Champ de Mars reading Albert Cohen's *Belle du Seigneur*. It was Madame Ziou's copy, as thick as a bible, and I was reaching the end. A dishevelled middle-aged man with a shock of wiry grey hair that stood out from his head like Beethoven's sat down beside me. He was watching a little boy on a tricycle and turning the pages of a magazine. Repeatedly he glanced at me and I did my best to ignore him as I read Albert Cohen's story of the death of love, but it was distracting and I became irritated by the intrusion.

'I'm sorry,' he said when I glared at him. 'It's just that I'm envious. I can't think of anything I would like more than to be

44

sitting on a bench on a day like this reading that book for the first time.'

'How do you know it's the first time?'

'You look too young to be on your second reading.'

I studied him. He had a round, almost juvenile face with dark, laughing eyes and a soft, girlish mouth.

The boy with the tricycle was now wrestling with his sister, trying to prise something from her fingers. The father stood up and went to arbitrate. I watched with *Belle du Seigneur* open in my lap.

'Laure can have the whistle until the long hand reaches twelve. Then Joshua can have it till it reaches two.'

The father handed the whistle to his daughter.

'How long is that?' the little girl asked.

'Too long,' her brother said tragically.

Then the little girl put the whistle to her lips and blew in short rhythmical bursts. This was too much for the boy and he threw himself on the ground.

'Go and blow the whistle over there, Laure. I'll call you when it's Joshua's turn.'

Then he lifted the boy onto his shoulders and ran about in circles until the boy's laughter made me smile.

We met again twice in the park before he asked me if I would be interested in looking after his children. He said that their current nanny would soon be leaving them. 'First come and meet my wife Chloë,' he said. 'Then you can decide.'

I told Odile about the offer and she encouraged me to take it, making me promise to come and see her every Sunday.

❧

I moved into the room above Chloë and Pierre's in the summer of our twentieth year. Pierre's wife Chloë had a cold manner that belied her generosity. She had striking powder-blue eyes and a glassy, unsettling gaze. She seemed to survey her children with a detached admiration. They went to her for the rituals of

45

mother-love: a kiss in the morning, when they left for school, when they returned and when they went to bed, but for gratuitous tenderness they went to their father.

It was Chloë who had the money and she was free with it. She took me in, gave me a room on the seventh floor with a kitchenette, a shower and a double bed and paid me more than the going rate for the hours I did. Over the two years that I was with them, she took me on as a project. The transformation was miraculous when I think about who I was when I delivered myself into her hands. From the outset she groomed me, carefully and meticulously smoothing off the rough edges, rubbing out my peasant origins. She seemed to take pleasure in her work and never stopped encouraging me along the path to my conversion. She pushed me in my studies, taught me how to behave, how to speak, how to dress. She gave me her old clothes, took me to the hairdresser, taught me to drive and sent me, with her children, to her house in Provence.

Chloë and Pierre seemed polite and remote with each other. He drifted carelessly in and out of a household which she ran with diligence and precision. Every morning she would leave me elaborate instructions stuck to the fridge. Then she would go to her legal practice near the Jardin du Luxembourg. She took a break for lunch at one, went to the Palais de Justice at two, pleaded until six and then came home. She never took a case that impinged on her private life – except, of course, for my brother's. When I entered her life, I brought chaos with me.

One evening, not long after I arrived, Chloë gave a dinner party. In the kitchen she told me that she didn't expect me to serve them. She wanted me to sit down and eat with them.

'You're here to help me look after the children,' she said. 'You're part of the family. I want you to remember that.'

I felt a wave of gratitude. It was an unfamiliar feeling which made me uneasy. She started to busy herself with the food. I murmured my thanks and turned away.

It was a hot night and all the windows were open onto the avenue. The flat was aglow with scented candles and the smell

46

reminded me of the incense that Father Antonio used for the festival of Santa Barbara.

Among the guests were the neighbours from downstairs, Jean Baptiste and his wife Loup. There was an urologist and his wife, a woman who had been to law school with Chloë and a couple who had a shop on the Seine that sold classical antiques. The conversation turned on the controversy of the moment: the Islamic headscarf and whether or not Muslim girls should be allowed to wear them at school. Pierre had been convinced by an editorial in *Le Monde,* which argued that it was contrary to the values of the Republic to allow pupils to display outward signs of religiosity.

'France has too many demons,' Pierre said. 'The *lycées* must remain secular places.'

I watched Jean Baptiste from the far end of the table. He seemed tired, extinguished beside Pierre.

'Let them wear what they like,' he argued. 'Win them over with education, not rules. Think of the age of these girls. They're adolescents. Don't make their natural rebellion play into the hands of the imams. If we win them over with reason, they'll *want* to be French.'

'They already are French,' Pierre retorted. 'That's why their behaviour is so absurd.'

Chloë served artichokes with lemon dressing. Jean Baptiste's wife Loup sat among us like a ghost, pale and demure. She wore a headscarf to hide the baldness brought on by her recent cancer treatment. Pierre and Jean Baptiste went on arguing, sucking on the leaves and tossing them into a big dish in the middle of the table.

'Anyway,' Pierre went on, 'since when has reason ever held any sway over religion?'

'In the Renaissance,' the antique dealer said, stubbing out his cigarette in an artichoke leaf.

'Only because it was packaged then as a new religion,' Pierre said. 'Today the only weapon democracy has against fanaticism is coercion. Look at the Soviets! They were the only foreigners in Beirut who didn't suffer from the epidemic of kidnapping. You know why? Because after the first time it happened to them, the KGB grabbed an Islamist off the street, cut him up into little pieces and left him on the steps of their embassy. That's the language these people understand.'

Pierre glanced at me and I sensed that all this was somehow for my benefit, that he had detected some violence in me, the peasant among them, and in defiance of his bourgeois friends was paying homage to it.

Jean Baptiste threw up his hands and then withdrew into a sulk. Loup, who was sitting opposite me, kept staring at me, leaving her food untouched on her plate. Chloë served up tiny birds wrapped in pastry parcels, some kind of root vegetable that I had never tasted and a salad with different coloured leaves. Pierre ate voraciously while he talked, stabbing the birds with his fork. When we had finished, I was still hungry.

I was surprised and thrilled when the guests, one by one, kissed me goodbye. Loup hung back until the other couples had gone. Her cold little hand clasped mine as we kissed.

'Would you come and see me? I'm just two floors down,' she said, pointing to the floor.

I told her that I would. Jean Baptiste was holding the lift door open. He seemed embarrassed by the urgency of her request.

'Come on, Loup,' he said. 'It's late.'

That night I lay in my bed in the room on the top floor of the grand apartment building. The sheets were cold and smooth. I looked at the moon through the dormer window at the end of the bed and thought of my brother, alone in his cave. The idea of him coming into this polished world suddenly seemed implausible to me.

A few days later I received another letter from Teresa asking me to come home. Jose was very ill. She said she could not describe his state but she knew that I would want to be with him. To my eternal shame, she was wrong.

Still, I went to Chloë and told her that I had to go home. For some reason I didn't tell her that it was my twin who was ill. I told her that it was my mother. This was the first of many lies.

Chloë paid for my trip back to the village. Before I left she gave me a present, which I unwrapped on the train. It was a brand-new Louis Vuitton suitcase made of leather with a brass combination lock. Like the peasant that I was, I kept on opening the case to breathe in its expensive smell.

I had not seen Jose for ten months.

I arrived late at night and decided to go and see him early the next morning in the hope of waking him. But the climb into the hills was exhausting and took me longer than ever before. City life had put lead in my shoes. I had to stop and rest frequently, and as I stood on the final curve before Jose's plateau, panting for breath, I smiled to myself at the thought of him running ahead of me, teasing me for my new sluggishness.

Nothing could have prepared me for what I saw when I crawled through the entrance to his cave. The place was filthy and it stank of piss. He had painted wounded animals all over the walls. Their teeth were bared and they were dripping blood. When I saw the hundreds of eyes on the ceiling above his bed, I felt a surge of fear.

I turned round to find him watching me from the entrance. His beautiful face was hidden by a beard and his hair was long and matted. His clothes were ragged and his hands were covered in cuts. We stood looking at each other and my heart beat as if I were facing a hostile stranger.

Look what you've done, his eyes said.

I had been thinking about this reunion all night on the train, rocking in my bunk as I had crossed France and all the next day as I crossed Spain. I had imagined throwing my arms around him, giving him his present, telling him stories.

But I couldn't move. I couldn't go near him. He turned and fled.

Back at our stepfather's house my mind swayed between fear and rage. My twin had rejected me. I was filled with self-pity and a new, unfamiliar guilt. All through dinner I chatted to cover up my feelings. I made Cassilda, Katarina and Sylvino laugh with stories about Paris. Sylvino was delighted by the idea of a man celebrating his victory and then falling from his horse and frothing at the mouth. He could not stop laughing and I knew that he would dine out on this baffling impression of Ivan the Ukrainian jockey.

When at last I fell asleep I dreamt that Jose could only breathe under water and was living in old Dino's tank. He had sprouted gills like a cockerel's comb on either side of his head where his ears should have been. The only way I could talk to him was by getting into the icy water with him, but every time I put my foot into the water, the level would drop, leaving my brother in danger of suffocation. *Please, Aisha*, he begged me. *Please come in.* And so I did and the water drained away, leaving him curled up on the floor of the mossy tank, gasping for air.

When I woke up, Katarina was at my side. She smelt as usual of camphor mothballs.

'I heard you shouting. You were having a nightmare. I brought you some tea.'

The tea smelt of lavender and thyme and I sipped it, letting her talk.

'Your mother's pregnant again,' she said with a sigh. 'Let's hope it's a boy this time. But it won't be. She's had terrible morning sickness. If it *is* a boy, pray Heaven he's not like your brother.'

I gave no answer, but sipped my tea.

'Why do you hate me, Aisha?' she said at last.

I looked at her puckered lips.

'I don't hate you. I just don't understand what you're doing in my life, that's all. I don't understand what you're doing in any of our lives.'

She looked at me with her black pebble eyes.

'All I ever wanted was to help,' she said.

I stared coldly at her. Even though I now had the words for

50

my hatred, plenty of words, I said nothing. To me she was an evil meddler who had murdered our parents' love, but I would never give her the opportunity to justify herself. When I went back to sipping my tea, she stood up and left the room.

Christopher has helped me to put my hatred of Katarina in perspective.

'I guess she's a distraction, isn't she? To prevent you from having to look at the truth.'

I find the truth hard to contemplate, even today. It sits like a cold steel ball at the core of my nature. It will never leave me.

Our truth was like a sentence, pronounced before we even entered the world. Those on whom it is pronounced are filled with shame: no mother-love, no mother-love, no mother-love.

❧

The next morning, before anyone was up, I went back to Jose's cave. The sun was still behind the Perdrilha hill, but the little chapel of Santa Barbara on our side was already glowing pink. I walked at a slower pace this time and managed to make the climb without resting. In the rucksack I was carrying blankets, cleaning fluids I had borrowed from our mother's house, a razor, shaving foam and shampoo.

As I slipped behind the cypress tree that grew in front of the cave, I heard him breathing. I listened for a moment, remembering the little boy who had slept in my arms. When I crawled in he sat up immediately. I held out a present I had bought for him. It was a transparent plastic ball with the Arc de Triomphe and the Champs Elysées. I shook it to show him how the scene filled with falling snow. He reached out and took it and I watched him shake it again and again, letting the snow settle completely each time.

Jose sat outside with his snowscape while I cleaned his cave. I dug up the corner where he had been pissing and brought in fresh earth to cover the spot. It was hard work. I burned his old blankets and made up his bed with clean ones. Jose let me scrub the animals off the walls but he wouldn't let me get rid of the eyes. I worked all day and when I had finished, my hands were raw.

In the evening I sat down beside him outside the cave. The setting sun shone on our faces. Words crowded together in my head, clamouring for attention, but I ignored them all. There was nothing to say. I sat beside him until the sun had gone.

At last he got up and went into his cave. Clearly, I would be punished for longer. While I gathered up my things to begin the walk back to the village, he reappeared with his bow and arrow. I felt a surge of happiness. I was to make a fire while he found supper.

He came back with a rabbit, which he cooked with wild thyme.

He wanted me to describe Paris. I held the small plastic souvenir of the Eiffel Tower on the palm of my hand and asked him to imagine that, but as tall as Santa Barbara's hill over there. He shook his head.

'I promise,' I told him. 'At night it lights up, from the ground right up to the tip. It's so tall that the clouds get caught on it.'

He stared at me open-mouthed.

'And there's a shining white cathedral called the Sacré Coeur, which stands on a hill above the city. At the bottom of the hill there are prostitutes and strippers: women, of all shapes and sizes, who take their clothes off for men and let them make love to them for money. There are busloads of English and Germans and Japanese men who come and watch the shows and slip money into the girl's panties. The girls wear brightly coloured feathers and bikinis made out of diamonds and they dance like this.'

I stood up to show him. He watched all agog as I wiggled my arse about and stuck my tits out. 'What do you think? Wouldn't *you* pay me money?'

But he had covered his face.

'Oh Jose, I'm teasing. I don't do that. I go to school. I can speak French fluently now. Listen.' And I sat down beside him and took his hand. 'I have a job looking after two children,' I told him in French. 'Their names are Joshua and Laure. He's five and she's six. Their father is a professor of philosophy and their mother is a lawyer for criminals. They're very rich but they're kind.'

He understood some of what I had said, including the word 'rich'.

He wanted to know: *how rich?*

'Much richer than old Dino. They have more money than all the people in this village put together.'

More money than Father Antonio?

I let go of his hand.

'Weren't you listening? I said more money than the whole *village*. That *includes* Father Antonio.'

An owl hooted and we sat together in silence in the fading light, our eyes wide to the sounds of the wood behind us.

I still wasn't ready to sleep with him in his cave and so I went home. The next day he let me near him to cut his nails. I had no scissors, so I used his knife, which was very sharp. Then I cut his hair and shaved him.

'There. You're handsome again,' I said, kissing his smooth cheek.

But he did not respond. He held himself perfectly still, as though my kiss hurt him, and I felt as though I had been punched in the chest.

While I was in the village our mother had another miscarriage and started bleeding heavily. She went to bed and Katarina predicted the Change of Life. Sylvino stopped talking to me, as though I were somehow responsible for his wife's condition. He was angry because he knew that he would never have a son. Whenever he wanted to tell me something, he would address Katarina.

'Tell her we're going shooting up there in the morning, so they'd better stay out of the way.'

'Shooting', I said. 'Thanks to you people there's nothing left

53

to shoot. I can't believe you shoot even the songbirds.'

'Ask her what's wrong with songbirds?'

'They're meant for singing, you peasant! Not for eating!'

Sylvino no longer rose when I called him a peasant, just as I no longer responded to him calling me a slut.

'Enough, Sylvino!' Katarina shouted.

Her new thing was to pretend to be on my side. But I knew that the war between Sylvino and me suited her. She had already seen that I could make money and wanted me to remember her as my ally. She courted my favour over the three weeks I was in the village, making baskets of provisions for me to take up to Jose's cave.

At the end of my first week back I began to read Stendhal's *The Red and the Black* to Jose, translating it from French as I went. As we ventured deeper and deeper into the story, we forgot my betrayal and sank back into the idyll of our childhood. In the day we lay in our old spot by the *rio* and at night Jose would make a fire in the mouth of the cave and we would sit beside it reading in the light of the flames. But as we came closer and closer to the end, we were both aware of trying to ignore the knowledge, like some creeping shadow, that I had abandoned him once and would do it again.

❦

When I returned to Paris on 1 September, I discovered that Jean Baptiste's wife Loup had been taken into hospital. I'm sure now that my devotion to her in the last days of her life was a form of penance, a way of eluding my guilt about Jose.

I visited Loup every day in my free time in order to read to her. The cancer had metastasized in the brain and the inoperable tumour was pressing on her optic nerve, impairing her vision. She would listen with her eyes closed, occasionally correcting my pronunciation. A horse chestnut was turning orange outside her room and I would open the frosted glass window so that she could smell the leaves and listen to them moving in the breeze. I read her *Belle du Seigneur*. At the time I didn't question Loup's reasons for wanting to hear a story about the emptiness of social ambition and the futility of romantic love. To me the book spoke of something powerful and exquisite and unknown, that I could feel all around me, beating its wings. This time I didn't get to the end of the story. Loup died one night in mid-October, before Solal and Ariane's idyll of passion had begun to turn sour.

I would often encounter Pierre as I was leaving the hospital. He would walk with me through the grounds to the exit. Soon we became aware that we were both engineering these meetings.

'That's a pretty dress.'

'It was Chloë's. She gave it to me.'

'How funny, I didn't recognize it.'

It was a cornflower-blue dress that she must have chosen to go with her eyes. I remember feeling irritated with Pierre for not having admired her in it.

'Aisha,' he said, 'it is very kind of you to visit Loup.'

'I like visiting her.'

We were walking along an avenue of plane trees. In a moment the use of my name had brought all our careful behaviour to nothing. I felt the cool bark against my back. Pierre was kissing me and I was kissing him back.

For weeks after the kiss, I avoided him. I would try to leave the flat before he got home and then I would sit in my room upstairs, thinking about him. I thought of the smell of coffee and wine on his breath, of the dimples which appeared in his cheeks when he smiled, and of his hair, which grew out of his head like wire and couldn't be combed. I liked the way the expensive suits Chloë bought him quickly became baggy and unkempt. I was touched by him: by the way he walked, slightly tipped forward, and by the fact that he was always late.

Then came the day of Loup's funeral. We buried her at Père Lachaise in the morning and afterwards Chloë held a lunch party at the apartment. Pierre tried not to watch me as I moved about the room filling people's glasses. Jean Baptiste drank too much and cried. Pierre comforted him while the other guests pretended not to see. When the sobbing grew too loud, people began to creep off, kissing Chloë on their way out. The afternoon was hot and airless and full of thunder. While Chloë was picking up the children from her mother's flat on the other side of Paris, the storm broke. The wind drove the rain in swathes, slamming the windows and smashing a pane. I hurried to close them and looked out at the avenue, awash with leaves and branches ripped from the trees – Jose always loved a storm.

While Pierre listened to Jean Baptiste recount his first meeting with Loup, I cleared up.

'It was in Courchevel,' he said. 'She was wearing an enormous fur hat with her little face peeping out. She looked so vulnerable. Like a small animal. That was the first and last time in my life anyone had made me want to look after them.' He began to cry again. 'Never again. What an idiot I was. Who did I think I had become all of a sudden? Loup was an aberration which lasted thirty years.'

Chloë called to say that she would spend the night at her mother's and drive back in the morning. Most of Paris, she said, was jammed. Apparently the Seine had overflowed and both expressways were closed to traffic.

Pierre and I took Jean Baptiste downstairs to his flat, helped him onto his marital bed, broad and high as an altar, and took off his shoes. Then, without a word, we went up to my room.

Although I had often lain in bed at night imagining some boy's hands on my body, I had, until Pierre, repelled all assaults on my virginity. The few boys in Coelhoso who had been brave enough or drunk enough to make a pass at me had been flailed by my legendary scorn. I don't think Pierre knew that he was my first lover. He seemed more nervous than I was as I stood before him in that room and took all my clothes off – except for, for some reason, my shoes, which stayed on the whole time. Pierre came quickly, leaving me little time to feel anything but curiosity.

We were leaning up against the wall and afterwards his legs gave way and he pulled me onto the floor and fell asleep, holding me in his arms. I determined, as I watched him sleep, that with him I would learn to love this strange act, so full of possibility.

When Pierre woke up he kissed me. Then he pulled away and I saw tears in his eyes.

'It's all right,' he told me. 'I'm not unhappy. I cry easily.'

'How easily?'

'With the right music, figure skating can make me cry,' he said.

The idea of this university professor weeping over a couple dressed in spangled lycra and whirling around to Tchaikovsky made me laugh. He told me then that I should laugh more often.

I got up, put my dress back on and made us a cup of coffee. The gutter outside my window was full of leaves, so Pierre started to empty it for me. I remember watching his hairy bottom and the big drum of his stomach and his curved penis bouncing on his balls as he went about scooping up the leaves and dropping them into a plastic bag.

'I've always liked it up here,' he said. 'No one can look in.'

He told me that it was in this room that he would wish to write his novel when he eventually got round to it.

'What about me?' I asked, handing him the mug of coffee. 'Where will I go then?'

'You could stay here with me,' he said with a smile.

As we sat there, drinking our coffee, me clothed and him naked, he began to ask questions.

'Where are you from?'

'Portugal.'

'I know, but where?'

'A small village near Bragança.'

'What is its name?'

'Coelhoso.'

'The place of rabbits.'

'You speak Portuguese?'

'A few words. I went to Coimbra once as a visiting professor.'

The idea of him speaking my language made me uncomfortable.

'What do your parents do?' he asked.

'They're peasants.'

'What kind? What do they cultivate?'

'Everything. Wheat, olives . . . everything.'

'They survive on what they produce?'

'Not really.'

'You help them?'

'My father's dead,' I told him. 'I don't get on with my stepfather. That's why I left. But I don't want to talk about it.'

I imagine that Pierre developed a theory about his place in my life, based on this meagre information. He tiptoed around the gaps in my past, guessing at a world of abuse and suffering. I did not tell him that I had a twin.

❧

Pierre often mentioned Chloë when we were together, as if her name, spoken with tenderness and respect, were a charm against the ugliness of what we were doing. I never voiced my shame to him. Not once. He made it clear that this would make things even uglier. Perhaps the experience of adultery was part of my conversion to bourgeois values. Pierre sometimes made it seem that way. For him, adultery was for other people. We had a passion, he explained, and a duty to that passion as serious as the duty to preserve the feelings of the people around us.

'When you build a fire in a forest to keep warm, you protect the environment,' he once said. 'It's a matter of *savoir vivre*.'

In the week before Christmas Chloë sent the children to her

mother's *manoir* in Normandy. It was better if I didn't go with them, she explained. Marthe, a young woman who had worked there since she was fourteen and who had known Joshua and Laure since they were babies, would take offence. I was to give the Paris apartment a good clean and look after Pierre while she went skiing with a group of friends. Pierre had always detested skiing. He said it was the most fatuous of all bourgeois pastimes.

My passion for Pierre blazed that week – if something so calculating can be called a passion. I had come to realize that he had more knowledge in that leonine skull of his than Teresa had in her entire library. I must have sensed that making love to him was the quickest way to access his intellect. At the time I was unable to tell apart my love for his brain and my love for his body.

While I spring-cleaned in my underwear, Pierre sat in his dressing gown, preparing a new series of lectures for his course in Classical Philosophy. The rest of the time we made love or read.

After sex I would lie on his chest and he would read to me from Virgil's *Aeneid*, stopping occasionally to comment on the world-view that lay behind some of the passages. We read Ovid's *Metamorphoses* and I thought of how much Jose would love these stories of men fashioned from the earth and women turning into trees because they didn't want to have sex.

That was how I discovered philosophy, in bed with Pierre, his deep professorial voice resounding in his chest. The early days of our affair come back to me as an interlude, whole and severed from the rest of my life. That week we were on a raft. We would make love and read and make love again. For a short while Jose didn't exist.

֍

I spent Christmas with Chloë and Pierre in Normandy. Pierre

59

and I had one brief fuck in a barn and the rest of the time he mooned about in a sulk.

I was happy playing with the children, making a snowman, walking on the long grey beaches, breaking the ice on the puddles.

When we returned to Paris a week later I discovered that Chloë had had my room repainted. The walls were lavender blue and there were white curtains with a matching counterpane for my bed. I had a new bedside light with a pale green shade. I sat down on the bed and swore that I would end the affair with Pierre.

The next morning I went downstairs to find Chloë. She was alone in the kitchen, making breakfast. I stood in the doorway.

'Thank you for my room,' I said.

She looked up and smiled at me.

'I'm glad you like it.'

'I do.'

'Good,' she said. 'I thought perhaps I should have told you. Let you choose the colours . . .'

'No, no, I couldn't have chosen. I would have told you to choose.'

As we laid the table she asked after my mother's health. I told her that she was fine, though I'd had no news of her since September.

'She had a miscarriage,' I said to fill in the gap.

Chloë expressed her sympathy, but was dissuaded from asking more questions. This was not the kind of subject that she felt comfortable with. She poured me a cup of coffee and came straight to the point.

'Pierre says that before you came to Paris, you were planning to go to university in Portugal. You know there are equivalencies. We think you should try and enrol here.'

'I'm happy working for you.'

'You can work for us *and* study. We'll get organized.'

'Thank you, but I'm fine.'

'Tell me, Aisha, what were you going to study?'

'Literature.'

'Is that what you'd like to do?'

'Not really.'

'What then?'

I hesitated. Her bright blue eyes were fixed on me. She never looked happier than when she was helping someone.

'Philosophy.'

For a moment she seemed to be wondering about me. Was I dangerous? I looked down and she must have thought that I was shy.

'Why philosophy?'

I hesitated.

'It's broader than literature,' I said.

She waited, unsatisfied by my answer.

'I want to grapple with the ideas behind the stories. Stories ask questions but they don't answer them.'

She smiled proudly at me.

'You should probably have Pierre, then,' she said. 'He's the best.'

⚜

I wasn't there when Chloë announced to Pierre her ambitions for me. I doubt he realised that she was indirectly responsible for prolonging our affair.

He came up to my room that evening and leaned against the door, looking at me with amusement.

'So.'

'So what?'

'So you're going to be my pupil.'

'It wasn't my idea.'

'She's remarkable, isn't she? I wouldn't be surprised if she knows.'

The idea shocked me.

'I think we should stop.'

'Come here.'

I stood still, looking at him. I felt lust, mixed with a creeping disgust for him and for my own ambition.

He came forward and took me in his arms and kissed me. When he pulled away he said, 'You'll have to work hard. I won't be any easier on you than the others. Just because I'm in love with you . . .'

The rest I didn't hear.

⁊

In. Love. With. You. I was flattered, smitten, struck dumb by those words said in that order. I had, after all, gorged myself on the great romantic novels. Ambition flows through those stories, the dark underbelly of romantic love. Emma Bovary, Ariane Deume, Julien Sorel.

I would enrol for the autumn term. Until then, Pierre would coach me.

That year I worked forty hours a week for Chloë, starting at midday and ending at eight, except for Wednesday mornings which I had off to go to the library. On Saturday mornings I looked after the children so that Chloë and Pierre could sleep in. I presumed, without resentment, that this was the time they set aside for sex. Sunday was my day off. In the morning I would visit Odile and we would play cards, mostly a game called *belote* that I never liked, and she would tell me about her filthy guests. Since I had gone, the revulsion she felt for the traces that they left behind on the sheets or the towels or in the bathroom seemed increasingly to outweigh the need for income. Since I had left, attendance had slacked off but she did not seem to care. She drew her pension and talked to her parrot and every Saturday went to the PMU to bet on the horses, just as her father had done.

I studied every night until at least two in the morning. I met no one except for the guests at Chloë and Pierre's dinner parties. I never went out with anyone of my own age. I was Pierre and Chloë's creature.

Chloë paid me four hundred euros a week of which I spent very little. By the end of my first year I had saved almost ten thousand euros, five thousand of which I had used as a down payment on a second-hand John Deere for Sylvino. I also learned to drive. Chloë paid for lessons with a Yugoslav baritone called Bruno who chewed gum and sang opera out of the passenger window.

Chloë and Pierre were a little afraid of their children. They saw future recrimination everywhere and crept about in its shadow, subjecting Joshua and Laure to daily multiple choice:

'Would you like to have your supper now, Joshua, or take your bath first? Would you like to go to the park and then go swimming, or shall we take the bikes to the Bois de Boulogne?'

Depending on his mood, Joshua would give the answer he thought they wanted, or the answer he thought they didn't want.

Laure was less contrary. She simply didn't answer or else would shrug and say, 'Don't care'. This worried Chloë in particular, who believed she would ultimately be made to pay for not having forced her daughter to express her desires.

Neither Pierre nor Chloë noticed that the children never objected when they were not presented with a choice.

'Today we're going to visit Odile,' I would tell them and they would run and get their coats. 'And grab something from the biscuit tin for the parrot please, Laure.'

Joshua liked video games and spent hours in front of the computer, playing a game called *Halo* in which the character's face is hidden by a mask. His parents were torn between the fear of what it was doing to his psyche and the fear of sharpening his appetite for it through rationing. Sometimes his mother would march up to the computer and pull the plug out, and Joshua would roll about on the floor, kicking and screaming because she had in an instant rubbed out two hours of progress.

I could always distract him with stories. He would lie in my arms and suck his thumb. Laure could take or leave stories.

She liked drawing.

'What shall I draw?' she would ask.

'Draw me a unicorn and a rainbow, and a castle and a tree, and a woman with a magic lamp.'

'And a tank,' Joshua said.

'A fish tank?' Laure asked.

'No, stupid. A tank. With a gun turret.'

'No.'

'Draw a tank.'

'I don't want to.'

'Please.'

'No.'

'When my brother was little,' I interrupted, 'he used to think that rainbows sucked up the water from the earth into the sky when it was thirsty.'

'That's stupid,' Laure said, leaning over her picture.

'Well, where I come from it sort of makes sense because rainbows always come after a drought.'

'What's a drought?' Laure asked.

'How old is your brother?' Joshua interrupted.

'He's the same age as me. We're twins.'

Laure looked up and stared at me.

'Who came out first?'

'I did.'

'Do you fight?'

'No.'

'Never?'

'No, never.'

She shot a guilty glance at Joshua and then went back to her drawing.

Laure liked being ill. She had discovered that this was the only way to get her mother's undivided attention and every month or so she brought on a fever that kept her in bed for three days. Her bouts of illness suited Joshua too, who was able to retreat unnoticed into his *Halo* trance.

One morning as I was squeezing oranges for breakfast,

Chloë walked into the kitchen in her dressing gown and stood there for a moment watching me. I smiled at her but something about her made me uneasy.

'Why didn't you tell us you had a twin, Aisha?'

I went on squeezing the oranges.

'Laure told me you had a twin brother and that you never argue.'

I stopped what I was doing and looked over at Chloë, feigning detachment.

'I just didn't think you'd be particularly interested.'

'How can you say that, Aisha? Of course we're interested in you.' And for the second time she added, 'You're part of the family.'

When she said it I'm sure she believed it.

❦

Teresa's letters were the only news of Jose I had. She would always urge me to work hard at my studies and not to worry about him. She was keeping an eye on him. She said that he was taking the books she was leaving him and reading them at a remarkable rate. One evening she had met him down at the mine and actually managed to coax him home for supper. After that, Jose ate regularly with them. She said that their two teenage boys loved and admired him. He would show up after dark with the book he had finished and she would give him another. Soon she had to get books out of the Bragança library for him. Teresa said that she wished she could hear what he thought of them. 'It's a great irony,' she wrote, 'that the only person left in the village I feel I could really talk to is mute!'

Her letters convinced me that Jose was no longer at risk and so I decided not to go home that summer. Even though I had enough money saved up to bring him over, I didn't. I was distracted, in both senses of the word, by desire and ambition.

Pierre and I became skilled at stealing time together. We met three mornings a week to have sex. Pierre had taken up jog-

65

ging to provide an alibi and would get up at six and put on his running shoes and creep away from his sleeping family. Instead of running around the Jardins du Ranelagh for half an hour, he would run round the block and come in through the side entrance of the building. He would take the service lift to the seventh floor and knock on my door. I would let him in and he would crawl into my bed and make love to me while I was still half-asleep, leaving before I was fully awake. I imagined him slipping back into his flat half an hour later, sweaty and weak from ejaculation, then climbing into the shower to wash my smell off his skin.

In July, Chloë went to Tunisia for two weeks with a girl-friend and Pierre came up to my bed every night after the children had gone to sleep. We fucked in the summer heat until we were ragged and worn, and lay panting at each other's side like two dogs. All the next day, I would fight off sleep in the library, the memory of physical desire coming back to me in waves.

When Chloë returned, the sexual withdrawal made Pierre resentful. He could not show her, so he showed me. I was relieved to have her back, to return to my books and the more balanced routine of our thrice-weekly meetings. My acceptance upset Pierre. He said that it was proof of a certain detachment in me, which frightened him. He began a new pattern of punishment, disappearing for days at a time and then returning full of desire and remorse. I preferred things as they were before.

In August we went to Chloë's house in Provence. I read Proust and taught the children how to swim. Chloë, who was in her fortieth year, discovered she was pregnant and disappeared for three days to have an abortion. When she came back, her face was drained of colour and she could not look any of us in the eye. Pierre took her for a long weekend to a luxury hotel in Antibes. When they came back, they announced their decision to return together to Paris to work. They would leave me the car and return on the weekends.

On the way to the station I sat in the back of the car with the children, avoiding Pierre's desperate gaze in the rear-view mirror. Chloë sat in silence, looking out of her window at the flourishing vines. She had lost her pallor and had a new calm about her that made Pierre more attentive. His anxiety seemed equally divided between the fear of losing me and the fear of losing her.

While Joshua and Laure waved goodbye to their parents I sped away from the station without looking back, feeling elated and free.

Every day I would think of Jose. I talked to the children about him so often that Joshua soon became obsessed.

'Would Jose do this?' he would ask. 'Does Jose like spaghetti?' They often asked me when he would come to Paris.

'Soon,' I said.

Joshua and Laure thrived on the mindless routine of that summer. Every morning we woke up and cycled to the *boulangerie* to buy bread and croissants: past the scary Alsatian on a chain, in and out of the eight poplars, down the wet gully where they shot the wild boar, up the hill, past the fat lady with the hair-band, around the mossy fountain and past the chickens to Eric and Marilyn's shop. Laure loved Marilyn because she had a tattoo of a dolphin on her flat stomach and Joshua liked Eric because he looked like a superhero and because he ignored him.

After breakfast we would play in the pool and after lunch, in the heat of the day, I would read to them or else invent stories, urged on to a greater and greater pitch of violence by Joshua, who preferred stories in which the hero died an impossibly painful death. Then the children would sleep and I would read, and when they woke up, as the village clock was striking four, we would cycle back to Marilyn and Eric's for an ice-cream. I had strawberry, Laure had *pistache* and Joshua had chocolate. In the evenings we swam in the pool and then played on the flat band of grass between the lavender beds. Laure and Joshua would usually fight before dinner. I would water the garden and then I'd tell them a story involving Jose and some baddy in the form of an evil farmer with an Alsatian with drooling fangs.

Pierre and Chloë came back every Friday night to spend the weekend. I remember the night of 15 August, Assumption Day. It was their wedding anniversary, a hot, airless night with a full moon. Pierre and Chloë had been to Avignon for dinner and came home a little drunk. I was out on the terrace reading when I heard them both giggling and whispering in the children's bedroom. A few minutes later, Pierre came out with a glass of cognac in his hand.

'What are you reading?'

I showed him the cover.

'Rimbaud. Lucky you.'

We heard Chloë knock something over on her dressing table.

'Aisha,' he whispered, 'please don't leave me.'

I couldn't see his face because of the glare of the moon behind him, but I could feel a chill settling inside me that I knew could only spread.

❦

When we returned to Paris I told Pierre that I no longer wanted to sleep with him. As he stood at my door in his running clothes, his body seemed to go slack.

'Let me in,' he said.

'No.'

'Please, Aisha. I have to sit down.'

'I don't want you to come in. We'll go out.'

'Aisha, please.'

'We'll go to a café.'

We went to the Jardins du Ranelagh and sat on a bench. The street cleaners were spraying the streets. The ground was littered with horse-chestnut leaves. Pierre sat in stunned silence.

I looked at my watch.

'You mustn't be late,' I said. 'You have twenty minutes.'

'I don't care.'

'You will if you lose Chloë.'

He took my hand.

'Don't you like our sex?'

'It's not that I don't like it. I don't want to do it any more. I feel like we were in a dream and we've woken up.'

'I haven't woken up. I don't want to wake up.'

I took my hand away.

'You didn't want to but you already have. You woke up weeks ago. When Chloë went off to have an abortion.'

He looked at me in horror for having said such an ugly word. Had I learnt nothing from him?

'That was none of your business,' he said coldly.

'You're married. That's my business.'

He smiled bitterly.

'Surely you can do better than that. You should be able to avoid that kind of banality by now.'

'It's reality.'

'You're a child, Aisha. You have no lessons to give on reality.'

At this I stood up and walked away. Pierre followed me.

'Relationships change,' he said. 'They evolve.'

I stopped and turned to face him.

'They do,' I said. 'It has to end. My twin brother is coming.'

'Is that why you're ending it?'

'No.' I hesitated. 'Yes.'

As I walked away, he opened his hands.

'I don't understand,' I heard him say.

When I had told him my brother was coming, I had felt a surge of adrenalin. At the time I didn't know why. I had no idea then how dangerous my summoning Jose would be. As I walked towards the telephone box, I mistook the heady feeling for power; some kind of erotic power over Pierre, perhaps, as well as over Jose. On the phone I told Teresa to put him on a bus as soon as possible. Then I crossed Trocadéro, weaving through the screaming traffic, walked into a café and ordered a brandy. After a second glass, the heady feeling had gone.

⊙⊹⊙

Three days later, Teresa drove Jose to Bragança and put him on the bus to Paris. When he pulled into the terminus at Trocadéro, I saw his face behind the glass and I waved and clapped and laughed. He stepped off the bus and I put my arms around him. He smelt of sweat and Teresa's salt cod. He held me tightly for a long time in that immense square and I felt a rush of fear. He had a suitcase with wheels on it that must have been a gift from Teresa. He picked it up and clasped it to his chest and his face lit up with joy. He was looking past me at the Eiffel Tower.

On the walk home to Chloë and Pierre's, his silence was heavy. I had never felt awkward with him before. I talked frantically in an attempt to fill the space between us, about Chloë and Pierre and the children, about Odile Moulin and her hotel, but I knew that I didn't fool him, nor did I fool myself.

When we stepped into the marble hall of the apartment building I could not look at him. I had noticed that his jacket was too short in the arms.

'I'm tired,' I told him as we stepped into the lift. 'Let's spend the evening alone. You can meet Chloë and Pierre tomorrow.'

I closed the metal gates and pressed the button to the seventh floor, my face burning with shame. I didn't notice Jose turn pale as the lift rose. When we stepped out into the top corridor, he threw up onto his boots.

I sat on the bed and watched his back as he washed his boots in the sink.

'Did Teresa give you those?'

He spun round and looked at me.

'Luis?' I suggested.

He nodded.

'They were his?'

No, he objected. They were brand new. A present. But even the joy of this present, he seemed to say, has been swept away by what you're doing to me now.

I stood up then and crossed the room and buried my face in his chest. He put his arms around me and I let him hold me long enough to know that I was sorry.

When it was time to sleep, he lay down on the floor beside my bed, fully clothed and with no blankets. I lay awake for hours that night, watching the night sky through the window and listening to his breathing. He was with me and yet I felt a distance between us greater than ever before. My throat was tight from the fight against tears. I lay there and remembered waking up from a fever as a child and finding him on the floor fast asleep, beside me. My mind roamed between the past and the future, from our village to this city and back again, searching for a clue to my fear.

The next morning was Sunday and I woke up late to find Jose gone. I jumped out of bed and pulled on some clothes. I imagined him lost in the big city. I had driven him away. I saw myself searching the streets for him for days, months, years.

I ran down the seven flights of stairs. Someone had forgotten to shut the lift gates and it was stuck on the third floor. I stopped running in the hall. Through the glass doors I saw him standing beside a tree on the other side of the avenue.

I showed him how to open the doors by punching out a code.

'You have to remember the number,' I told him. He pressed the four digits and the door clicked open. Then he did it again and again and again.

'Where did you go?' I asked him, leading him away.

He had been to the river to watch the boats. I imagined him sitting on the bank of the Seine as the sun came up, watching the barges glide past.

71

'Did you see any dogs?'

He shook his head.

'Some of them have dogs on board that ride on the bow,' I told him.

Until then Jose had never seen a boat, except for the tugboat made out of matchsticks that I had given him. He had never imagined that they could be so big.

'People live on them,' I told him. 'I'll show you a place where there are lots of them.'

We went to have breakfast in one of the cafés on Trocadéro. Jose had hot chocolate and a *croissant*. I was happy to watch him and shut from my mind his impending encounter with the rest of my life. I had not yet told Chloë and Pierre that he had arrived.

That day we walked arm in arm around Paris. There was a chill in the air and the light was golden. We walked along the Seine from the Place de la Concorde to the Louvre and looked at the houseboats. Jose stood and stared at a woman who was sitting on the deck of her barge reading a book.

He wanted to know when she would leave, when she would sail away.

'Oh, she won't leave. These boats aren't meant for the sea. They stay here, in Paris.' I distracted Jose from disappointment, as I had always done. 'Let's go and visit my friend Odile,' I said, taking his hand.

On the bus to Odile's, Jose was enjoying the machine for validating the tickets. The driver became so irritated by the noise that he asked him to stop. His tone was aggressive and I could see that Jose was shocked. Again, I began to worry about how he would fit into my life here.

Odile opened her arms and welcomed him and did not balk for one moment at his silence.

'Come in,' she said, holding out her hand to him. 'There's someone I want you to meet.'

She led him into the kitchen and straight to the parrot's cage. The blue and gold macaw had lost much of her plumage on her right side and she stood with her good side facing us, dipping and weaving on her perch. As soon as Jose leaned down and looked into her cage, Kiki stopped her neurotic dance. He looked up at Odile.

'He wants to know if he can take her out,' I said.

'Oh, I'm afraid she won't come out. She's very suspicious and she bites.'

Jose looked at me.

'He has a way with birds,' I told her.

Odile shrugged.

'Why not? Have a go.'

Jose opened the cage and held out his hand. The parrot cocked her head and looked sideways at him, then shuffled along her perch, stopping at the entrance to her cage. Jose reached in and took the bird in a hold that was both firm and gentle. The bird moaned sadly and Jose opened his hand. She hopped onto his wrist.

'Well,' said Odile, 'I would never have imagined. Even Thierry couldn't do that. And she loved Thierry.'

We sat together in Odile's kitchen and ate her meatballs while the parrot perched on Jose's shoulder opening and shutting her wings.

I did not take Jose to meet Chloë and Pierre that day, or the next. I went to work without him, letting him wander the streets until I had finished. I didn't start at the Sorbonne until 1 October and so I began to teach him French. We read *The Red and the Black* again, this time lingering over every word. Jose sat beside me, frowning over the text, absorbing my translation. I felt a narcissistic pride in him, believing that his remarkable memory was a version of my own, enhanced by years of isolation.

On sunny days we would catch the bus to our favourite park on the hill at Saint-Cloud, overlooking Paris. We would sit on a wooden bench, which had been donated by a certain Madame de Ganay in loving memory of her husband René. It looked out over the curling river, the thick green stripe of the

Bois de Boulogne and the city beyond, shining in the sun like a pale mosaic.

⽞

On 11 September Pierre came looking for me. It was lunchtime in Paris when he knocked on my door and the people of New York were still sleeping in blissful ignorance of what was to come. I was cooking spaghetti and Jose was sitting in the corner, reading over the words he had just learnt. He looked up and smiled at Pierre, who turned away rudely, thinking he must be my new lover.

'I have to talk to you,' Pierre whispered.

'This is my brother,' I told him. 'Jose, this is Pierre.'

'Your brother,' Pierre said, a warm smile appearing on his face.

Then he crossed the room and shook Jose's hand.

'Pleased to meet you.'

'Jose doesn't speak,' I said. 'Are you hungry?'

'No,' Pierre said, holding up his hands. 'I don't want to disturb you. I'll come back another time.'

At the door, he gripped my arm.

'We have to talk, Aisha.'

'Everything is always urgent for you,' I told him. 'It's a form of tyranny.'

'You used to see it as a form of desire,' he said, letting go of my arm.

I looked at him standing there on the landing. Workmen renovating the building were on their lunch break and had left the corridor stripped bare. White dust sheets covered the floor. He looked forlorn standing there in that pale, austere setting. I thought of the heat our bodies had made in that little room, the heat from our eyes and our mouths as we lay facing each other, all enfolded in the mirage of fusion.

I told him to come back in a few hours.

When, that afternoon, the suicide bomber flew the first

hijacked plane into the first tower, my brother was sitting on the banks of the Seine reading Stendhal and Pierre was on his stomach, my legs around his ears, giving me oral sex. When the second plane hit the second tower, Jose was still reading, I was sleeping in the afterglow of orgasm and Pierre was walking in that crisp, radiant autumn day feeling overcome with what he later described as an inexplicable emptiness.

He missed out on the intellectual tumult in the staff room as his colleagues watched the attacks live on television because he was walking in the Jardins du Ranelagh feeling sorry for himself. When he finally appeared in class at six that evening, he was unaware of how the world had shifted in a single afternoon. I'm sure that the contrary position he took on the matter of the attacks on America was built on his feeling of shame at having 'missed' them and on his strange, post-coital state on that apocalyptic day.

The prevailing view among his colleagues in the faculty, that America had earned her punishment, irritated Pierre profoundly and he began to make enemies for the first time in his life.

The following weekend I took Jose to meet Chloë and the children. Chloë clasped his hand and gazed into his eyes, making me think of some elegant celebrity pressing flesh for the UN. Pierre held Jose responsible for the end of our affair and could hardly bring himself to look at him.

Chloë, who was delighted with my brother's good looks, was soon showering him with presents, spoiling him as she had spoiled me. At first she simply left out Pierre's tired shirts for him. Then she began to buy him things of his own: cotton pyjamas, a watch, a leather briefcase for his books. She was thrilled. It was as if, with the arrival of my twin, her project had taken on a bolder, grander design.

Every afternoon after school, Jose took Laure and Joshua to the Jardins du Ranelagh, while I went to the library to finish my reading list. Jose played football with Joshua, carrying Laure on his back to hobble himself. When the library closed,

I would go to meet them. Laure learnt to speak on Jose's behalf. She would boast about his muteness to strangers.

'He doesn't talk,' she explained to people. 'Because he doesn't *want* to.'

❦

I attended my first lecture at the Sorbonne on 6 October. The subject was Freud's theory of the death instinct and the lecturer was Professor Pierre Magnand. When I arrived, the lecture had started and the amphitheatre was full. I went to the back of the huge, echoing room with its domed ceiling and marble walls, and watched Pierre stride up and down the podium, one hand holding the microphone and the other driven into the pocket of his shabby linen suit.

Freud, Pierre's voice boomed, had the wisdom to change his mind: *Il n'y a que des imbéciles qui ne changent pas d'avis.* He paused to let his students laugh. The young Freud's thought, he went on, rested at first on the theory of the libido and the pleasure principle, on Eros and the life instinct. As the old man approached death and its reality began to settle within him, he came to believe in the equal drives towards life and death. All cellular life, he reasoned, was a pull in both directions, towards creation and destruction. At the time I did not guess at the relevance of that particular lecture to my own destiny and to that of my twin.

At first the language of philosophy was a struggle for me and I would pore over the books, trying to unravel each sentence, tears of frustration in my eyes, wishing that I still had Pierre to help me. I would read late into the night, the dictionary of philosophy that Chloë had given me open beside me, while Jose slept on his futon on the floor. Chloë wanted to find a room for him in a nearby building but I discouraged her because I was so happy to be back in our old, complicit silence. Our first autumn in Paris had me fooled. I thought we were back together.

At the end of term Pierre held a seminar on Plato's *Symposium* in which he focused on Aristophanes' version of the Genesis myth. In the beginning, Plato wrote, there were three sexes: man, woman and a third sex that was both. These primeval creatures were round and had two heads facing in opposite directions, two sets of genitals – male and female – four arms and four legs and they rolled about at great speed. They were so powerful that they began to wage war on the gods, so the gods started to destroy them. At last Zeus took pity on them and decided that the solution would be to divide and rule, so he cut our ancestors down the middle as though he were halving an apple, or as Plato puts it, *as if he were cutting an egg in two with a hair*. From then on, each half sought out its opposite. Whenever they met, they threw their arms around each other in an attempt to merge into one. I wonder if it occurred to Pierre when he read the story to us that I was one of those creatures.

⚬⟊⚬

For five months Jose and I shared my room on the seventh floor. Every evening I taught him French and in the day, while I was at my lectures, he studied. The first French book he read without my help was *The Stranger* by Camus. When I returned home one evening he looked up at me from the red IKEA chair that Chloë had given him and I saw an expression on his face that I had never seen before.

'What? What is it?'

He held out the book to me.

'I know. It's good, isn't it?'

But he shook his head.

'You didn't like it?'

He nodded vigorously.

'You did. But it's sad.'

It was, of course, more than good or sad. He wanted his own words to tell me what it was.

He was despondent all evening and I could not shift his mood. After that he no longer wanted me to read to him. He wanted more books to read by himself. And so I got them for him. Every other day I would return with a new one. He read them all but he was becoming more discerning. He liked Maupassant but not Zola, he liked Camus but Rousseau sent him into a rage. His headaches returned. He would sit in his red chair, head lolled back, an icepack over his eyes, groaning. I told him I thought he was reading too much, that it was bad for his eyes, but he would not stop. I began to creep about in his presence, fearful of a new kind of frustration which I could feel gathering momentum inside him.

❦

By the end of Jose's first six months in Paris I found myself being increasingly careful with him. He read all the time and his reading made him moody. He started to write things down for me instead of communicating with me in the usual way. The note-writing upset me and I began to avoid his company, staying out late with people in my class. By the end of term, we were barely communicating at all.

At the beginning of March 2002 I suggested that he get a job. He was sitting in his chair reading a bible he had got out of the library. I also wanted to ask him for his socks because they needed washing, but he no longer allowed me to do his laundry.

'What do you think, Jose? We could ask Chloë if she could find you something. You could do gardening,' I suggested cheerily. 'Or work in a zoo. Wouldn't you like that?'

Jose looked up from the bible and smiled absently at me. The sight of him going through the motions made me catch my breath. He went back to his reading.

The next day he went out and found himself a job. When I came home that evening, he handed me a note. As I read it, I flushed and had to turn away.

I got a job at Quick. I'm on French fries.

I turned and smiled at him, trying to hide the injury.

'Quick the hamburger chain? Where?'

It was the Châtelet branch. His manager was called Hamed. He was from Iran.

After his first week at Quick, Jose had terrible burns all the way up his arms from the boiling fat. Hamed was kind to him and helped him to stay calm when things got busy. He made Jose laugh.

For the first time in our life, I found myself feeling disgusted by my brother's physical presence. When he came home from work, he smelt of stale fat. I recoiled from his breath. I longed for him to find his own place. I did not consider the fact that on his salary he would never be able to afford to live in Paris.

Jose introduced me to Hamed. We went to a Vietnamese restaurant on the Ile de la Cité. Hamed paid for us. The fact that we were twins kept him amused. His handsome Persian face was all aglow in the little red table lamps as he pointed out our similarities.

'Same eyes,' he said. 'Same mouth, same nose, same dimple.' He pointed at his cheek. 'Here. Same . . .'

'Different genes,' I interrupted.

Hamed ignored me. I looked at Jose, who was lost in thought.

'And you have the same hands,' Hamed said. 'Look.'

He took my hand. His palms were warm and rough. I wondered if his hair smelt of chip fat and his breath of rotting meat like Jose's.

Jose didn't seem bothered about going home without me. He was engrossed in his Bible and would be able to read well into the night without disturbing me. I went with Hamed to Blanville, a desolate suburb to the north-east of Paris. He took me to his flat on the fifteenth floor of a tower block and showed me a photograph album full of pictures of his mother and his sisters back in Tehran. His father had been killed in the Iran-Iraq war, just after he was born.

'I am the only son,' he said. 'I must provide for them.'

When I picture myself going back to Hamed's flat and watching him put the key in the lock, I'm at a loss to understand who I was then. I don't know why I went to bed with him. Pierre, of course, would argue that it was an attempt to get closer to Jose: a kind of ancillary incest.

I didn't enjoy the sex, on any level. I was used to looking into Pierre's eyes while we made love and plotting the progress of his desire. Hamed's eyes seemed blind. His dick was alien and a little cold and he used it like a probe.

So many of my choices then did not feel to me like choices. I was adrift, washed from one experience to the next, unable or unwilling to say Yes or No. I sometimes wonder if this posture of surrender was some obscure homage to our defiled mother.

The next morning Hamed drove me into Paris. He let me out in the middle of the road, at Châtelet, and I darted past the cars to the river without looking back. The day was cold and grey. The Seine had flooded its banks and the stark trees rose out of the water, their arms raised. I crossed the bridge to the Concièrgerie and thought of Chloë, competent and elegant in her gown, her heels clicking along the corridors of the Palais de Justice. I missed Pierre. Sex without him had been a lonely business.

That afternoon I sat at the back of the amphitheatre and watched Pierre lecturing. I thought he looked even more dishevelled than usual. He had told me that seeing me or not seeing me made no difference to him; he still suffered. I decided to give in my notice to Chloë and look for another job.

That night Chloë came into the kitchen where I was doing the washing up. The children were in bed and Pierre was next door in his study, lying on the ottoman with headphones on, listening to music.

Chloë poured herself a glass of red wine and offered me one, which I declined. She leant against the counter and asked me how things were going for my brother.

'Fine,' I said. 'He's making friends.'

'Are you all right, Aisha? You look tired.'

'I'm fine. I have to tell you something.'

Chloë set her face into a sympathetic smile.

'I have to leave,' I told her.

'Leave?'

'I have to give in my notice.'

'Why?'

'The flat is too small for the two of us.'

'We'll find a place for him,' she said. Then, as though the problem was solved, she drained her glass and put it down on the counter.

'No. I want to leave. You've been so kind to me and for that I'm grateful . . .'

Chloë looked at me, shocked by the change of tone.

'Of course, if you're not happy, Aisha . . .'

'I'm not unhappy. I just want a change,' I said.

And I could tell that, for Chloë, people like me did not seek the luxury of change. She did not believe me.

'Can't you tell me what it is, Aisha? Are you in trouble?'

'I'm not in trouble.'

She looked at me with her piercing blue eyes. Then she shook her head and I guessed that it was not often that people eluded her like this. Still, I was a peasant, a different species. Perhaps I was just reverting to type. She left the room without another word and went to take one of her long baths.

❦

A month later Jose went to live with Hamed in his flat in Blanville and I returned to Odile's. I missed my brother and would then remind myself that it was not the Jose who worked at Quick and was now reading the Koran I missed, but the old Jose, who had lived in a cave and caught rabbits for my supper.

My brother came into town from Blanville every day except Sundays. He started his shift at Quick at six o'clock in the evening and worked until two a.m. He had been promoted from chips to burgers and the burns on his arms were healing. Since he was not allowed to receive visitors during working hours, I would pick him up at two in the morning and we would walk along the left bank of the Seine, past the Palais de Justice and the deserted Place Dauphine, quaint in its proportions as the set of an opera. Then we would walk right to the end of the gardens of the Ile de la Cité and sit on a bench and watch eddies in the water. During those months I found myself missing him when we were apart and then experiencing an almost physical feeling of loss in his presence.

Hamed had introduced Jose to a group of friends from his estate. One Sunday afternoon in March, at Jose's request, I went to Blanville to meet them. My brother and I sat outside Hamed's building and waited. I hated Blanville. It was the ugliest place I had ever seen. The tower blocks, scattered over bald and muddy hillocks, were made of grey, striated concrete. The children did not play but hung about in groups, tagging or cat-calling young women or burning dustbins. To me they were not children but sinister little sentinels, paid by the dealers to watch for outsiders. I looked at the gaudy pink blossom on the trees struggling out of the tarmac and felt the first stirrings of the dumb optimism that comes with spring.

At last Hamed appeared, smelling strongly of aftershave, and we walked to the karate club to meet the others. Hamed had changed since I had last seen him. He had cut his hair and coated it in gel and moulded it into hundreds of little points. He moved differently too, as if one leg were longer than the other. He talked incessantly, about Jose and his progress at Quick, about the bonus system and about how he might soon have become manager if he had been able to talk. Beneath his joviality, I could feel his hostility towards me.

While we waited outside the club, Hamed started shadow-boxing with my brother and I smiled in spite of myself. At last Z, Raoul and Dab came out of the karate club. They greeted me chivalrously, shaking my hand and putting their fists on their hearts. On the way to the café, I saw that they had made a kind of mascot of my brother. They touched him frequently, ruffling his hair or patting his shoulder as if he might bring them luck.

In the café Jose sat beside me facing his new friends. When I asked him, Z was reluctant to reveal the name behind his initial because he hated the cult around the footballer Zinedine Zidane.

'Zidane is not a good Muslim,' he said. 'He's a clown.'

I learnt that Raoul's parents were French and Dab's were Portuguese and that both boys had recently converted to Islam.

When he saw my confusion, Z said, 'Don't you read the papers? Watch the news? Islam is the new revolution . . .'

'Yeah, and Islam accepts everyone,' Hamed said mockingly. 'Even Catholics. Eh, Dab? Eh, Jose?'

He punched my brother playfully on the arm and my brother smiled.

I could tell that I intimidated Raoul and Dab. They hid their shyness by chatting to each other in fast, confidential banter. Z, however, talked incessantly at me, his little black eyes shining from deep in their sockets. He talked mostly about the attacks on America and about how the Americans had had it coming to them. I noticed how he would glance maniacally at his friends after each statement. There was something unhinged about him.

'I used to deal drugs,' he said. 'Then I found Islam. There was a man in prison, a great man, who brought me back to my faith. I try and help people now. Help them stay off drugs and alcohol. I try to give something back to the community,' he added, as though quoting from a pamphlet. 'Karate's good. Channels the aggression. All right, Jose?' he asked, sweeping my brother's hand and making a fist in the air.

I later discovered that Z had sought to be recruited by real Islamic militants, who had turned him down. He was unpredictable and prone to outbursts of violence. People humoured him but they didn't take his piety very seriously. He drank alcohol and couldn't speak Arabic because his Algerian parents, whom he had long ago repudiated, had clung to the dream of turning him into a Frenchman.

We sat in the inhospitable neon of the café and talked and drank Mecca-Cola. Z raised his glass in a toast:

'Ten per cent of profits to Palestinian children!'

Through it all Jose watched me. He was proud of me and he was proud of his friends. It was the first time I had seen him experience the pleasure of being with other people. A few months later they would all be arrested and he would be alone again. Or rather he would not be alone: by then he had found the sheikh.

I stayed away from Blanville after that. The place frightened me and I told myself that we had not escaped our barbarous village to end up there. I didn't like Jose's new friends either. Telling myself that he had seemed happy, I threw myself into my work.

One day, after a seminar, Pierre caught me as I was leaving the classroom.

'Aisha, I want to talk to you.'

I watched him put his papers into his briefcase and remembered his small, soft hands on my skin.

'I was wondering, have you considered opting for the extended essay? As you may know, you can offer this as an alternative to sitting two of your four papers. I think you should think seriously about it,' he said, without looking up. 'The applications have to be in by the end of this month.'

'I'd thought about it.'

'You'll have to choose a subject. Do you have any ideas?'

'I'd like to do Freud.'

'You must know that Freud is tricky. They mark severely because many of them don't consider him a philosopher. Do you know what aspect of his work you would focus on?'

'The death instinct.'

Pierre looked up and his professional mask fell away. He smiled.

'*Civilization and its Discontents*. Very good.'

He shut his briefcase and rested his hands on it and looked at me sadly. I stepped over to him and kissed him.

This time we hardly spoke. Nor did we read. Every Tuesday after Pierre's evening lecture we went to a hotel near Notre Dame called L'Esmeralda. We had sex on a noisy spring mattress and then parted. This time there was an unspoken agreement that the only thing between us would be sex.

I suppose this suited me. Pierre's silence reflected the reality of our relationship: that he didn't really exist for me, neither his suffering, nor his guilt, nor his love.

When I think of Pierre I'm filled with remorse.

Christopher believes, like his mother Natasha, that the only truly bad thing in matters of the heart is to waste someone else's time.

❦

There was a hot spell at the beginning of April. Jose had been moved to the daytime shift and I sometimes met him in the evenings. We would walk in the Jardin du Luxembourg until the park attendants with their little capes and whistles ushered us out for closing time. I was happy with my life then and no longer suffered in his company. As it turned out, my brother had already started talking but I had no idea of this; he still kept silent in my company.

That month Hamed was sent back to Tehran for working on a student visa. In his absence, Jose went on living in his flat. Without Hamed to look after my brother, Z felt free to exploit what he had identified as Jose's criminal potential.

Was it a blessing that Jose got caught on his first run, or a curse? If he had been caught after several burglaries, he might have been sent to prison and I would still have him. I can easily imagine him living in captivity. He was built to withstand persecution, and physical violence had no effect on him. He was inured to pain of most kinds. His persecutors would prob-

85

ably have come to respect resilience like his. In prison, he might have acquired status. Perhaps it was freedom he had not been equipped for.

I don't know exactly what happened that night. I know that Jose was useful to them for his agility. He could scale a wall and jump great distances. There were three of them: Raoul, Dab and Jose. Z, who had planned it all, was waiting to receive the equipment in the basement of C Block. They got through the chain-link fence that surrounds the industrial park, then Raoul and Dab waited outside the computer ware-house for Jose to let them in. On the way out, Dab lingered to spray his tag on the side of the building and triggered the alarm. Only Jose came back after custody two days later.

While he was in the police cell, I went to Chloë and asked her to take on his defence. She agreed and lent me her car to pick him up.

They brought him to me in handcuffs. His head was bowed and his face was red with shame. He signed for his things: his belt, his shoelaces, a small, dog-eared, leather-bound book with a bookmark made of plaited silk and a bead bracelet that I didn't recognize. Outside, I held him.

'Did they hurt you, Jose?'

I felt him go tense in my arms and I let go.

'What is it?'

It was then that he shouted at me. The voice was so terrify-ing to my ears that I couldn't move.

'Let me live my life!' he screamed.

Then he turned and ran.

I was so shocked by that sound that I stood for a long time outside the police station, until the policewoman standing guard at the door asked me to move on. I got into Chloë's car and drove it back alone.

If it hadn't been for Chloë, Jose would probably have been sent to prison on remand, like Dab and Raoul were, but she pleaded 'reduced responsibility', arguing that my brother was a half-wit (the term she used was 'highly suggestible') and say-

ing that he had been exploited by the others for this very reason. As it was his first offence, the charges were dropped but
he had to see a social worker once a week.

Every Monday night we went to a mental health centre run
by the social services in the fifteenth *arrondissement*. I sat in
on the sessions until the psychiatrist – a man only a few years
older than us, with dyed blond hair and multicoloured socks –
told me that it would not be necessary for me to attend any
more.

'Your brother can talk now,' he said calmly. 'There's no need
for you to talk *for* him.'

I stared at his smug little face and thought of Katarina. He
was a meddler too, but I had to obey him: he reported to the
magistrate and if my brother missed an appointment, he
would be sent straight to a remand centre. The psychiatrist's
name was Fumaroli. It was he who would encourage Jose's
relationship with the sheikh and come to identify him as the
missing father-figure in my brother's life.

That summer I saw little of Jose. I could not bear the sound of
his voice. Whenever he opened his mouth to speak, it felt to me
like a betrayal. I studied for the following year and helped Odile
in the hotel. Occasionally he would come and visit me there. I
would seek out Odile's company because I didn't want to be
alone with him. We would sit in her kitchen and Jose would take
Kiki out of her cage and let her perch on his shoulder. He would
talk about what he was reading. He quoted passages learnt by
heart from the Koran or from the New Testament. The new
voice grated on my nerves. To me it sounded like something that
had been trapped and should not be let out.

One evening in September the three of us were in Odile's
kitchen. Odile had made hot chocolate. Whenever I think back
on it, I hate myself for having sabotaged that moment. It
should have been a happy scene for us. Odile offered the kind
of loving environment we'd never known.

Jose had a copy of the Koran in his lap. The sight of it
enraged me.

'You're becoming a zealot,' I told him.

'What does that mean?' he asked.

Odile held out the jug of hot chocolate.

'Will you have some more, Jose?' she asked kindly.

Jose held out his bowl.

'It's a fanatic. How can you drink that in this heat?'

He did not answer but said, 'I would like to go to Fez.'

I stared at the chocolate moustache around his mouth: now he had dreams of his own.

'Why Fez?' I asked coldly.

'It's supposed to be a lovely city,' Odile said.

'You've got chocolate around your mouth,' I said.

Odile handed him a dishcloth and he wiped himself.

'Fez was the seat of Muslim learning,' he said.

'So?' I asked.

'I'm going to become a Muslim.'

'That's ridiculous!' I turned to Odile for support. She was giving him a concerned look that irritated me. 'You can't convert,' I said, turning back to him. 'It's mad.'

'What do you want to convert for, love?' Odile asked gently.

'Because it's a beautiful religion,' he said.

'You have your own religion,' I told him. 'Why do you have to borrow someone else's?'

'Our religion worships suffering,' he said.

'What do *they* worship? Death by glory.'

'I'll give you something to read,' he said patiently. 'You'll see.'

He pulled a little book from the back pocket of his jeans. It was the small leather-bound book I had seen in the police station.

'Here,' he said, handing it to me. 'Read these. You must give it back because it belongs to Sheikh Laraoui.'

'Who?'

'He's my friend.'

At that moment I wished I'd never brought him to Paris. Odile was standing very still.

'A sheikh,' she repeated stupidly.

'Yes,' Jose said.

'From Arabia?' Odile asked.

'No. He's from Morocco. He studied in Fez.' He nodded at the book in my hands. 'The poem I like is on page seven.'

'I thought sheikhs came from Saudi Arabia,' Odile was saying.

I stared down at the book, wanting to run from the room.

'A sheikh is a priest in the Sunni religion. In the Shiite religion it is called an imam,' Jose was explaining.

I looked up at him. He was smiling at Odile. It was the most beautiful sight.

I opened the book and turned to page seven. The poem was in French with the Arabic translation on the opposite page. It was something about trying to be like melting snow. I could feel my brother watching me and waiting, and I felt as though the inside of my head was heating up under his gaze.

'It doesn't make sense,' I said angrily.

Then my brother put his hand out and touched my hot cheek.

'What?' I asked, pulling away.

'Not *sense*,' he said, smiling.

'What's the *point* of it?' I snapped.

'Nothing, Aisha,' he said gleefully in his ugly new voice. '*Nothing* is the point.'

For the first time in my life I wanted to hit him.

❦

After that evening at Odile's, Jose disappeared into the sheikh's world. I missed him and at the same time I was filled with anger every time I thought of him. Once I called Hamed's number and then hung up on the third ring. I told myself that he could call me if he needed me.

The second of November was the day I defended my extended essay. I have so often raked through my memories of that morning. I knew the mythology of twinship. I knew that I was supposed to have felt something: a sudden knowledge, sharp as pain. The fact that I had felt nothing, nothing at all, tormented me for years.

When it happened, I was sitting in the corridor of the Sorbonne, waiting to be called in by a panel of judges. That morning I had put on a new pair of shoes which had given me blisters, and I limped as I walked up the aisle of the Great Hall towards three men and a woman, all dressed like magistrates. I stood before them and defended my ten thousand word essay called 'Death Instinct: an Anatomy of Doubt'.

When it was over, I met Pierre round the corner at the Brasserie Balzar and we had lunch. We both chose lamb's liver and spinach and we shared a bottle of Mercurey. Over lunch he told me that he had a surprise for me. Instead of going to the Esmeralda after lunch, he took me back to what had once been my room.

He had turned the studio into his study. He had replaced my double bed with a divan like a psychiatrist's couch, and he had hung the walls with old maps of the world. He was as excited as a child. This, he told me, was where he would write his novel. He clutched my waist and pulled me to him, convinced that it was to me that he owed his happiness.

While we were fucking we heard the phone ringing in the flat downstairs.

I don't know how much time had passed before we heard Chloë's footsteps in the corridor. The light was fading, so it must have been about five o'clock. We could hear tears in her voice. For a few moments we lay side by side, perfectly still.

'Pierre,' she said, 'open the door. Please.'

We heard the soft thud of her forehead on the door. At last Pierre stood up, picked up his trousers off the floor and put them on. Then he walked over to the door and opened it.

Chloë stood before him. Her eyes were red from crying. If she was shocked to see me there, she did not show it.

'Aisha?' she whispered.

I stepped forward. When she walked up to me I thought she was going to hit me. Instead she took me in her arms.

'Jose is dead, Aisha. He killed himself.'

I don't remember how I got out of that room. I only remember Pierre standing by the door with his mouth open and Chloë trying to hold on to me. I think I lashed out at her to release me. Then I ran. She had said that Jose was in a morgue in Saint-Cloud. I don't remember hailing a taxi, but that was what I did.

They had found Jose's christening medallion, the medallion which had his identity engraved on one side and on the other the old man with the staff who was supposed to protect him on all his journeys, however long or however short. The police typed my brother's name and date of birth into their computer, found the record of his offence and the name of his lawyer and called Chloë.

It was dark when I arrived at the morgue. As soon as I stepped into the building, the smell, like the smell of human shit only sweeter, made me throw up. The porter helped me to a chair in the long corridor and gave me a sugar cube. I sat in a cold sweat while he cleaned up my sick with a mop and bucket and some powerful lemon disinfectant that made my eyes water.

'It's all right, love,' he said to me. 'Stay there till you feel better. There's no hurry.'

His voice was that of a woman who has smoked all her life.

He came back and stood over me, rolling down his shirt sleeves.

'Feeling better?'

I nodded and he made his way back to his desk in the entrance.

'I think I'm going to be sick again,' I said.

He turned round and came and sat down in the chair beside me.

'Now listen,' he said, nodding at the lifts, 'who *was* that in there?'

I stared at him. The skin of his face was yellowish and his neck was loose like an old woman's.

'A relative, your boyfriend?' he prompted.

'My brother. My twin.'

The porter took both my hands.

'It isn't going to be easy, but I want you to remember something. That is not your brother in there. What's in there is just meat. Like in a butcher's shop. Your brother is anywhere but in there. Do you understand me?'

I looked at his sagging grey eyes and thought that I was seeing a woman in a man's body.

'Your brother will come to you in the next few days. You'll see.' He laid my hands tenderly on my lap. 'Now,' he said, 'are you ready?'

I gripped his wrist and shook my head.

'Come on, love,' he said. 'You can do it. I'll help you to the lift.'

'I can't.'

The porter gave me a tired smile.

'Yes, you can.'

Something in that smile of his gave me the strength to stand up and walk to the lift. He pressed the call button. When the lift door opened, he took my hand and for a moment I felt calm. As the lift descended, our separate identities dissolved: this stranger of indeterminate gender who was holding my hand loved me simply because I was human.

We came out of the lift and the smell of chemicals made me retch again. The porter held me around the shoulders and walked with me through some swing doors, then through a plastic curtain and into a chill, tiled room where a dripping tap echoed in the silence.

The porter was right: what I saw in that room was not Jose.

I can't remember much of the journey home. I remember sitting on the overground Métro to Passy, holding Jose's christening medallion in my fingers. The porter had asked me to sign for it and then handed it to me in a plastic bag with a three-figure number printed on it. I think it was raining as I walked back to Odile's hotel.

When she opened the door it was clear that she already knew. She took me in her arms and then led me up to bed.

As the porter had predicted, Jose came to visit me in my room at Odile's. I could not see him but I felt him lie down on top of me. I could hardly breathe from his weight.

In my head I began to sing to him. I sang as I had when we were children. I sang his favourite: the prayer of Saint Teresa.

> *Let nothing disturb you,*
> *Nothing frighten you*
> *All things are passing,*
> *God never changes . . .*

I sang until he grew lighter. It was only after he had gone that I began to cry.

❦

My brother set fire to himself on the morning of 2 November 2002 at the age of twenty-two. I think he would have been aware of the numerical symmetry. He chose our favourite place to do it: the park at Saint-Cloud.

That November morning the view of the city from René's bench was shrouded in mist and you could not see the river. The ground was slippery underfoot and there was a smell of burning leaves in the air. The sky was filled with layered cloud and the woods, from a distance, looked like purple smoke. In the Romantic Garden, moss grew in the shade of the tall, ragged evergreens, and the bright yellow chrysanthemums planted here and there looked like pieces of litter. That morning a light rain hung in the air and a lone park-keeper wandered about with his hands in his pockets, his breath in plumes.

The only visitor at the time was an old tramp who had managed to spend the night on a bench, undetected by the keepers. He was contemplating the statue of Adam and Eve before him and wondering why they were both holding apples. Eve was striding forth with an expression of agony on her face and holding a piece of cloth over her private parts – as if, the tramp thought, she was having her period – and Adam was entirely preoccupied with her and her period pains and not about the Fall of Man or the fact that he was going to have to plant potatoes for the rest of his life. 'Women,' the tramp was often heard saying in an exasperated voice.

The tramp would have seen my brother's tall, skinny figure making its way down the steep steps to the site of Napoleon's château, destroyed by the Prussians in 1870. He might have stood up and started towards my brother in order to beg his first cigarette of the day.

Like our father, Jose killed himself. I often wonder whether he thought about Fausto when he made his decision, for unlike Fausto's leap from the roof beam, Jose's death had involved careful planning. He had caught a train and then a bus to Saint-Cloud, he had walked to its most impeccable stretch of lawn, sat down on the edge of the ha-ha, or 'wolves' leap' as the French call it, poured petrol onto his head and body and set himself alight.

When I discovered the manner of his death, I mistook my horror for an elaborate retrospective dread. I believed that all my fears had finally revealed themselves to me, that on some level I had known all along that he would kill himself, even that he would self-immolate. I believed that I had somehow helped it to happen. Only now is it clear to me that it was all fantasy, part of that same terrifying omnipotence.

A week after Jose's death I went back to Saint-Cloud. The police had told me that a tramp and a park-keeper had been the only witnesses. I found the tramp sitting on his bench in front of the statue of Adam and Eve with their apples. He shared his wisdom with me – about the statue and about women in general – while he smoked a cigarette. When I asked him about that morning, he glanced uneasily at me and then lowered his eyes and wouldn't say a word. He sat there pulling urgently on the cigarette as if I might snatch it away from him, then he got up and walked off down the alley of perfectly conical yew trees.

I found the park-keeper in the lodge. His name was Sebastien and he was what the French state called a *cas social*: a state employee of limited mental capacity who was the subject of a quota system that had been introduced in the 1970s. Although Sebastien could not read, he could recite the history of the château and its gardens, from its construction by Catherine de' Medici to its destruction in the Franco-Prussian War. My brother's act had ruined for him the only place where he had ever felt at home. A ward of the state, Sebastien had been doing his job ever since he was sixteen. At the age of forty-three, it would be impossible for him to find anything else.

When I stepped into the lodge he was sitting on a high stool, his hands wrapped around a mug. I introduced myself as the journalist from the magazine *Psychologies* who had called that morning. My greeting was returned by a tiny white-haired woman with red glasses who was sitting behind the ticket desk.

'This is Sebastien,' she said, coming round from behind her desk and putting a hand on his shoulder. 'Sebastien?'

But Sebastien was gazing into his mug.

'Shake hands,' she ordered kindly.

He took my hand without looking at me. It was big and rough. The little room was overheated but still smelt of damp.

'Do you mind if we walk?' I asked him.

He looked nervously at the little woman, who nodded at him. He put down his mug and put on his anorak and we stepped out into the cold.

There was frost on the ground between the cobbles. On the way down the steps to the foundations of the destroyed château, I slipped and Sebastien caught my arm. His grip was surprisingly firm.

We walked along the alley of yew trees.

'Is this Le Nôtre's work?' I asked him.

'André Le Nôtre,' Sebastien said in his childish tenor. 'He laid the plans for this four-hundred-hectare garden between 1660 and 1700.'

I had not eaten all day and I suddenly felt sick.

'Where did it happen?' I asked him.

He stopped.

'There,' he said, pointing at the ground a few metres away. I looked for traces on the ground but there were none.

'They re-turfed it last week,' he said.

I looked at him. His face was round and child-like and he had flaccid lips and pale, staring eyes. He swallowed. Poor man. He wanted to leave this place, to be sure that all his life had not been leading up to this, to the witnessing of this horrific act.

'What did you see?' I asked him.

He rubbed his nose and then drove his hands into the pockets of his anorak.

'Well,' he began, using the same gentle, pedagogic tone he used for his guided tours, 'I saw a young man.' He indicated my brother's trajectory with a nod of his head. 'He walked from the Gates of Honour over there to the Avenue of Statues. Then he walked south, past the Dogs' Pond to the Lyre's Border and then . . . Then he walked straight onto the Green Carpet. Right here.'

Sebastien swallowed again. He seemed unable to breathe through his nose.

'Then?'

'Then he sat down in the middle of the Green Carpet.'

'And?'

He opened his mouth in a bitter grimace.

'*Why?*' he whined. 'Why do you want to *know*?' he pleaded. I looked at him coldly.

'We're doing a series of articles on suicide,' I said.

Sebastien was distressed. The only words he knew were the

ones they had taught him to say about this place.

'But *why*?' he asked plaintively.

'Because it's a psychological condition. We're a psychology magazine. We have to treat subjects like this. In order to understand.'

'Understand *what*?' he whined.

'Why something like this happens.'

Sebastien turned his back on me and mumbled, 'He was on fire.'

'What did you say?'

'He was burning,' he moaned. 'He was sitting still and then he stood up and moved around in circles . . . All in flames. Then he fell down on his knees.'

He turned on me. He was red in the face and his slack mouth was wide open.

'He was all *burnt*,' he wailed, throwing out his hand petulantly. 'There was black on the Green Carpet.' He shook his head. 'Please,' he moaned, 'I want . . . I want to go. Can I go now, *mademoiselle*?'

I would have liked to have taken him in my arms then and held him, but I could not move. It felt as though I was observing him through a one-way mirror. I knew that he thought I was something evil, come to haunt him.

'What did you do?' I asked him.

'I put my coat on him.' He looked at his feet. 'It got burnt. They gave it back to me.'

I turned and looked at the spot again. I could just make out the dark lines around the new turf. When I turned back, Sebastien was walking away as fast as he could on the icy cobbles.

I walked slowly towards the lodge. My brother had died in the ambulance on the way to hospital. I had seen his body in the morgue. The pain had left a rictus on his face, a terrifying parody of his smile. Only his legs were not charred.

On the other side of the park gates, I stopped and looked back at the lodge. Sebastien and the little woman were watching me from the doorway. I was too far away to see their faces. She put her arm around his shoulder and led him back inside.

❧

The morning after he died I woke to find Odile sitting beside my bed.

'Shall I open the curtains?' she asked.

When I didn't answer she took my hand.

'It was my fault,' I said.

'No, it wasn't. He fell into bad company.'

Then I began to scream.

Four days later, in the afternoon, Odile and I took a taxi to the crematorium. It was close to the airport and the planes flew just above the black trees, their ultrasound piercing the white air. That was the first time I saw the sheikh. He and his wife were the only ones present. Z, Dab and Raoul were in prison and Hamed was still in Tehran. Chloë and Pierre had been told about the funeral by Odile but they had not come.

Odile and I stood together facing the sheikh and his wife on the other side of the conveyor belt. The sheikh slightly bowed his head at me and I looked away. Odile squeezed my hand tightly as Jose's coffin began to move towards the purple satin curtains.

When I had told the teenaged undertaker near Odile's hotel that I wanted no music, he had warned me that music served another purpose than that of simply providing atmosphere. 'It covers the noise of the mechanism', he had said. That afternoon, as Jose's coffin rolled towards the curtains, I understood what he had meant. All we could hear was the squeaking of the wheels beneath the conveyor belt and the sporadic hissing of the flames jetting from the furnace walls. At last Jose's coffin disappeared and Odile let go of my hand.

Outside I watched the sheikh and his wife go out through the main gates. They walked along the railings, him ahead and her several steps behind.

In the taxi on the way home Odile said, 'It's a pity your mother couldn't be there.'

'I haven't told her.'

'Oh, my dear. Why not?'

'She didn't love my brother.'

'But what do you *mean*, she didn't love him?'

'She didn't love him. In fact she hated him.'

She looked at me aghast.

'She kicked him out when he was still a child and he went to live in a cave.'

'A *cave*? But how did he *eat*?'

'He hunted and foraged and later he grew things. He was very good at living in the wild,' I said. 'He was happy. Then I brought him here. If I hadn't brought him here he would never have met the sheikh and he'd still be alive.'

'Was that him? The man in the white robe?'

'Yes.'

'I don't understand,' Odile said, gazing out of the window. 'How did those dreadful people get hold of him?'

Suddenly I was sick with rage: at Odile sitting goggle-eyed beside me, at the sheikh and his pious-looking wife, but above all at my brother. How dare he remove himself from this world? How dare he leave me alone?

Odile took my hand and we sat in silence until we reached the hotel. That night I couldn't sleep. I got up early the next morning and began a week of fruitless investigation into my brother's suicide. I went about like a mad woman, frightening people with my anger, frightening myself. I went to Saint-Cloud and met the tramp and the park-keeper Sebastien. Then I went to see the psychiatrist Fumaroli.

I waited for him outside in the cold. It was night-time and the street was poorly lit. Mothers came out of the mental health centre with their anguished teenage sons all muffled up in their parkas. The boys hung their heads while the mothers seemed to hold theirs up in defiance. I saw no fathers and no daughters.

I thought of our own father. Had he carried some fatal gene that had worked its mysterious way through Jose? Fumaroli had said that Jose suffered above all from the absence of a father. (He had inferred that a girl could do without one.) Sheikh Laraoui, he had suggested, was a paternal figure for Jose, someone who embodied order and discipline, the purveyor of language, without which my brother could not make sense of the world or interact with it. I embodied the maternal embrace, the desire for fusion. I was blindness, muteness, darkness, the negation of life.

While I waited for Fumaroli, I had fantasies about greeting him and then stabbing him in the heart with my fountain pen. When at last he came out, he was with a female colleague. I clutched my pen in my pocket and stepped back into the darkness. They walked off together down the street and I followed. At the entrance to the Métro station, they separated. He went down the steps into the Métro. I followed him through the turnstile and onto the platform. He had a mincing walk. He let his umbrella tap along the platform. He went right up to the entrance to the tunnel and stood there, waiting for the train.

'Do you remember me?'

He looked at me and his alarm gave way to recognition, then mistrust.

'Yes.'

'You heard about my brother.'

He stood taller, knowing that he was under attack.

'I did. Yes. I'm very sorry.'

'Sorry about what?'

'Sorry for your brother. And for you.'

'What use is that? You didn't help him much, did you? Didn't you see in all those months of talking, of analysing . . . his dreams, his life, his relationships, with me, with, with . . . the *sheikh*!' I was so close to him, spit landed on his face. He leaned back. His dyed blond hair had been sculpted at the front to look like Tintin's. I wanted to hurt him. I clutched my pen in my pocket. 'Didn't you *see* that he was suicidal? How can you have missed that? He set *fire* to himself, for God's sake. He set himself on fire! He must have been psychotic, mustn't he? You don't do something like that unless you're seriously mad, do you? Didn't you pick that up? Did you think he was just a troubled soul looking for a father? What did you call it – "incomplete sublimation"? God, what rubbish! What dangerous rubbish!'

'Listen!' he shouted. 'I will not talk to you about this here. If you want to see me, please make an appointment.'

'What do you mean, see you? See you professionally? Why would I do that? You're dangerous! You should be struck off!'

I was a crazed girl with wild hair, shouting, and so a well-dressed woman came over to see if the poor man needed help. I spun round, arms raised. The well-dressed woman held out her arms, corralling me. I screamed at her, 'Get away from me!' and the woman stepped back. I turned to Fumaroli and pointed at him, but my warning was drowned out by the noise of the train. Too loud . . . Brakes on metal. I put my hands over my ears. Fumaroli's face was tapering in an ugly way. It looked like he was being sucked back into the tunnel. I turned and ran.

That night I lay in my bed at Odile's, fists and teeth clenched. I tossed and turned all night, cursing my brother for what he had done. I decided that he had only come to Paris to plot his revenge on me: I had abandoned him, and so he would abandon me. But forever.

I lay curled up in a ball like one of Plato's creatures. He and I were part of each other. He had no right to remove himself from this life.

In the morning my eyes were dry and sore and my body ached. I got up before it was light, packed my things and left Odile's hotel. I stood at the reception desk for what seemed like a long time, my hand poised to write her a note. In the end I simply wrote down my name and then crossed it out.

I caught the train to Blanville. Jose always left the key to Hamed's flat under the mat and I let myself in and went and lay down on the narrow bed that smelt of him.

I DON'T KNOW HOW LONG I lay on Jose's bed. I know that I didn't eat for several days and that it was Sheikh Laraoui who found me.

When the crying stopped I lay still for a long time. I began to drift in and out of sleep. My mind was like a withered balloon floating on the ceiling. Sometimes it felt as if I was floating and sometimes, often at night, as if I was falling. In the day, my senses were either muffled or hideously acute in isolation one from the other. The smell of cooking in the building made me sick, and the cries of young children outside in the schoolyard became as painful as gulls shrieking in my ear.

After some time I began to hallucinate. I saw the eyes on the roof of Jose's cave. They blinked slowly at me. I was Jose, lying in his cave. He had stopped eating. He wanted to die.

Our head was dry and shrinking and the pain was forcing our eyes shut. We were all body. Our stomach was hot and swollen and our mouth was bitter. Our heart was racing and our lips were quivering. However strong our will to stop it, the mechanism went on working.

The eyes watching us changed to mouths, hundreds of mouths moving – but silent. Each mouth was different from the other. It was a terrifying sight. I bit down on my own lips to still them.

❧

The sheikh had a key and one day he let himself in. He must have been looking for the book of poetry that he had lent Jose. When he saw me, he stopped in the middle of the room as though giving himself up to my scrutiny. I blinked at his tall figure, clothed in white, and thought he looked clean and cool as a river. Then he moved. He opened the window, looked at me again and went out. When he came back some time later with a tray, I screamed at him to get out.

He was shocked by my voice and stood still for a moment, holding the tray. I could hear him breathing, a thin whistle escaping from his lungs. When his face cleared, and he seemed about to speak to me, I screamed at him again. This time it was an inarticulate sound, just to scare him. Gently, he put down the tray on the bedside table and left the room.

When he had gone, I got up. The pain in my head took my breath away. I sat down on the edge of the bed and looked at the tray. Then I picked up the tray, went to the open window and threw it out. I watched the plate and the food and the cup and the tray float for a moment on the November mist and then disappear. I noticed that the windows were suicide-proof and only slid open a little.

I put my face into the opening and breathed in the cold air. I closed my eyes and saw my brother staggering about in flames, then dropping to his knees. I saw the gape of his mouth on his blackened face. I opened my eyes.

I slid the window shut and looked round the functional little room. My brother had been living alone here for months, but there was hardly any trace of him, except for the few belongings from his cave and his smell, rapidly fading, on the sheets. I went back to the bed and lay down.

∻

The sheikh returned the following day. This time he knocked. The lift was broken and he would be out of breath from the climb. When I did not answer his knock, he turned and walked back down the piss-drenched staircase.

His knocking seemed to become more and more frequent. It began to enter my dreams and at last seemed incessant, like the pain in my head. There were no curtains and in the day I lay with my head under the pillow, longing for night. At night I lay in the dark and listened: a cry, and I would picture youths scattering; a dog, barking; a moped with no silencer; the thud, thud of some domestic mechanism above me, a spin cycle perhaps; and then the sheikh, knocking. In the dark, each noise reminded me that the world was empty, that Jose was no longer in it.

I remembered, as a child, fantasizing about his death. I recalled the excitement as my mind hovered on the edge of the unthinkable. I remembered pretending to be dead, his distress.

I had been punished.

The sheikh was knocking again. I lay on my side, clutching my aching stomach.

'Go away,' I whispered.

'Ayesha,' he called.

My name is Aisha. In Portuguese, not Arabic. But I have no voice. My voice was his voice. His voice was mine.

'I am going to let myself in,' the sheikh was saying. Then I heard his footsteps receding down the corridor.

My bladder was full but I was too weak to get up. At last I rolled onto my side and swung my legs out of bed. When I stood up I thought that I was going to faint. My legs buckled but I did not pass out. I could see the rough grey carpet close to my face. It smelled of dust and chemicals. There, right in front of me, was a moth, a beautiful brown moth, with black eyes on the tips of its wings. I blew on it and it crawled forward a few steps. My breath was disgusting. My skin smelled of fried onions and my gums tasted of blood.

I went on all fours to the bathroom. The white tiles were cold beneath my hands. I saw a pubic hair that must have been Jose's. He had never made love. I rested my cheek on the toilet seat and closed my eyes. Even our doomed father had the edge on him there. He had felt the heat of physical passion flooding his heart, creeping up his neck to his face. He had felt it with Cassilda and I had felt it with Pierre. If Jose had known this feeling, would he have destroyed himself?

107

He had always been without fear. I remembered the first time he had dived from the high rock behind the mine. He had glanced at me once and then thrown himself into the void as if, for him, the membrane between life and death didn't exist. For him only my death existed.

I lifted the toilet seat. There was a pungent smell of stale urine. I retched into the bowl. Jose couldn't keep house. The place was filthy. After his arrest, he would not let me come and clean up for him. He said I was to let him live.

Let me live my life, he had said and a few months later he had killed himself.

I sat on the toilet and a trickle of pee came out which felt like the blade of a knife. I had felt this pain before, when I was a child. I had sat on a pot all night trying to pee, and each trickle had made me cry out. Katarina had forced me to drink a bitter tea made out of cherry stalks.

'Drink it!' she had shouted.

In the morning I was cured.

I sat and listened to the voices of little children singing outside. I guessed that they were walking in a crocodile behind their teacher. Soon the boys would start to piss in the staircases and spray their tags across the concrete. They would run their first errands for the dealers, the *caïds*, and then they would start to bait the police. When they were caught they would be humiliated and locked up, then released and locked up again. And the girls – what would they do? They would fall for the boys and weep and wait and weep and wait.

I closed my eyes and saw my sister Barbara, standing at her stove in her new house in the village. I could see her big lumpy arse in her favourite beige trousers. Barbara loved gold, and her husband covered her in it. Every time he went to Bragança he would bring something back for her charm bracelet. I had given her two of the charms: an Eiffel Tower and a little telephone with a dial that turned. I thought of her grin when I gave them to her. That girl was loved.

I flushed the toilet and went back to bed.

When I opened my eyes again the sheikh was leaning over me.

'Go away,' I whispered, breathing my pestilent breath over him.

He went into the bathroom and turned on the tap. He came back and held a glass to my lips.

'Drink,' he said.

But I kept my lips closed.

The sheikh went and sat down on the red chair that Chloë had given Jose. It was a swivel chair and the sheikh looked ridiculous perched on it in his long white jellaba with his brown moccasins sticking out below the hem.

'What are you doing here?' I hissed.

He did not answer, so I turned my back on him and faced the wall. I wanted to be alone with my thoughts. I was thinking about Barbara in her kitchen.

❧

Another night passed. Every time I woke, the sheikh was sitting there, watching me.

The sheikh leaned over the bed. He put his hand on my forehead.

'You must drink,' he said.

I could not move. My eyes were boiling inside my head.

He slid his hand behind my neck and lifted my head forward to meet the glass.

I closed my eyes and drank. The liquid flowed over my throat.

Forgive me, Jose.

The sheikh put his cool hand on my forehead.

❧

The sheikh did not, in spite of what he had said, try to talk to me. He either read or just sat still on the red chair. He would go away but never for long. In the middle of the night, he would get up and leave, and then return an hour or so later. I drank but I still would not eat his food.

In the end I was the one who spoke first.

'You killed him,' I whispered.

The sheikh looked at me but said nothing.

'You made him talk,' I told him. 'Talking didn't help him. It made things worse.'

'What do you mean, it did not help him?'

He blinked at me, waiting for an answer. His eyes had dark brackets around them that gave him a mournful look.

'It made everything worse for him,' I said. 'All it did was set him further apart from people.'

'From whom? From you, perhaps,' he said, smoothing the creases from the lap of his robe. 'He had nothing but your words, Ayesha. From the beginning, he had only your words. You gave him his thoughts with your words.'

'He had his own thoughts.'

The sheikh shook his head.

'Of course he did,' I said. 'You hardly knew him. How long did you know him? Six months? A year?'

The sheikh ignored my question. He went on in his soft voice:

'Because your brother did not speak, you guided his mind from infancy. He had to break free of you. He was a man.'

'What does that mean?'

'A man is acquainted with death,' he said.

'What is a woman, then?'

'A woman serves life. She is a servant of the earth. She gives birth, she makes a home.'

I was reminded of the smug righteousness of Father Antonio.

'You teach that because it suits you, not because it's true,' I said. 'Men and women are no different from each other when it comes to death.'

'A woman behaves as if there were no death.'

'Until it happens,' I said.

'Until it happens,' he repeated softly.

'You killed him.'

This time he said, 'I can understand why you would think that.'

'If he hadn't met you, he would still be alive. We were happy.'

'Were you?' he asked.

He was leaning towards me, his face full of gentle inquiry. This was the man who had taken my brother from me and put him far from my help.

I turned my back on him and faced the wall.

He spoke to me in his preacher's tone.

Does man think that he will be left alone to himself, free?
Was he not an emitted drop of semen,
Then formed into an embryo?
Then He fashioned, shaped and proportioned
And assigned it sexes, male and female.

I turned and faced him again.

'Is that how you brainwashed my brother, with archaic ideas like those?'

'It is from the Qur'an and so it is of course archaic. But it shows that we are both right. Men and woman are not different from each other, but it is God's will that they behave differently.'

I could see a scar low down on his cheek, close to his mouth. I imagined the old man in a fight. I imagined myself cutting him with a knife.

'He killed himself,' I hissed. 'Don't you understand what you've done?'

The sheikh rested his hands on his knees.

'That is why I am here,' he said.

'You tried to convert him,' I said.

He shook his head.

'I told him that he had much to learn still, even about his

own religion. If you are not in possession of all the elements you cannot make a good choice. But he was in a hurry. He went to see Sheikh Omar in Paris about the matter of conversion.'

'Why was he in a hurry?'

'That I don't know.'

'Why was he in a hurry?' I asked again.

'I do not know.'

'You wanted him to convert.'

'I wanted nothing.'

'I don't believe you,' I hissed.

He looked calmly at me, apparently immune to offence.

'Would you like me to tell you how I met your brother?' he asked.

'I don't care.'

He leaned forward and interlocked the fingers of his hands.

'It was Z who brought him to the mosque. One Friday, after prayer. I was standing with my back to the door, talking to someone. I believe I had already sensed your brother's presence in the room, even with the noise of the people putting their mats away. When I saw him standing next to Z, it was as though I recognized him. Do you understand?'

I stared coldly at him but the sheikh was not discouraged. He leaned further towards me on his chair.

'Your brother's face . . .' he began.

I sighed, knowing what was coming.

'The clarity of his gaze was unlike any I had seen before.'

Of course: Jose's intensely probing gaze that had always unsettled my mother and Katarina, and had made the other children want to hit him.

'Then later that day,' the sheikh went on, 'it occurred to me that I had seen it before. On the face of a baby or of a child too young to know that it has a self . . .'

'*L'idiot savant*,' I suggested sarcastically.

The sheikh glanced at me and then went on talking without looking at me.

'When I shook his hand and asked him if he was new on the estate he smiled at me.' The sheikh paused, remembering my brother's smile. I hated him for possessing a memory of that smile, for ever having seen it. 'That evening I went home, full of happiness at the idea that someone remarkable might have walked into my mosque.'

'He would still be alive if he hadn't.'

'Perhaps. But we cannot know that.'

The sheikh stood up and went over to the window and looked out at the desolate geometry of the estate. 'I remember that Z greeted me with the usual formality and respect, his hand on his heart, but I felt the misgiving that I always feel in his presence.' The sheikh turned and looked in my direction. I fixed on the ceiling. 'All around him, people seem to fall and only he remains standing.'

'Doesn't your religion teach compassion?' I said. 'Even for people like Z?'

'We are told to love our enemies as a close, affectionate friend.'

As if my question had convinced him of my interest, the sheikh returned to the red chair and sat down.

'Until Z told me your brother's name and where he was from, I had assumed he was a Muslim . . .'

'What did you care if you weren't interested in converting anyone?'

Again, he ignored my spite.

'When Z told me that he was Catholic, he said "for the time being" and gave a grin, and I wanted to take your brother by the arm and tell him to leave the estate and get as far away as possible.'

'You should have,' I said. 'Why didn't you?'

'I tried to guide your brother away from Z . . .'

'But you didn't,' I interrupted.

'I did not. I began to understand that Jose's compassion was indiscriminate. I began to realize that I had no lessons to give him.'

It was a shock to hear my brother's name in his mouth.

'Get out,' I said. 'I don't want to hear any more.'

Wearily, slowly, the sheikh stood up.

'You were irresponsible,' I said. 'It was Z who got him arrested.'

'I believe that the experience brought him closer to God.'

'That's ridiculous!' I shouted. My head rang with pain. 'That experience made him bitter and withdrawn. It was after he was arrested that he turned against me. I was the only one who had always loved him and always defended him.'

'Defended him against what?' he asked.

'Against everything!' I shouted. 'You have no idea. People were cruel to him!'

The sheikh looked at me,

'You are right,' he said. 'People are cruel.'

I closed my eyes. The hunger was taking away my strength.

'It is time for you to eat,' he said.

'I don't want to eat.'

He walked to the door and turned round.

'If you don't eat you will die. Do you want to die?'

'It's none of your business.'

'I am going to get you some food.'

When the sheikh had gone, I sat up and looked at the empty room. I wished there were some trace of my brother there. I remembered the small leather-bound book of poems. It was in the suitcase that Chloë had given me, but I was too weak to get up and fetch it, so I sat there, my head throbbing, hoping that I would have the strength to refuse the sheikh's food.

I lay back and closed my eyes. My headache was burning, reddish-black, behind my eyelids. My caged stomach was growling. I curled up, longing for sleep. Outside, the light was fading and I could hear the children coming back from school. I wished that I had read those poems of Jose's and at least tried to understand them. I might then have guessed what he was going to do.

I was woken by the sound of the sheikh's key in the lock and then I smelled the food. My stomach roared: milk and honey.

'My wife wishes for you to eat her food,' he said.

There was no need for his caution as he stood over me with the tray – I didn't consider for one moment refusing the food.

There was a plate with daisies on it and I knew at once that it was his wife's best. There were two earthenware dishes: one with meatballs in a tomato sauce and the other with plain couscous. A steam smelling of fresh laundry rose from the couscous.

'Slowly,' he said gently.

The meatballs tasted of mint and cumin. In a small glass dish was something that looked like yoghurt. It was ice cold and it tasted of rose petals. I ate everything as if I was scared that the sheikh would snatch it away. I did not look at him when he picked up the tray.

'Please thank your wife.'

He stopped and turned towards me.

'It was the most delicious food I have ever tasted.'

'That is what your brother told her.'

Then he left the room and I was suddenly terrified of being alone again.

I got up and went into the bathroom. I looked at my face in the mirror above the sink. It was drained of colour except for the shadows under my eyes. My lips were cracked. My mouth was full of ulcers. There were traces of blood on my teeth.

I did not know how long I had been standing there, looking at my reflection, when I heard the door.

'I have brought you some tea,' the sheikh called.

I put on Jose's track-suit trousers, tied up my uncombed hair and went back into the room. He had left the tray beside the bed. On it were a teapot and glass. I went to the door and looked out. The corridor was empty. I closed the door, knowing that he had already got the better of me.

❧

The sheikh did not come back to get the tray until the next morning. It occurred to me that he knew what he was doing, that this was the conquest as he had planned it.

'Sit down,' I told him.

He remained standing, but he looked tired and out of breath.

'You drank the tea,' he said.

'Yes. Why don't you sit down?'

'Are you inviting me to sit?'

'Yes.'

He sat and rested his palms on his knees.

'You wish to talk about your brother,' he said. It was not a question.

'What happened after your first meeting? I want to know how you got him to start reading the Koran.'

'I didn't get him to do anything. He was on his own path.'

'Tell me what happened after Z introduced you to him.'

Then the sheikh began his account of my brother. It was as though I were listening to some sacred biography. In a calm, dispassionate voice, he drew out this simplest of narratives, lingering over apparently innocuous details as if they might one day overflow with meaning. He told me how on their meeting he had asked Jose and Z to have tea with him, how he had taken them home and his wife had served them, how the three of them had sat cross-legged around the tray while Z poured the tea and how he had discovered for the first time that Jose was mute. 'Until then I had not noticed the lack of words,' he said. 'Language seemed to pour out of his eyes.'

The sheikh told me that he had noticed the scars on Jose's arms and wondered what they were. Jose had seen him looking at them and had held out his hands as though, the sheikh said, he were offering them for handcuffs. Z had explained that they were burns from chip fat and the sheikh had put down his tea glass and examined the scars. 'He must have seen my distress because he shook his head and smiled and rubbed his wrists as if to say that I should not worry, that he no longer felt any pain.' The sheikh's eyes shone as he told me this, as if the detail were further proof of my brother's saintliness.

'When he left, my good spirits went with him,' the sheikh said. 'I found myself thinking often about the mute boy. My wife had said that he had the eyes of an angel. The next time I saw him was in the playground, surrounded by little children. There is nothing for them to climb on because it has all been removed for safety reasons. Everything has gone: the climbing frames, the sandpit and the swings. Jose was entertaining them by walking on his hands. He must have seen me coming towards him upside down.' The sheikh smiled at the memory. 'I asked him if he could read French and he told me that he could and so I gave him one of the photocopied sheets I was carrying. It was a poem by a Sufi poet whom I admire. I suppose it was here that it all began. I was sure that Allah had kept this boy innocent for a purpose. I told myself that if I was wrong, I would be punished.'

'You have been punished.'

He looked at me and said quietly, 'Perhaps I have.'

'You know you have. Otherwise you wouldn't be here talking to me,' I said.

'I came because you had put yourself in danger.'

'I didn't ask for help. I wanted to die.'

He looked at me and I suddenly felt ashamed. My suffering was a travesty of my brother's. I wished I could take my words back.

After a long silence I said to the sheikh, 'I don't understand why you fixed on my brother. He wasn't even religious.'

He looked steadily at me.

'He had a special gift.' He paused. 'A gift for the spiritual.'

I leaned back against the pillow.

'What does that mean?'

'He was not contaminated by the material world. He did not suffer from all the usual blindness: pride, ambition, envy. This made him able to see straight through to . . .'

He hesitated. I felt triumphant.

'To what?'

'To the Divine. Or, if you like, to universal love.'

'Universal love,' I repeated with disgust.

He rubbed his eyes wearily.

'Why don't you try to explain?' I snapped.

He was looking at me as though trying to remember who I was.

'What is it?' I insisted. 'Is it because I'm a woman?'

'No.'

'What then?'

'Jose could love all things.'

'No, he couldn't. I can think of plenty of people he didn't love. People who had done him harm.'

'Do you *know* this?'

'Of course I do.'

'I believe that by the time I met your brother, there was not a drop of hatred in him. He showed compassion towards everyone he met, whoever they were. But I have told you this . . .'

'Of course Jose was loving. He's always been loving, ever since he was little. But he was also vulnerable. And he was easily led.'

The sheikh looked down at his hands and said, 'He was full of compassion for all things.'

'He was capable of anger too. Once he lashed out at me.'

The sheikh looked up at me.

'Only once?'

'Surely your point was that he was not capable of anger at all. Well, he was. He felt anger towards me at the end. And he expressed it. He shouted at me. He told me to let him live his life.'

'Perhaps he told you that out of love. Perhaps he was warning you.'

'About what?'

'About his decision to kill himself.'

'Why?' I paused, watching him carefully. 'Did he tell you

that he was going to kill himself?'

The sheikh rubbed his eyes again.

'No,' he answered sadly.

Then he looked back at me, his expression neither kind nor stern. He just seemed weary as he sat there, waiting patiently for my next question.

'If you feel no responsibility for his death, then what are you doing here trying to justify yourself to me?'

He let the silence settle then gave his answer, 'When twins are born, it sometimes occurs that one has all the power. I believe that this was the case for you.' The sheikh leaned towards me, his hands clasped in front of him. 'By power I mean, of course, power to succeed on this earth. Your brother told me that he should have died at birth . . .'

'He told you that?'

'He said that he had been kept alive by the midwife.'

'Witch more like,' I said.

'You dislike this woman?'

'We both do. I mean, Jose hated her too. She persecuted him just as much as our mother did.'

'Perhaps it has been difficult for you to go through this life carrying your brother.'

I flushed.

'How dare you?' I shouted. 'Jose was my life!'

'I don't disagree with you. I'm only asking that you consider the burden that you had taken on.'

'It wasn't a burden! We loved each other. Love between a brother and sister who only had each other. Not Universal Love. He wasn't a burden. He's gone and I miss him.' I was fighting tears then. 'Please. Go away. Leave me alone.'

But the sheikh did not move. He sat and watched me bury my face in my hands. When I had stopped crying he said, 'My wife Rachida would like you to come and stay with us until you are stronger. We have a room for you. It is small but comfortable.'

I did not raise my head when he picked up the tray.

'We are also in Block A,' he said. 'On the tenth floor. The flat is number 101. The door is orange. We hope you will come, Ayesha.'

'Aisha.'

'Aisha,' he repeated.

Then he left.

My brother never knew rage, perhaps because he never knew desire. I think he was born without it. That was his curse – or, as the sheikh would have it, his gift. I was always driven by desire, the desire to escape our village, to have knowledge, to be admired. I had desire but my brother had love. When the sheikh had gone I lay alone in that room and ached for lack of love.

❦

The sheikh did not return. He sent his wife Rachida to fetch me. I thought this might be Muslim decorum, or perhaps it was strategic: it would have been harder for me to have refused hospitality from a stranger, and by sending his wife he was not forcing me to capitulate directly to him.

I needed help to walk down the concrete stairs, as my legs trembled after a few paces. The lift, which had been broken ever since Hamed had brought me to Block A eight months before, had still not been repaired. Rachida held me firmly by the elbow and I, aware of my foul breath, turned my head away.

It was Rachida who looked after me. The sheikh kept him-self scarce. This too, I imagined, was strategic, and I forced myself not to ask after him. Rachida put me in their son Khaled's room and waited on me hand and foot. I could tell from the way she behaved towards me that she had loved my brother.

On my first night at the sheikh's it began to snow. At two o'clock I heard him get up and go out to the mosque for the call to night prayer. He did not sing from a minaret because there was no minaret on the estate, but according to my broth-er he had a beautiful voice that carried well, even from the ground and without a microphone. I opened the window above the bed to listen. The man's voice was not beautiful: it was old and cracked.

I got out of bed and inspected Khaled's room. Posters of footballers, some caught striking the ball in mid-air, others more improbably sedentary, arms folded in polo-neck sweaters. On the only bookshelf were stacks of manga comics. There was an illustrated copy of the Koran in Arabic. The book was tattered and the illustrations looked old-fashioned. I turned to the front and saw that it was printed in Rabat in 1956. I flicked through it: these were the same stories as the ones Jose and I read in our *Children's Bible* – Adam and Eve, Cain and Abel, Noah's Ark, the plagues of Egypt, Moses and the Ten Commandments.

I climbed back into the child's bed and lay curled up, my teeth chattering. The sheikh's voice droned on. Outside the window, the snowflakes, caught in the orange lights of the estate, looked like floating ash.

At last the droning stopped. Some time later I heard the sheikh close the front door behind him. I waited, thinking for a moment that he might knock. I missed the calming presence at my bedside, the soothing voice. I heard him open the door to his bedroom along the hall. Then I lay there listening to the comforting sound of a hushed conversation between husband and wife. For the first time since Jose had gone, I fell into a deep sleep.

I woke to find Rachida leaning over the bed and sliding the window shut.

'It is cold in here. You will get sick,' she said. 'I will bring you some tea.'

I started to get up but she held up her hand.

'You must stay in bed. You must rest.'

A few minutes after she had left the room I heard Khaled call goodbye to her and then the sound of the TV.

I lay and dozed until she returned.

'There's yoghurt and honey, some bread and jam,' she said,

laying a tray on my lap. Then she left me alone.

Soon I was a curiosity on the estate. Rachida's friends, after a spell in the kitchen, would put their heads around the door to greet me. Some would offer their condolences, kissing their fingertips and then touching their hearts. One woman left some pastries, which Rachida, late one evening, brought to me on a tray.

'These are from Fatima,' she said, sliding the plate onto my lap. 'She also lives in Block A. She did not know Jose,' Rachida admitted, pulling a stool close to the bed. 'But her son Mouloud knew him.'

She looked at me with open tenderness. Embarrassed, I ate one of the pastries.

'You are feeling better,' she said, beaming at me.

I didn't look at her. I felt a hardness towards her which was only exacerbated by her kindness.

'How long did you know my brother?'

'Not long,' she sang. 'A few months. You did not have to know Jose for long to love him,' she said. 'Five minutes was enough.'

I considered jealously how in only a few months he had carved out a life for himself here in Blanville, a life which hadn't included me. This woman, with her lovely kind face, had been one of his devotees. These people traipsing through this flat to get a look at me were fighting over him, staking their claims to his memory.

Rachida rose and picked up the tray.

'You must be tired, Ayesha,' she said gently. 'I will leave you.'

'It's Aisha.'

'Aisha,' she said with a smile. 'I will not forget.'

In that first week I was a hostile stranger living in their midst. They crept around me, scattering from view when I emerged from Khaled's bedroom to wash or go to the toilet.

One evening towards the end of the second week, as I walked past the kitchen, I overheard the sheikh talking to his wife in Arabic. Their voices were hushed and urgent. Occasionally they would break into French. I stood still and listened until I heard Rachida say, 'But she looks so *like* him.'

'I know,' the sheikh consoled. 'I know.'

The following afternoon I got up, put on some clothes and combed my hair. When I came out of Khaled's bedroom the flat was empty. The sitting room, arranged around the television, smelled of furniture spray. Behind the sofa was a huge photograph, spanning the length and breadth of the wall, of some Mediterranean port set on a vast, glimmering bay.

The warm smell of vanilla wafted in from the kitchen. Jose had eaten Rachida's food, had complimented her on it. Perhaps he had sat with the sheikh in this room, beneath that absurd photograph, discussing mystical poetry. The front door opened and I hurried back into my room.

Moments later I heard the sound of the PlayStation and came out again. The sheikh's son Khaled was sitting on the floor close to the TV screen, playing a car-racing game. When I greeted him, he said 'Hello' without raising his eyes from the screen. In his parents' absence his manners were less careful. I sat down on a chair in view of the screen and watched him play.

'You're good at this,' I said. 'How long have you had it?'

'Couple of months,' he said, leaning into a sharp turn.

He had bought the game while Jose was alive.

'Would you like a partner?'

He hit Pause and turned to look at me.

'Can you play?'

I shrugged.

'I can have a go.'

He crawled forward to retrieve a second joystick.

We played five times and he won each time by a smaller margin.

'OK,' I said, 'I've had enough of being beaten.'

He took back the joystick without a word, winding the wire conscientiously around its middle. He struck me as a clever, lonely boy. In the two weeks that I had been living there he'd never, as far as I knew, invited anyone home. He was almost fifteen but still looked like a child.

'Did you and Jose ever play that game?'

'Of course,' he said, hitting the Start button for a solo race.

'Who won?'

'Jose mostly,' he answered, without looking up.

I smiled.

'Thank you for lending me your room. It's nice.'

'I like it better in the sitting room anyway,' he said. 'I can play with my PlayStation at night.'

I sat and watched the screen with him until the sound of the key in the lock made him spring to his feet. In seconds he had hidden all evidence of the game and was leaning over his schoolbooks in a perfect show of diligence. Rachida took off her coat, went into the kitchen with her shopping trolley and then came to greet us. She kissed her reluctant boy on the top of his head and smiled at me.

'You like the picture?'

I stared at her, nonplussed.

'The photograph,' she said. 'I got it for very little money. When the Italian restaurant closed down, they sold everything in an auction. It was a bargain,' she said opening her hands. 'It makes the room look bigger, no?'

'Yes,' I said. 'It's very nice, very bright.'

Rachida pointed to it like a tour guide.

'The bay of Naples,' she said. 'Now all my friends want the same. Come, I have made something that I want you to try.'

I followed her into the kitchen and sat down at a small red Formica table. She pulled a tray from the oven.

'Jose loved these,' she said. 'We call them Gazelle Horns.'

She put a plate of the pastries on the table in front of me. I looked up at her. Strands of her hair had escaped from her head-scarf and her face shone with perspiration. My brother had only been dead for three weeks and she was trying to win me over with cake. I summoned all my indignation but it wouldn't come.

124

She wiped her brow with the back of her hand.

'Please,' she said. 'Try one.'

I bit into the cake. Of course it had been Jose's favourite. It was as sweet as anything could be. I ate it slowly, taking tiny bites. The sense of taste flooded back. In the next moment, her arms were around me and I was crying. Her bosom smelt musty. Soon the silky material of her shirt was damp. I clung to her like a child and sobbed, while she rocked me slowly back and forth, humming softly to me in Arabic.

❦

Rachida was the reason I stayed: Rachida and the fact that I didn't have the will or the energy to go anywhere else. I spent my time living like a child – one of Rachida's children, waiting for the small rituals of each day with a kind of passive pleasure that I had never known in my own childhood.

I waited for mint tea with Rachida after the morning's cleaning, for Moroccan satellite news at one o'clock, for Khaled's return from school and the pastries that she made for us, for homework and PlayStation and the quiet, pleasant hours we'd spend together before the sheikh's return from the mosque. After three weeks with them I had cauterized memory and desire. I didn't think of Pierre, of my degree, which I'd abandoned, or of any of my former ambitions. Nor did I think of my past life with Jose. It felt to me as though Jose and I were somehow continuing our life together, there within that alien family. I didn't even need to speak of my brother: he was with us all the time.

The sheikh and I never returned to the conversation we had begun in the room upstairs on the fifteenth floor. In his own house he no longer seemed to possess the same authority. Home was his wife's domain, and in her presence he became a benign shadow. He rarely addressed me directly, but would hear short accounts of my progress from Rachida over supper. He would sit with us at the table and listen, ceremonious and aloof.

125

One afternoon Hamed rang on the doorbell. He had returned from Teheran only the day before and had a gift for Rachida. It was a large hunk of beef, wrapped in blood-stained newspaper. Rachida was thrilled. While she was thanking him, Hamed kept glancing at me to see the effect he was making.

'For tajine,' he explained. 'It is good meat.'

'Thank you, Hamed!' Rachida said. 'How generous! There is so much. You must share it with us. Come for dinner!'

That evening he returned. We pushed aside the furniture in the sitting room to make room for the dining table. Rachida set the tajine dish on a white cloth in the centre of the table and we sat around it, scooping polite ellipses of the delicious stew with our bread. Hamed was more pleased with himself than ever. The sheikh, who was sitting beside him, hardly said a word, while Hamed boasted about how open-minded, how free he was of prejudice, the only Shiite in a Sunni mosque. I sat next to Khaled and hardly spoke, like a sullen child waiting to be excused.

'The beauties in Teheran are incomparable,' Hamed said.

'Surely they are covered,' Rachida said. 'You can't see them.'

Hamed scoffed, 'Of course you can! Iran is not Afghanistan. They wear the veil and they cover their bodies. But many show enough of their hair to guess what it's like. And their eyes –' Hamed glanced at me. 'Their eyes and their lips tell everything!'

The sheikh looked at his lap. He didn't like the turn the conversation had taken, but he said nothing. Rachida rose and picked up the tajine dish.

'Thank you, Hamed. You see, there is still some beef left. Would you like me to wrap it for you to take home?'

Hamed held up his hand.

'Keep it,' he said. 'Please.'

When I stood up to help Rachida, she stayed me with a hand on my shoulder.

'So, Khaled,' Hamed asked when she had gone, 'how's it going?'

I knew Khaled well enough to know that this was not the kind of question he liked. It was too vague. Consumed with shyness, he fixed his eyes on the tablecloth. The sheikh didn't make his son answer, so the four of us sat in silence waiting for Rachida to return. At last Hamed turned to the sheikh.

'I have a computer for you,' he announced proudly. 'For the mosque. It's a good one. Very powerful.'

'Thank you, but I do not need a computer,' the sheikh said in his gentle voice.

'You can use it for records,' Hamed suggested.

'It is not necessary for me to record anything.'

'For people's details,' Hamed insisted. 'Addresses, phone numbers. That sort of thing.'

The sheikh looked at Hamed. When he answered his tone was quizzical.

'Why do I need their phone numbers? If I need to talk to them, I can do so when they come to worship. If they don't come, then I will have no need to talk to them.'

Hamed puzzled for a moment over this remark, then he let it go.

'You could use it for writing your *khutba*,' he said.

'I have a pen for that,' the sheikh replied.

Rachida returned with a large plate filled with a selection of her pastries.

'Aisha beat me today,' Khaled chimed suddenly. His father was gazing absently at him. 'At PlayStation.'

The sheikh almost smiled.

'I will bring it round to the mosque anyway,' Hamed said. 'You can give it to someone who needs it.'

'I don't know who would need it,' the sheikh said.

'Thank you, Hamed,' Rachida interrupted. 'It is very generous of you.'

'It is not stolen then?' the sheikh asked, looking Hamed in the eye for the first time. Hamed's face flushed and his big adam's apple bobbed in his throat.

Instead of answering, he rose, took his jacket from the back of his chair and put it on. He wrapped his black and white Palestinian scarf around his neck and said, 'You treat your enemies better than your friends, Sheikh Laraoui.'

The sheikh seemed to be waiting for him to explain himself further, but Hamed turned to Rachida and bowed, then he swept out of the room.

Khaled put his hand over his mouth to stifle a laugh. Rachida looked at her husband. Her face was free of reproach, but the sheikh defended himself anyway.

'He will bring us no good,' he said.

I put a pastry into my mouth, happy that he had gone.

๏๏

January was very cold. The pipes froze and we were without hot water for three days. On the morning the plumber was supposed to arrive, I offered to do the laundry for Rachida so that she could stay at home and wait for him, and she accepted.

'Here,' she said, taking off her headscarf in the hall. 'Put this on.'

I took the piece of green material.

'A hijab,' I said, smiling.

'For warmth,' she said. 'Here, I'll do it.'

She wrapped the silky cloth around my head and stood back to admire her work. She turned my shoulders to the mirror beside the front door. 'See? It is pretty like that. Berber style, with the knot at the top of the head and the neck showing.'

'You don't wear yours like this,' I said, looking at her smiling face in the mirror. With her wild hair free, I could picture her at my age. She must have been very beautiful.

'My neck is too old,' she said.

'So it's vanity, not religion,' I teased, turning round to face her.

She smiled.

'I wear it because people have become afraid of it and I want to show them that they have nothing to fear.'

'A campaign,' I said.

She shrugged.

'I suppose so.'

'Does the sheikh like you to cover your head?' I asked, pulling on Chloë's old coat.

'The sheikh does not mind whether I wear it or not. He likes to believe that the hijab is one of the more practical rules of Islam, to avoid sunstroke in the desert. He says that it is important not to confuse practicality with morality.'

I picked up the two bags full of laundry.

'Sounds reasonable,' I said. 'But you're more lovely without the scarf.'

She busied herself by straightening my collar, then she stopped and rested her hand on my cheek and looked at me with sad eyes.

'Thank you, Aisha,' she said and I knew that she was seeing Jose in me.

I followed Rachida's directions and walked across the estate to the launderette. It was the first time I had been outside since I had come to Hamed's flat more than a month before. The sky was white and the smell of snow hung in the air. Water dripped from the trees and the snow had turned to slush on the ground. I stepped along a walkway of planks that had been laid through a muddy wasteland, the site for more housing. Jose had told me with great eagerness, as if the news would please me, that the five new buildings would be named after French philosophers. There would be Descartes, Pascal, Sartre, Bergson and Foucault. To his dismay, I had laughed at the absurdity of it. Jose did not see the ugliness of Blanville. It was, above all, a place that had welcomed him. For him, the beauty of the Coelhoso hills was associated with banishment and the tower blocks of Blanville with acceptance.

My shoes leaked and my socks were wet by the time I reached the launderette. It was on the far side of the estate, on the ground floor of Block C. The sign and the stone facing had been ripped off the front, leaving a naked concrete façade with wires sticking out. The two large windows were cracked and had been repaired with tape. As I approached the door, someone ran up behind me. I spun round. It was Hamed, grinning at me.

'You look like the perfect Arab housewife,' he said.

I don't know if it was the remark, or the smug grin, or simply the fact that he was standing there, but my hand shot out and slapped him in the face. For a moment he looked as if he was going to hit me, then he jammed his hands into the pockets of his jeans and dredged up a weak smile.

'Why did you do that?'

'I felt like it.'

I glowered at him. Not once had he had the courage to mention Jose.

'How are things going with the sheikh?' he asked. 'You seem . . . comfortable.'

With his honey-coloured eyes and his thick black eyebrows and his square chin and straight nose, Hamed was a handsome man. I felt nothing but disgust for him and the memory of my own body prone beneath his.

'You're a coward, Hamed,' I said.

I did not wait to see the effect of this blow to his Persian dignity. I turned my back on him and stepped into the launderette.

Among Rachida's laundry were two wool jellabas belonging to the sheikh, which were to be washed separately. I put them on a gentle cycle and then loaded the rest of the laundry, with my wet socks, into another machine. I put my damp shoes back on and went and sat down on the bench in the middle of the room. When I had been watching the cycle for some time, a man came in. He sat down at the far end of the bench and began to read a newspaper. He seemed out of place in Blanville: an affluent-looking, middle-aged white man, with crew-cut hair and an extravagant moustache. He wore a tan leather jacket, beige trousers and highly polished, brown leather shoes. On his wrist he wore a heavy gold bracelet.

The man gave a theatrical sigh and rolled up his newspaper and began tapping it against his ankle, which was resting on his opposite knee. His bracelet slipped down onto his hand. Dark hair grew up to the knuckles.

The man turned and gave a meagre little smile beneath his moustache.

'You must be Jose's sister, Aisha.'

'Who are you?'

He stood up, took a card from his pocket and sat down next to me on the bench. I ignored his card.

'I asked who you were.'

'I'm the police officer investigating your brother's death. My name is Paul Ortoli,' he said, returning his card to his pocket.

'My brother's death has already been investigated,' I said.

'It was no ordinary suicide, was it?'

I stared at his moustache.

'Was it?' he asked again.

He was sitting too close. His breath smelt of coffee and alcohol. He had small grey teeth.

'What *is* an ordinary suicide?' I asked.

He inspected his nails.

'Self-immolation is generally viewed to be a religious act.'

I would have left then if it hadn't been for Rachida's laundry.

'We've been looking at the company your brother kept.'

He stared at me for what felt like a long time, and I guessed that this was some kind of technique he had learned.

'You were twins, weren't you, Aisha?' He paused. 'You must be very upset.'

I kept on staring at his ridiculous moustache.

'We think that your brother might have been influenced. We understand that your host was converting him to Islam.'

'I don't think so.'

He was smirking at me. I looked at the web of little red veins on his cheeks.

'You don't?'

131

'No. He lent him some mystical poetry, but that was about it.'

Again the policeman gave me his pinched smile.

'They have you in a headscarf, I see,' he said. 'That didn't take long.'

I sighed in a show of boredom, but I was angry and my heart was beating too fast.

'What about you, Aisha? Is he converting you?'

I would have told him to stop using my name, but I found that I was scared of him. Mercifully, the wash cycle ended then and I stood up and began to unload the machine. I hugged the wet clothes and crossed the room and loaded them into two dryers. I put in some coins and the drums began to turn. Then I went back to unload the sheikh's two wool jellabas, which I folded and put into a plastic bag as Rachida had instructed. All the time I was aware of the policeman watching me.

I went and sat down on the bench again, this time with my back to him.

'I thought you should know, we have good reason to believe that Sheikh Laraoui had undue influence over your brother, that he pushed him to carry out his act.'

The elaborate diction made me sick. I turned and looked at him.

'His act?' I repeated.

'We believe your brother went off in Sheikh Laraoui's hands.'

'Like a firework?'

He was not amused. His eyes seemed to have gone a shade darker, as if they were absorbing the light rather than reflecting it.

'Is he converting you?'

'No.'

'Why the headscarf?'

'To keep my head warm.'

'You know this man is the worst sort of religious extremist. He's very plausible and that makes him particularly dangerous.'

'I'll bear that in mind.'

'We understand that they intended to send your brother to Pakistan for military training.'

'Military training for what?'

'For the *Jihad*.'

'Who are *they*?'

'This is not a joke, Aisha,' he said, standing up.

'I asked who *they* were?'

'We'll be in touch,' he said, and he walked out, his pimp's shoes smartly striking the tiles.

'And who are *we*?' I called after him, but he had gone.

❧

When I returned I found Rachida lying on the sofa. She looked up at me with glassy eyes. I felt her forehead.

'You're hot.'

She closed her eyes.

'I have a fever.'

Rachida's 'flu lasted for a week. It amused me to see that she was not robust in the least. She had a slight fever and behaved as though she might die. In the day she lay in her bed under a blanket with Disney's *The Lion King* printed on it, looking up at me with forlorn eyes. I put a cool flannel on her forehead and sat beside her and told her stories. I was astonished to discover that she knew none of the stories from the *Thousand and One Nights*, so I told her Aladdin. I did not tell her about my encounter with the policeman in the launderette.

When Khaled came back from school, his disappointment at finding no pastries was overridden by a certain excitement at the disruption of his routine. He danced around me in the kitchen, clamouring for a game.

'Any game,' he said. 'You can choose.'

'Later,' I said. 'I have to make supper for you and your father.'

'Make hot dogs,' Khaled suggested. 'They're easy and he likes them.'

'But they're made of pork,' I said. 'I thought you didn't eat pork.'

'Not these hot dogs,' he said, pulling a packet from the freezer compartment of the fridge. 'You boil them in water.'

I made a face.

'They're good. When Mum's ill we have them with bread and ketchup.'

When the sheikh returned from the mosque, Khaled and I were playing chess. I told him that his wife was sick. After he had looked in on her, he came and sat in his favourite arm-chair. I noticed that he looked tired and pale.

'You have your brother's gift with young people,' he said to me. 'Like him, you do not attempt to be anywhere other than where you are.' He rubbed his eyes and added wearily, 'Khaled knows when I am elsewhere in my thoughts. Don't you, Khaled?'

Khaled looked at his father as though seeking a clue as to what to answer. Finding none, he returned to his move.

'Khaled's good at chess,' I said.

The sheikh looked fondly at his son.

'Rachida has always been frail in damp weather,' he said. 'She comes from the mountains, so she is strong, but not in weather like this.' He looked out of the window at the rain, which had been falling relentlessly since my return from the launderette.

'Mate,' Khaled said.

He had beaten me. I held out my hand.

'Well done,' I said to him, smiling. 'You're too good for me.'

He took my hand but looked downcast.

'You weren't concentrating,' he said.

'I was.'

'You weren't.'

'You must learn to win graciously, Khaled,' the sheikh said. Then he stood up. 'I will cook supper.'

I followed him into the kitchen.

'It is called a Berber omelette,' the sheikh said, rolling up the sleeves of his jellaba.

'Khaled wanted me to make hot dogs.'

'This is better,' the sheikh said. 'Sit.'

So I sat at the red Formica table and watched him prepare the food. He took a knife from the pocket of his robe, opened the blade and ran it under the tap. Then he took an onion and held it in the palm of his hand, cutting through it with strikes in all directions, turning it into hundreds of tiny geometric pieces. Carefully, he peeled three tomatoes so that their skins fell away in a long spiral. The sheikh's competence in the kitchen hinted at a life before Rachida. Like Khaled, he seemed invigorated by her collapse. I watched him stir the onions in the tajine dish and tried to imagine him as a young man.

The sheikh looked up and said, 'You can make the salad. Do you know how?'

'Rachida showed me.'

'Good.'

As we worked together in silence I imagined that Jose was watching us. I suddenly felt ashamed of being there, on his territory.

'I went to the launderette today,' I told the sheikh. 'While I was there, a policeman accosted me.'

The sheikh put down the frying pan and looked at me.

'Please describe him.'

'Dark, crew-cut hair. Moustache.'

He sighed.

'I'm sorry, Aisha,' he said. 'He is not a pleasant man. I hope he did not offend you.'

'He's not pleasant, but he didn't offend me. Who is he?'

'His name is Paul Ortoli. He is not a policeman. He is head of something called the Islam Section of the secret police. He is what is called a spook.'

'How do you know him?'

'I have known him for many years. I once made the mistake

of helping him. It was in a case involving drug dealers. I thought that I was helping Blanville but I was wrong. The drugs are still here and I, along with many other people, am under surveillance.'

'Why?'

He sighed.

'It is a long story. Not a very interesting one. I was useful to him once. I no longer am. He resents the fact that I witnessed his rise to power. He would be happy to see the back of me.'

I poured oil onto the salad.

'He said that Jose was being trained for the *Jihad*.'

The sheikh smiled.

'Paul Ortoli is one of those men who wished never to grow up. He has a wife and child whom he never sees because he spends all his time at work or in his surveillance van. He leads a miserable life. When I feel anger towards him I try to remind myself of this fact.'

I watched the sheikh stir the beaten eggs into the onion.

'I want to thank you for having me to stay,' I said.

He turned round and looked at me, his eyes shining.

'You are welcome, Aisha.'

Over dinner he talked about his daughters Rabia and Fatima, who were both married and living in Morocco.

'Rabia's husband is a pharmacist in Marrakech and Fatima's husband works in a bank in Casablanca. Neither of them was drawn to the spiritual life but they are good girls.' He looked at his son. 'I still have some hope for Khaled.'

Khaled looked up. He was like his mother, with her dimples and her quality of attention.

'I'm going to build aeroplanes,' he said.

'That, I admit, is a clever alternative,' the sheikh said.

Khaled seemed to glow under the unfamiliar benevolence of his father's attention.

'It must have been hard for Rachida when her daughters left home,' I said.

'It was,' the sheikh said. 'In particular when Rabia left. She was the first.' The sheikh studied me a moment as if to measure my interest, then he went on. 'We named her after a woman mystic who lived in Basra during the eighth century.' Khaled and I watched the sheikh being carried off by his thoughts. 'It is a pity that our Rabia does not have that woman's gift for happiness.'

After dinner I tidied up the kitchen while the sheikh read his son to sleep. As I listened to the soft, guttural sounds of the old man's Arabic, I knew what Jose had sought and found there in that family.

✤

One afternoon a few weeks later, Rachida was at the sink peeling potatoes and I was at the table kneading dough for bread. I paused for a moment to ask her how she and the sheikh had met. When she turned round and dried her hands on her apron, I saw that she was happy to have been asked.

'I was eight and he was twelve when his father brought him to my village. They were both riding a donkey. It was the donkey that I liked!' she added mischievously. 'My friends and I ran along beside it as they came into the village. It was all white.'

She rubbed her brow with her wrist.

'The sheikh and I are cousins through our grandmother, and we were always supposed to marry. That day when he came to meet me for the first time I noticed the way he held on tightly to his father's hand and wore a very serious expression. I saw that this seriousness was only a mask and it was this that pleased me.'

'You mean that it was a mask or that you had seen it?' I asked.

'That it was only a mask,' she said. 'After that, he was sent away to a school for Koranic studies in Fez and we did not see each other for many years.'

She sighed.

'You look tired, Rachida. I'll finish the potatoes. Come and sit down.'

I guided her to a chair and then took her place at the sink. I had my back to her when I asked her about the policeman with the moustache.

'He is harmless,' she said wearily. 'He is like the rest of them. They sit in their filthy vans and listen to what is being said in the mosque and try to force members of my husband's flock to inform against him. In some ways it is a good thing. It proves that my husband does not support terrorism.' She paused. 'Still, he has too many worries for a sick man.'

I turned round.

'Is he sick?'

'It is his heart. The doctors say it is encased like this.' She cupped her hands. 'There is a layer of scar tissue around it and that is why it does not work properly.'

'Can't they operate?'

'They can, but the sheikh does not want them to.'

'Why not?'

'He says he will not take time off.' She hesitated, then lowered her voice.'But that is not the true reason. He does not like hospitals. He thinks if they open him up he will die.'

It was a familiar kind of mistrust. Where I came from, you only went to hospital to die.

Rachida started to knead the dough and I went back to the potatoes.

'And you, Aisha, are you all right?'

'I'm fine.'

I emptied the sink and threw away the peelings.

'Come and sit with me.'

But I did not move. Her compassion felt like something that had to be resisted.

'Come and sit, Aisha. Please.'

I sat down opposite her, enduring her kind gaze.

'Are you all right, Aisha? I want you to be truthful.'

I shook my head.

'I'm all right, Rachida. I just don't know what to do, that's all. I don't know how to live, what to do next. That's why I'm still here, because I don't know what to do.'

She reached across the table and took my hand.

'I will tell you something,' she said. 'You are like your brother. You have something of his gift. You came to a place of great ugliness and saw beauty in it.'

I shook my head.

'No, I didn't. I hated this place.'

She ignored my protest.

'You came here, Aisha, in order to heal. You did not see the ugliness then. You saw us: me, Khaled, the sheikh – the words that we speak, the food that we make . . .'

'You've been very kind to me . . .'

She leaned back in her chair and turned away, as though I was distracting her.

'I wanted to tell you that the night before Jose died, he stayed with us . . .'

My heart sank at the mention of him.

'He often slept here when he came to dinner. He slept on the sofa. He and my husband liked to talk late into the night.'

I tried to imagine my brother talking late into the night, and wondered what on earth he talked about. I would never know. I wished he had talked to me. I wished I hadn't spoken for him. The sheikh was right: I had stolen his voice from the start.

'Very early the next morning,' Rachida was saying, 'Jose came into the kitchen. My husband and Khaled were still asleep and I was getting ready for the day.' Rachida rapped her knuckles on the table. 'Your brother sat down at this table. I was making flat bread but I covered the dough with a damp cloth and began to make him tea. He said he had been awake all night reading.'

'Reading what?'

'He was reading some poetry that my husband had given to him.'

'What poetry?'

139

She saw the urgency behind my question and took a soothing tone.

'It was sacred poetry.' Then she went on. 'That morning, the morning of his death, he sat there, where you are sitting now, and I thought to myself, he has discovered my secret.' She paused. 'That I am most happy when I am alone in the kitchen preparing for the day, while my family sleeps and it is still dark outside.' She smiled at me. 'When Jose sat with me that morning I knew that he too was happy. I could feel it filling this room. That is what I wanted to tell you. That I know he was happy when he died. He went to heaven with his heart full . . .'

'I'm sorry, Rachida,' I said, shaking my head. 'I can't listen to this. You're talking about someone I never knew.'

She came over to me and took me in her arms.

'Hush, Aisha. You are angry that he died without you. Perhaps you are angry that you did not die in his place.'

Suddenly I couldn't bear to be held and I pulled away.

'I wasn't *with* him!' I shouted. 'He was here. With *you*. He was thinking about killing himself and I had no idea. What was I *doing*?'

She looked down at me and I saw that all the pity had drained from her face. No one raised their voice in her house.

'You were living your life,' she said coldly. 'And he was living his.'

Then she left the kitchen and I felt bereft. I stared at the ticking clock on the wall. On its face was a picture of some famous mosque. The fridge whirred. What was I doing there, in this ugly place, with this strange family? I looked at my hands in my lap. They were long and heavily knuckled, like my brother's. I'd always hated them.

Rachida and I never mentioned my outburst in the kitchen. For a week afterwards, we crept around each other, showing politeness and consideration, but the ease had gone. I knew that I had to go. Then suddenly, before I could summon the will to leave them, all our lives fell apart.

❦

A week after that painful conversation with Rachida, I was woken by a scream. I sat up and opened the window, thinking that it might be the victim of a *tournante*, a new atrocity favoured by some of Blanville's teenage boys. I pictured the young girl trapped in the tunnel between the two tower blocks. The game was to take it in turns to rape her.

When the scream came again, I realized that it was inside the flat. I jumped out of bed, pulled on Jose's track-suit bottoms and rushed out of my room.

The little entrance hall was filled with people. Rachida was shrieking in Arabic and Khaled was standing in the corner in his pyjamas, watching her. The sheikh was standing between two policemen in uniform. He looked pale and his eyes were wide. He seemed to be heaving for breath. To my horror I saw that he was wearing handcuffs.

'What's going on?'

The sheikh didn't acknowledge me, so I turned to Rachida. 'Who are these people?'

But Rachida went on shrieking. Her target was Paul Ortoli. He was standing by the door, his hands thrust behind his belt buckle, which was shaped like a horseshoe.

'He's sick!' Rachida shrieked in French. 'Can't you *see*?'

I went and put my arm around Khaled's shoulders.

'If he dies it will be your fault!' she yelled. 'You'll have a riot on your hands! Is that what you want? A riot in Blanville?'

Ortoli took a step towards Rachida. The sheikh spoke in an attempt to stall him, 'Hush, Rachida. I will be back soon.'

'Is that what you want?' Rachida shrieked. 'Because that is what will happen if you hurt my husband. The whole place will burn!'

Ortoli was smiling at her as he took another step towards her.

'I appreciate that the sheikh is a man of influence . . .'

'Aisha!' the sheikh hissed. 'Look after my wife.'

I let go of Khaled, but it was too late. Rachida was screaming, spit flying.

'How *dare* you come into this house? How *dare* you?'

Ortoli's hand, the one with the heavy gold bracelet, flew from his belt and slapped her in the face, the force of the blow sending her head sideways. The sheikh lurched forward and was yanked back. I rushed to Rachida. I held her face and inspected her lip, which was bleeding. She looked down, unable to meet my eye.

I turned and looked at Paul Ortoli. He was pointing at Rachida, as if petrified by his own rage. Then he dropped his arm and turned to his assistant, a tall, skinny man in a dirty white T-shirt and black jeans with an inky tattoo on his neck.

'Take him to the car please, Florian.'

Florian ushered the uniformed policemen towards the door.

'Do you have a lawyer, sheikh?' I asked gently.

The sheikh's chin was raised as he struggled to draw air into his lungs.

'It's all right,' I said. 'We'll get you a lawyer. I know a very good one. And we'll press charges for the violence done towards your wife.'

A high little laugh issued forth from beneath Ortoli's moustache.

'If you're thinking about the woman whose husband you fucked,' he said. 'I'd think again if I were you.'

I turned to see if the sheikh had heard him, but he was being led away.

When they had gone, the three of us sank to the floor and sat there in stunned silence, listening to the cars drive away. Rachida had still not looked at me. I stood up and led Khaled back to the sofa.

'Sleep a little,' I told him. 'It's still early.'

'What time is it?'

'It's not yet seven.'

'I can't sleep.'

'Just try. I'm going to stay with your mother.'

'Where have they taken him?'

142

'To the police station. They'll bring him back in a few hours. You'll see.'

'My mum's right. There'll be big riots if they hurt him . . .'

'They won't hurt him.'

'How do you know?'

'They wouldn't dare. He's a religious man, an important figure in the community.'

'Once they arrested a man my dad's age and he had a heart attack and died at the police station. They rioted for a whole week. There was smoke and burning cars everywhere. I was four.'

'Your father's strong,' I told him.

'No, he's not. He's got a weak heart.'

I rested my hand on his forehead and began to stroke his hair. He lay there, looking up at me, holding his breath as though afraid of the caress or afraid that I might stop. After a few minutes I took my hand away. He rolled over resignedly and closed his eyes. I lingered a moment, concerned for this lonely, sensitive boy. Even with loving parents like his, he seemed badly equipped for life.

There was a smell of burning rubber. I wondered if word had already got out about the sheikh's arrest. Then I realized that it was Sunday morning. Every Saturday night a few stolen cars were brought back over the ring road that separated Blanville from Paris, as the Styx separated the living from the dead. The cars would be driven in wild circles all night long and then, as the sun came up, torched.

I found Rachida crying in the kitchen. She explained that Ortoli had found the excuse he had been looking for. His men had searched the mosque and found Hamed's stolen computer, still in its box.

❧

The next morning, despite Ortoli's warning, I went to Chloë's office to ask for her help. I had suggested to Rachida that she might come with me in order to show the bruising on her lip. But she preferred to show her battle scars to the jury of Muslim housewives who sat in her kitchen, clicking their tongues censoriously. I told her that unless she showed her face to a doctor, she could not bring charges against Ortoli. But she just shook her head and sighed as if I were foolish and naïve. Her stubborn resignation irritated me, so I decided to concentrate on helping the sheikh. On the train into Paris I pictured him standing in his white robe amongst his persecutors, fighting for breath.

As I walked along the railings of the Jardin du Luxembourg, I no longer recognized the city I had loved. Its stately beauty now seemed ridiculous and its self-importance bored me. Leisurely housewives and the retired stamped their feet in the cold morning as they queued around the block for a Botticelli exhibition at the Senate.

I reached Chloë's office to find that she had not yet arrived. I was shown into the waiting room by her assistant, a young woman with short, sand-coloured hair and pink rims around the eyes. She seemed distressed by the news that I didn't have an appointment and her thin fingers plucked nervously at her earlobe.

'Could I have your name please?'

'Aisha Ribiero. Maître Magnand knows me. I'll wait for her.'

The young woman hesitated then closed the door gently behind her.

Chloë's waiting room was filled with white orchids in pots. There were white blinds on the windows that diffused the daylight. On the walls were several framed posters. Among them was a poster of a painting by Paul Klee. It was of a man sleeping in an orchard. He had used his coat as a pillow and he looked as though he was floating above the emerald-green grass. I remembered the daily war Chloë waged against what she saw as the ugliness of modern life. She disliked food packaging and would empty pasta, rice and cereal into labelled glass jars.

I heard the front door slam, the assistant's plaintive voice, then Chloë's heels on the parquet. The double doors opened.

She stared at me with her blue gaze. I stood in the middle of the exquisite room and I let her take in the grey cashmere coat I was wearing that had once been hers. She had cut her fair hair into a bob and she looked different, somehow more aware of her own beauty. It occurred to me that she might now be having an affair.

'What are you doing here?' she asked.

'I wanted to talk to you.'

She folded her arms.

'I don't want to talk to you.'

She stood aside to let me pass. I did not move.

'I wanted to ask you for your help. It's for someone else. He needs a lawyer.'

'A new boyfriend?' she suggested sarcastically.

I shook my head.

'I know I did wrong . . .'

She cut me off.

'You betrayed my trust. I did everything I could for you . . .' Then, as if she was suddenly struck by the offence of my presence, she shouted at me, 'How *dare* you? How dare you ask for my help?' She lowered her voice. 'Come into my office,' she hissed. 'I have some things to say to you.'

I followed her along the corridor. The assistant, clutching some files, leaned back against the wall as we passed. Chloë opened the mirrored doors at the end. Her office was painted dark red and smelled of the same cedar candles that she had at home. A large black lacquer desk sat at an angle in the centre of an ornate rug. The walls were lined with files in burgundy folders. Here too the white blinds were down, as if Chloë herself were a precious piece of parchment.

She sat down in a leather armchair and motioned for me to sit opposite her, on an ornate wooden chair with uncomfortably high armrests.

'Now that I have you here in front of me, I realize there's

nothing to say. Stupid, isn't it?' She paused, taking me in. 'You have no conscience, do you?'

'I did wrong.'

'You know *that* at least.' She leaned further back in her chair and folded her arms. 'Why are you here? What do you want?'

'Before my brother died he became friends with a sheikh, Sheikh Laraoui of Blanville.'

'I know,' she said, softening a little at the mention of Jose. 'I should never have let you send him to that terrible place. I noticed that you didn't go and live there with him.'

'I live there now,' I said.

'Too late.'

I looked at my lap.

'Yes.'

'The children loved him, you know,' she said.

'I know they did.'

'They often ask about him.'

'I'm sure.'

'I should have kept him and got rid of you.'

I looked up.

'You couldn't have *kept* him, Chloë. He wasn't yours to keep.'

'I don't mean it like that. And you know it. I never treated you as an inferior. Did I ever make you feel like a servant? Did I? Didn't I make you feel like one of the family?'

'You tried. But I *was* a servant.'

'You're ungrateful!' she hissed. 'You manipulated me from the beginning. Asking to study under my husband. Getting me to help you get him into bed.'

She shook her head and gave a little laugh. I stood up to leave.

'Sit down!'

I sat.

'I haven't finished.' She sat back in her chair and folded her arms again. 'I'm intrigued. Why on earth did you think I would help you? Are you trying to take some kind of revenge on this sheikh?'

'No. He's been arrested and he needs a lawyer.'

She stared at me in disbelief.

'Is this the same sheikh who tried to convert your brother?'

'I was wrong. He didn't try to convert him.'

She shook her head.

'I think you're mad.'

'You won't defend him then?'

'Certainly not.'

'Why not?'

She picked up a silver pen from her desk and began to roll it between her fingers.

'First of all, I don't approve of religion. I never defend religious people. On principle.'

'He doesn't deserve to go to prison . . .'

'And secondly, ideas like his are responsible for most of the violence in this world, in particular the violence done to women.'

'He doesn't condone violence.'

'Why has he been arrested then?'

'Someone put a stolen computer in his mosque.'

She threw down her pen.

'What are you *doing* with these people?'

'The sheikh is a good man. He helped me after Jose died . . .'

'What is the matter with you?' she shouted. 'Your brother killed himself in an unimaginably violent way after listening to this man's ideas and now you're defending him! I don't see how you can be anywhere near him.'

'I couldn't,' I murmured.

'I don't understand.'

'My brother didn't kill himself because of the sheikh.'

She hesitated, then asked gently, 'Why *did* he kill himself, Aisha?'

I stared at the silver pen on her desk. Pierre had one just like it. I looked up at Chloë. A wave of tiredness washed over me.

'Aisha?'

'I don't know,' I said at last. 'I don't know.'

Summoning all my strength, I stood up. My visit had been pointless. This time she didn't stop me.

'I'm sorry, Chloë,' I said. 'I'm sorry for everything.'

'Wait till I tell Pierre that his star pupil has thrown him over for a sheikh.'

She was triumphant. I thought of poor Pierre, punished, chastened.

Then she did something astounding and yet entirely characteristic. She opened a drawer in her desk and took out her cheque book. I watched her take the lid off her pen and begin to fill out a cheque.

'What is your sheikh being charged with?' she asked.

'I don't know exactly.'

'Well, it makes no difference,' she said, without looking up. 'Now, I want you to leave, Aisha. And please don't come back,' she said, holding out a cheque.

I didn't feel any resentment towards her, only this great tiredness at the prospect of having first to cross that room and then make the journey back to Blanville. I turned and walked towards the door.

'Wait,' she said. 'I owe you money. You're entitled to your salary for the month you left.'

I walked out of the room without looking back.

On the way to the front door, I passed the assistant, who raised her poor pink eyes to mine then returned to her computer screen. The waiting-room doors were ajar and I slipped inside. I took the framed Paul Klee poster off the wall and walked out with it.

❦

When I got back to Block A, Rachida was sitting at the kitchen table surrounded by four women, only two of whom I had seen before.

I greeted them all and they murmured greetings in return, but I felt as though I was part of their problem.

148

'I'll be next door with Khaled,' I said.

Rachida nodded.

Khaled was playing a new combat game. Wordlessly, he handed me a joystick. I put down the Klee picture and sat down beside him. I knew Khaled did not like me to choose male fighters, so I chose Tiger Lily, an Asian girl in a bikini who carried a mace. He selected Tex-Mex, a body builder with long blond hair.

After a few minutes, Khaled snatched the joystick from me and handed me his.

'Try this one,' he said.

But it did not help. He beat me again.

'I'm sorry. I'm not very good at this,' I said.

He glared at me and then went on playing. The victory jingle rang again. I heard the women leave, one by one. Again Khaled beat me. He sighed and took back the joystick.

'I'm sorry,' I said.

Khaled winced at this second apology.

Rachida was crying again. Khaled folded his arms and stared sullenly at the figures on the screen.

'She'll be all right,' I told him. 'You all will.'

But he did not want to discuss his mother's tears. He picked up the joystick and began to play again, so I left him and went back to Rachida in the kitchen.

I sat down opposite her and reached across the table for her hands. She let me hold them, but I did not feel that she had given me permission to comfort her.

'I had no luck with the lawyer,' I told her.

Rachida withdrew her hands and stood up and went to the window to look out.

'He does not need a lawyer,' she said, keeping her back to me. 'He has been taken to Vincennes.'

'What happens in Vincennes?'

'It is a detention centre. A place where they keep you when they are going to deport you.'

'They can't deport him.'

'His *carte de séjour* expired six weeks ago,' she said.

She was pressing her forehead against the glass.

'They can't deport him for that,' I said.

She turned round.

'They can, Aisha! They can do what they like. There is a new law. It has become much easier to expel people. His papers are not in order. That is all they need. In twelve days my husband could be put on a plane and sent back to Morocco.'

'He needs a good lawyer,' I said.

'He *has* a good lawyer! He has a lawyer from SOS Racisme. The man is defending him for nothing. He is a black man from Guadeloupe. He deals with cases like my husband's all the time. When I told him about his *carte de séjour* he said, That is unfortunate. In the present climate, he said, that is very unfortunate. Then he began to speak with hope, but it was too late. I knew that my husband had no chance.'

'Rachida, for God's sake. This is France . . .'

'Please!' She held up her hand to silence me. 'You don't know what you are talking about!'

And she walked out of the room.

That night I dreamt of Jose. We were in an underground car park and a tinny tune that I did not recognize was being played through old-fashioned speakers. Katarina was there, dressed in her black housecoat with the daisies on it, and she was holding a skipping rope. She had tied one end to a ring in the wall and she held the other, turning the rope so that Jose could skip. I was supposed to run in and take over, but for some reason I couldn't move. Katarina began to scream at me. 'Come on, Aisha! Help your brother. He needs to rest.' I could see Jose was getting tired but I was paralysed. My feet wouldn't move. 'You *selfish* girl!' Katarina shrieked. 'You only think of yourself!' Jose was dripping with sweat and red in the face, but I still couldn't move. I knew that if I ran in to relieve him, Katarina's rope would cut me to shreds.

The next morning I went to the detention centre in Vincennes. It was a bright, cold day with a deep blue sky and frost shining on the trees. I was irrationally hopeful as I walked from the Métro, along the edge of the woods, to the detention centre. I don't know what I believed: that somehow my presence, the proof of my support, would help the sheikh's cause. On the way I bought him a bar of chocolate and a copy of *Le Monde*.

The detention centre was a long, squat building of grey concrete with narrow loophole windows. I ran up the steps and pushed through the swing doors. There was a smell of cooking, of charred meat and cabbage. A young gendarme was sitting behind a table in the entrance, a register open before him.

'I've come to see Sheikh Laraoui,' I said.

The young gendarme looked tired. His juvenile face was puffy and I guessed that he was suffering from a hangover. He turned the register towards me and told me to print and sign my name and my relationship to the sheikh.

'Relationship?' I repeated.

'Only next of kin are allowed to visit,' he said.

I wrote *daughter*.

'Leave your identification, please,' the gendarme said, patting the desk. 'Then pass through there.'

I handed over my *carte de séjour* and walked towards the metal detector.

'Wait, *mademoiselle*. Excuse me. Hey!'

He knocked over his chair as he stood up.

'You can't go in.'

I stopped on the other side of the metal detector and turned round.

'Why not?'

He held up my card.

'You're not next of kin.'

'I am.'

'Not to me, you're not. You don't have the same name.'

'That's my married name.'

'Then come back please and show me further identification.'

I looked towards the staircase. A tall, thin African man was sitting on the bottom step, watching us.

I walked back through the metal detector.

'I can't let you through,' the gendarme said. I turned and saw him holding up my ID card. 'Please step this way,' he added. 'This way please, *mademoiselle*.'

'What kind of a place is this?' I asked, walking back through the metal detector and snatching my card from his fingers.

My act wakened him from his stupor. His expression cleared, as though I had just come into focus. He held out one hand in a calming gesture and with the other he pressed a bell on the wall. I could hear ringing in the distance, like the fire alarm at school. Then a bell started ringing above my head.

'He hasn't done anything!' I yelled, backing towards the entrance. 'You can't lock him up! It's illegal!'

The gendarme stepped towards me. I turned and ran.

I walked in the woods. My shoes still leaked and my toes were soon wet, then numb, but I kept walking until I was lost. I felt humiliated. Of course I had been prevented from visiting the sheikh: I was nothing to him.

I walked around a frozen lake to a little wooden bridge. An old woman was standing half-way across it, throwing bread to the ducks. I stood beside her and watched the birds moving daintily over the ice. Some slid comically on landing. I looked at the old woman's profile. She was intent. This was her task, not her amusement. Her eyes were watering from the cold and the tip of her nose was red. As she distributed the bread in tiny morsels, she kept moving her mouth as though miming a prayer. What more did I know of the sheikh than of this woman? Nothing. Only that he had loved my brother.

I offered the old woman the chocolate I had bought the sheikh, but she declined. My presence seemed to bother her, so I left her and walked back around the lake. At last I spotted a huge, prehistoric rock rising out of the tree line. The rock was made of cement and the black dots scattered over it were monkeys. It marked the primate house of Vincennes Zoo. I had been there once with the children and we had stood before that rock for a long time. I remembered Joshua shrieking with delight: 'Look! Aisha! Look at their little *fingers*!'

When I returned to Blanville, Rachida was sitting on the sofa with Khaled, watching TV. Neither of them seemed to derive any comfort from the other's presence. They seemed cut off from one another. The room smelled stale.

Rachida looked up as I walked past them to Khaled's door.

'Where are your new shoes?' Rachida asked.

I had told her that I was going to buy new shoes.

'I didn't find any I liked.'

She nodded slowly and then returned to the screen.

In Khaled's room I lay down on his bed. Now I was lying to Rachida. It was time to leave.

༺࿐༻

Two days later, on 3 February, I returned to Odile's. Rachida had tried, weakly, to convince me to stay. She had stopped cooking and was feeding Khaled the kind of food that he liked: turkey hot dogs, frozen pizza, tinned ravioli. I think it was shaming for her to have me there to witness this domestic breakdown. She took my number at Odile's and promised to call me with news of her husband's case.

I arrived at the Hôtel des Acacias at four in the afternoon. It was already dark outside and the sixteenth *arrondissement* was deserted. No children played in the Jardins du Ranelagh. The rich ones, like Joshua and Laure, had been taken skiing or to the Caribbean Islands for the winter holidays, and the poor ones were in their cramped ground-floor apartments, playing on their computers. There was a smell of wet earth and wood smoke in the air.

Odile was standing behind the reception desk looking at a magazine through a pair of pink spectacles on a plastic chain. She took a moment to raise her eyes. This was her way with customers.

153

'Hello, Odile.'

The glasses dropped down over the cliff of her bosom.

'Aisha! I thought you'd gone back to Portugal. Where have you *been*?'

'Blanville.'

'Good God!'

She closed her magazine and opened the hatch of the desk and came round to take me in her arms. She smelled of talcum powder. Then she picked up my suitcase and put it behind the front desk. Her arm around my shoulder, she guided me like an invalid towards the kitchen. I sat down at the table and watched her glide about in her caftan. I remembered sitting in this kitchen with Jose. It was the last time I saw him alive: when, daubed with a chocolate moustache, he had told me that he wanted to convert to Islam.

'I've been worried about you,' Odile was saying. 'I even called Chloë. She wasn't friendly. I asked after the children. She knows perfectly well who I am, but she always pretends not to remember me. Not like her husband. He's kind,' she added wistfully. 'I know he's a professor and very brilliant but he's approachable.'

She made me a bowl of hot chocolate and sat down with me at the table.

'You must stay as long as you like.'

'I have to get a job, Odile.'

'You can work here,' she said cheerily.

'I have to earn money. Rent my own place. Lead a normal life.'

'I'd love the company,' she said.

I touched her hand.

'I'd like to stay until I find a job if that's OK.'

She rested her hand on mine and gave a deep sigh.

'I remember when you brought Jose to meet me for the first time. Do you remember? Kiki liked him. He was the only person who ever managed to hand-feed that bird.'

I had noticed how people liked to appropriate the dead in this way.

'I remember,' I said.

'And then those . . . people got hold of him,' she said with disgust.

Those people who rescued me, I thought. And I pictured poor Rachida and Khaled, bereft on that sofa, and the sheikh, alone in his cell.

That night, to celebrate my return, Odile made *coq au vin*. Fanta sat on top of the microwave and watched us with her poor, weeping eyes while we sat with trays on our knees and ate in front of the television. Celebrities swaying in a long row sang an anthem about world poverty. Odile poured us each a glass of Calvados and proposed a toast to Jose and her dear departed Thierry. Then she embraced me, a little teary-eyed, and went to bed. I sat up and watched television, afraid to be alone in my room.

My room was on the top floor and had a view of zinc roofs, chimneys, aerials and audaciously won graffiti. I did not unpack Chloë's suitcase but left it open on the chest of drawers, telling myself that I might leave at any moment and blinding myself to the fact that I had nowhere else to go. I fell asleep that night with the light on.

The next morning I followed Odile around the hotel like a shadow. She was happy to have me back and kept up a stream of chatter. Seven of her fifteen rooms were occupied, mostly with foreigners, and so she was busier than usual. After lunch she told me to have a break, so I went out for a walk. I stayed away from the Jardins du Ranelagh, trying to keep to the streets where I had not been with Jose. My walk took me to a part of the sixteenth *arrondissement* that I had never seen before. I stood on the kerb, looking across at a small hairdressing salon. Then I crossed the road and went in.

I told the young woman that I wanted my hair cut short. She looked reproachfully at me then, as if experience had taught her not to intervene in cases like mine, marched off to fetch me a blouse.

While she did my bidding in silence, I watched my haunted

reflection as my hair fell to the floor in thick clumps.

When she had finished, my eyes filled with tears.

'You were right,' the young woman said, raising a mirror so that I could see the back. 'The cut brings out your eyes. You look better. Honestly,' she added, jauntily.

But it was not my vanity that had brought tears to my eyes. It was the sight of my reflection and of my lost twin's face staring back at me.

❧

Every day I waited for Rachida's call but it never came. I threw myself into the daily chores of the hotel, turning my mind away from everything I had lost. The following Sunday I woke up early and caught the train to Blanville. After only two weeks' absence, I was out of breath from the climb to the tenth floor. I stood on the doorstep, listening for the sound of Khaled's PlayStation and wondering why Rachida was taking so long to come to the door. Instead of Khaled or Rachida I found myself looking down at a little fair-haired girl who must have been about five. Big, dark eyes stared out of a dirty, pasty face. A woman's voice yelled from inside.

'Who is it, Stephanie?'

Stephanie turned and then looked back at me. I smiled at her.

'Is Rachida here?' I asked.

The little girl was looking worried and I began to wonder if I had the right floor. But it was the sheikh's flat.

'Who is it?' the woman's voice called angrily.

'I used to live here,' I whispered.

'It's a lady who used to live here!' Stephanie called out.

A young woman with dark, greasy hair came to the door.

'Get inside,' she said, pushing the child roughly out of the way. Then she raised her chin at me and said, 'Yes, what is it?'

I looked down at the unloved child who was still hovering, trying to get a look at me. As if in defiance, her mother grabbed a handful of the child's dress and threw her back inside the flat. 'Will you get *in*, I said!'

I heard a thud as Stephanie hit the floor. I waited for tears but none came. Then I heard the sound of the TV.

'What do you want?' the mother asked.

'The family who were living here . . .'

'They moved.'

'Do you know where to?'

'Who are you?'

'A friend.'

The woman was now looking at me with open hostility.

'Is your name Aisha?'

'Yes.'

'Wait here.'

And she shut the door in my face.

I glanced up and down the corridor. A new tag had appeared since I had left. The name 'Demon', scrawled inelegantly in black, now covered all the key spots, including the lift doors.

The mother reappeared and handed me a brown envelope with my name written on it.

'They were sent back to where they came from,' she said. From the expression on her face, she clearly thought that I should have gone with them.

While I was looking at the envelope, she stepped back inside and shut the door. I stood there for a moment, listening out for the sequel to the poor child's unending misery, but there was no noise inside the flat except for a burst of studio applause.

Outside, I tore open the envelope. I read the sheikh's letter sitting on the steps to Block C.

Vincennes Detention Centre,
1 February 2003

Dear Aisha

I write this letter without the certainty that you will ever read it. A few days ago you attempted to visit me here at

Vincennes. I heard your voice downstairs in the hall. I would like to thank you for having tried to see me. The gendarme who guards me would not tell me why you had been refused admission, but I assume that it is because we are not blood relations. I do not blame him. He is only doing what he believes to be his duty. He is always polite to me and tries to make my stay here as comfortable as possible. I will give this letter to him when it is time for me to leave.

I have been here for four days, in this place that does not call itself a prison. Indeed, I am not a prisoner but a detainee. I am allowed to make and receive calls from the payphone in the corridor, and to be given clothes and books. Rachida is allowed to bring these things to me but I have told her not to bother. I know that I will only be here for another week or so and wish to use the time to think and pray.

I know from Rachida that your attempts to find me a lawyer came to nothing and I wish to thank you for your efforts and to let you know that it would have made no difference to my fate if you had succeeded. Maître Ducray, the lawyer who is representing me, has had a great deal of experience with cases like mine and he tells me that in the present climate I do not stand a chance. My heart bleeds for my wife. She will reproach me nothing, of course, but it was she who advised me many years ago, when we Moroccans were still invited guests, to request French nationality. Something always got in the way. Perhaps it was my pride: I would not ask, in case they did not give. In a little over a week I will be put on a plane and sent back to Morocco, where I have not been for twenty-nine years. I do not know what I feel about this unexpected turn in my life. I am putting my trust in God.

Since it is doubtful that we shall ever meet again I wish to tell you something which I was unable to tell you to your face. I have come to understand that I have been suffering from a form of delusion with regard to your brother. The Sufis believe in a guide, showing the path to God. I believed that Jose was

158

my guide. I thought that the extremes of hunger and loneliness which he had experienced in his cave had brought him to enlightenment. Like all the heroes and heroines of mystical Islam, I thought that Jose had managed to conquer the body and reach a place free of desire. After his death, I told myself that his final act of self-annihilation was a carefully staged return to the Absolute. I cut my mind off from the madness, the anguish and the agony of his final action by telling myself that he had come to the edge of no pain and stepped off. Today I know that this is a comfortable illusion.

We cannot understand a man's suicide. We cannot know his suffering. Until we are standing where he stood, his act will remain unknowable to us. This much I have understood.

You are full of fire, Aisha. I think of you defying the guard downstairs. I picture you walking away with your long stride and I recall Jose's depiction of you as a little girl in your village, your eyes wild with rage, a rock in your hand, ready to defend him against the cruelty and ignorance of the other children. I know that since his death you have measured the effect on your brother of that omnipotent love of yours and I believe that you are beginning to understand its real nature. We are all free. We tie ourselves to each other in order to ward off our fear of death but our gift is our separateness and it is this separateness that enables us to truly love.

As I sit here, waiting for the life I have built to come to an end, I am filled with a new kind of hope. I welcome the hunger that is starting to bite in my gut. I believe it will clear my head and help me begin to shrug off this loneliness that I have been feeling ever since Jose's death. It is a shameful feeling and one to which my religious life was supposed to have made me immune.

When you came to stay with us in Blanville, the business of everyday life seemed to sweep away the need for talk. I was glad of this at the time. It seemed to me that through the simple rituals of each day, you were coming back to life. I did not want to interfere with this healing process. Now that

159

events have separated us, I wish you to know how much your life means to me. I wish you to know how urgently I want you to go on living. It is time for you to bring that fire out into the world. More than ever I believe that our duty is to life in all its imperfection. Every day I pray to God for your happiness.

Your devoted friend,
Omar Laraoui

I folded the letter carefully, returned it to its envelope and put it into my coat pocket. A group of five teenage boys on scooters were conspiring on the far side of the courtyard, their front wheels meeting in star formation. When I stood up someone shouted out a word I did not catch. There was a burst of laughter. Their pubescent voices were cracked and ugly. I wrapped my coat more tightly around me and walked around the ransacked playground to the archway leading to Block B. Their motors revved behind me and I knew that they planned to trap me in the tunnel. I did not quicken my pace. *You have fire in you.* In the tunnel their engines roared louder. As I approached the exit I turned to face them. The five scooters approached slowly and in single file.

The sheikh was mistaken: I was full of rage and I understood nothing.

I clenched my teeth. My nostrils stung from the reek of urine. The boys glided past, their mutant teenage faces turned to look at me. I had disappointed them by not showing fear. To mask his shame, the leader pulled his scooter up into a wheelie. The others copied him and they roared out of the tunnel.

Outside, I sat down on a low wall and began to cry. I unfolded the sheikh's letter and looked through my tears at the long, slanted handwriting. He had held up the horror of my brother's death to me, telling me to shed my illusions as he had done. Then he had gone away, leaving me all alone with the madness, the anguish and the agony. I looked up at the tall grey blocks around me. Here in this desolate place, I had found his help. Now I was adrift again.

❧

That night I read and reread the sheikh's letter, looking for a clue as to what to do next. I hated him for leaving me alone with only this token of his wisdom.

I searched my things for the book of poems he had lent Jose. I found it in a side pocket of Chloë's suitcase. When I opened the book a photograph fell from between the pages. It was of Hamed, Dab, Raoul and Z, standing in front of one of Dab's graffiti murals. On the wall behind them a cartoon woman with big lips and enormous breasts brandished a rocket-launcher. Raoul's pit bull, Saba, was in the foreground, her head raised in a jagged bark. These four delinquents were as close as Jose had come to friends. I thought of how his love must have settled on their small vulnerabilities: Hamed's vanity, Dab's nervous laughter, Raoul's bravado and the way Z had of casting around uneasily for approval every time he opened his mouth.

I stood the photo against the lamp on my bedside table and turned to page seven to reread the poem.

Be melting snow.
Try and be a sheet of paper with nothing on it.
Be a spot of ground where nothing is growing,
Where something might be planted,
A seed, possibly, from the Absolute.

Wash yourself of yourself.
A white flower grows in the quietness.
Let your tongue become that flower.

This time the words tugged at my heart. I thought of Jose's mind opening like a flower as he read them. I thought of his silence and of the beauty of his smile.

161

That night I waited in vain for sleep. The rain beat down on the zinc roofs. Jose was in the room with me.

I whispered his name into the dark but he didn't answer. The sound of my own voice terrified me. I lay motionless in my bed like a child, too scared to turn on the light. Now I was afraid of him.

I lay there thinking of how I had managed to cut myself off from all the people I had loved or could have loved. I thought of the sheikh, Rachida and Khaled, Chloë and Pierre, Joshua and Laure, my teacher Teresa and her sweet, gentle Luis. No one, except for Odile, even knew where I was. My mother, my stepfather and Katarina only knew that I was alive because of the small monthly payments going into their bank account.

⁕

I began to feel waves of nausea every time I went outside, as if my senses were suffering from a kind of overload. My heart would beat too quickly. Any strong smell would make me retch. My eyes ached in the daylight and at night would not close. I stopped sleeping.

One Sunday I went in search of Pierre. It was raining as I walked to the Métro. On the train, crossing the Seine at Bir Hakeim, my senses were still disturbed. The wheels clattered too loudly over the metal bridge and the churning grey river below looked viscous. Two girls behind me were chattering in Portuguese. They spoke with the heavy accent of my region, Tras-os-Montes, and I was suddenly filled with nostalgia for my savage little village.

I walked under the Eiffel Tower and into the Champ de Mars. The rain had stopped and there were puddles in the wide gravel paths. The traffic noises sounded distorted to me, as if a divine hand had turned up the treble. There was the sickly smell in the air again.

Suddenly I spotted Joshua among the children. He was playing near the sandpit. He had grown so much in only three months. I wanted to call him and open my arms so that he could run to me, but I moved beneath the trees and out of sight. He was playing tag with three other boys. There was no sign of Laure or of Pierre. I grew calm as I watched Joshua play, relieved that I had not encountered Pierre after all. I closed my eyes and smelled the rain on the dusty trees.

'Aisha?'

He was standing beside me clutching a newspaper. He had lost weight and his eyes were dull.

'I didn't recognize you,' he said. 'You look so different. The hair. What are you doing here?' He glanced uneasily towards Joshua and his friends.

'I'm . . . I was looking for you.'

'Why?'

I stood and looked at his hand clutching his newspaper, at the stain on his sweater. I looked at his unshaven face.

'I don't know.'

Again I felt a wave of nausea and a strange subsiding feeling in my stomach.

'You don't look well,' he said. 'Will you sit down?'

We were moving towards the bench where we had first met. As we approached, it rose up to meet me.

'Aisha,' he was saying. 'Aisha, talk to me.'

The birds were deafening.

'Aisha . . .'

⁖

When I came to, I was lying on the bench with my head in Pierre's lap. He told me to stay there while he took Joshua home. After he had gone, I considered leaving but found that I didn't have the strength to move. When he returned, there was an eagerness in his step. He seemed to be enjoying himself.

His flat was a plush studio which belonged to Jean Baptiste's new Mexican wife Carla. It had a view of the Eiffel Tower.

163

I lay on the ottoman from his old study while he told me about Carla.

'She's the opposite of Loup,' he said. 'Strong, passionate, impossible.'

'How is Laure?' I asked. 'Why didn't she come to the park?'

'Laure is angry with me. Since I left, she won't go anywhere with me. If I want to see her, it has to be in the flat. It's her way of instigating my return. She's clever.'

Pierre's books were scattered all over the room in piles that formed a network of low walls. He weaved his way through them and handed me a glass of water.

'I'm sorry it's all I can offer you,' he said. 'I don't eat here much. I haven't got used to shopping yet. Are you hungry? I'll go and get us something.'

He watched me drink the water.

'You're not pregnant, are you?'

I put down the glass.

'No,' I said, trying to smile. 'I should go.'

'Stay a little. You're very pale. I'll go and get you something to eat. What about prawns?'

He knew I liked prawns.

I shook my head.

'I'll get some steak,' he said. 'You need protein. I'll make *steak tartare*. You've never had my *steak tartare*. Mine's rather good. In fact it's the only thing I can make. Apart from a Bloody Mary.'

He smiled and pointed at me.

'Stay there.'

Then he left.

The Eiffel Tower loomed dead centre and improbably large in the aperture at the end of the street. In fact, the view from the window – the wet cobbles, the quiet street, the little square with the plane trees, the quaint *tabac* on the corner – all looked fake. The rain began to fall again. I understood why I had come looking for Pierre. I had to reassemble myself. The nausea, the sleeplessness, the sifting insides, the racing heart were all symptoms of panic in the face of some terrifying dis-integration. Pierre would help me. I lay back and waited for him.

The telephone began to ring. It was so loud that I could feel the tone resonating in my chest. It became painful. I sat up and made my way to the phone, picked up the receiver and put it down again. I was breathless and my head ached. I thought of my father, lying in his cell. The phone began to ring again. The door opened. It was Pierre.

I slept on his sofa. When I woke, it was dark and Pierre had made supper and lit candles. I couldn't eat his *steak tartare* but I had some bread and butter.

He sat beside me on the ottoman and took my feet in his hands and began to massage them. I felt nothing but I let him do it. I was grateful that he wasn't interrogating me. That night he let me sleep in his bed while he slept on the ottoman. I was relieved not to be alone at Odile's. I was afraid that Jose would come back.

The next day was Sunday. Pierre woke me bearing a tray with croissants and *brioche* and hot chocolate. He sat down on the edge of the bed.

'You look thinner,' I told him.

He patted his pot belly.

'Hardly.'

'How has it been?' I asked him.

'Chloë's tough. You know that. It's better to be on her side.'

'What about the children?'

'Laure's appalled. She watches me all the time as if she's scared of what I might do next. She thinks it's my fault. Joshua's too young to apportion blame.'

'Do they know it was me?'

'We didn't tell them but I think Laure guessed. Joshua miss-es you.'

'Are you getting divorced?'

'We're on a trial separation. Supposedly. But Chloë has a boyfriend . . . So yes, I think we'll end up getting divorced. It should be fairly straightforward. All of it is hers. The houses, the cars . . . I don't need much.'

'Do you have anyone else?'

He hesitated.

'I've been sleeping with an actress.'

He was giving me a questioning look. I nodded slowly, feeling nothing. He went on:

'By profession and I suppose by temperament too, she seems to like watching herself.'

'You're not in love.'

'God no! I won't do that again.'

I looked at his brave smile.

'You're not unhappy?'

'I don't think so. Sometimes I feel sorry for myself. I'm not very adaptable. I'd got used to my life with Chloë. It was comfortable. I miss the children. Little things. Like bathtime and the sound of them running along the corridor, watching them sleep. But then, occasionally, I feel overwhelmingly happy. And free.' He paused. 'But what about you, Aisha?'

I told him that I was working for Odile again. I said nothing about my time with the sheikh and his family.

'Come back to university,' he said. 'Finish your degree.'

'I can't afford to study,' I said.

'I'll help you. You could live here.'

I looked around the cluttered room and smiled.

'Where?'

'We'll make room,' he said excitedly. He reminded me of Joshua.

Pierre's room was a sanctuary that day. He made no demands on me, letting me look at his books while he sat at his desk and corrected essays. I was not able to concentrate enough to read. Instead I flicked through his books to see what wisdom he had noted or underlined. His Tocqueville fluttered with labels and its pages were etched with notations. I stared for a long time at the picture on its curling cover: a faded sepia photograph of three nineteenth-century farmers dining in a field in Nebraska. They were sitting at a table in deep, dry grass eating watermelon. All three of them were looking at the camera, their knives poised. I wondered who the photographer had been. Their stance suggested an intruder.

I thought of our family picnics by the *rio* in the summertime, before Jose ran away. We would catch and cook the fish and then Jose and I would go off and explore, each with a slice of watermelon. We would sit on the bank and watch the dragon-flies land on the sweet fruit in our hands. My brother would catch water snakes, hold them in the air while I squealed for their liberation and then he would let them go. I remembered how we caught the fish. Our mother and Katarina would pound a root that grew by the river, moulding its pulp into balls, which they would throw into the water. A few minutes later the fish would all rise, dazed, to the surface and my brother and I would pick them out with our hands. I wondered if Pierre knew about this method of fishing.

In an essay by Emerson, he had underlined: 'The wise man through excess of wisdom is made a fool.'

In the first volume of Montaigne, he had underlined a quotation from a letter by Seneca: 'We are educated, not for life, but for school.'

I looked over at him, sitting in the light of the window. He raised his head and smiled at me. I wondered if he had recognized himself in those words. With all this erudition, Pierre had no clue. All these books did was to help him hide from life.

'I have to go. Odile will be worried.'

He looked over at me, seemed to consider arguing then decided against it. He replaced the lid of his pen, stood up and took his jacket from the back of his chair.

'I'll walk you home,' he said.

On the way back to Odile's, I felt sick again. I focused on the business of pulling the cool, damp air into my lungs. Pierre's incessant chatter made me feel very tired. It occurred to me as he walked beside me, holding my arm, that although I still didn't know what I wanted, I knew what I didn't want.

When I got back to the hotel, Odile was in the sitting room, working on her embroidery. She did not look up when I walked in.

'You should have telephoned,' she said.

'I'm sorry.'

'I was counting on you for breakfast this morning.'

'I'm sorry, Odile.'

She looked up at me, longing to ask where I had been.

'I saw Pierre,' I told her.

She made a little gasping noise.

'He and Chloë have separated,' I said.

She put down her embroidery.

'Are you . . . Are you and he?'

'No.'

'The poor children,' Odile said, gathering up her embroidery. 'Does he see them?'

'Yes.'

Odile gave a big sigh and took off her pink spectacles.

'Poor man.'

She looked up at me.

'You're to be careful with him,' she said. 'He's bound to fall in love with you.'

I suddenly felt like running away from Odile and her embroidery and her threadbare, ornate furniture and her porcelain clocks ticking away and her reproduction Old Masters and her cycling trophies and all her dark, creeping plants.

'I'm tired. Good night, Odile.'

'Have you eaten? I left some for you. Lasagne. It's in the fridge!' she called after me.

That night I fell asleep with the light on. It was a deep sleep, undisturbed by Jose. The rain on the roof woke me just after six. For an hour, I lay in my bed as though pinioned. Even raising my head seemed impossible. When the alarm went I could not lift my hand to stop it. I lay there, letting its buzzing run me through. The air was too thick and the world was too loud:

168

the rain, the plumbing, and now the banging on my door.

'Aisha, love! It's time to get up.'

When I didn't answer, Odile opened the door and looked in.

'What is it, dear? Are you ill?'

The smell of Odile's perfume, as she leaned over me, made me feel sick.

'What's the matter? Oh, love, don't cry . . .'

Her touch burnt my skin.

'I'm getting the doctor.'

Then she left me alone.

The doctor was a man with bushy eyebrows and black hairs sprouting from his nostrils and ears. His hands were ice cold. My body ached all over, as though I had run for miles. When he had finished examining me he wrote out a prescription for Lexomil.

'I'm referring her to Sainte Anne,' he said.

This was not some prayer. He was sending me to a psychiatric hospital.

❧

Sainte Anne was a suitably lugubrious setting for an asylum. The buildings were red brick or biscuit-coloured stone and the gardens were filled with dusty laurel bushes and ragged yew trees. Pierre, who came to visit me every day, was an unwelcome distraction from my thoughts. I had the permanent feeling of being on the edge of some discovery that was hovering in front of me, just out of reach. My head ached constantly as a result of this mental tantalization. He sat beside me on a bench and uncurled my clenched fists and held my hand in a dismal show of solicitude.

Snatches of Jose kept coming to me like clues. I saw him on the green chair, our mother turning on him, her face distorted with rage. I saw him standing in a circle of chanting children, his hands over his ears. I saw him lying in his cave beneath all those painted eyes. Sometimes I saw him with the sheikh, walking through the estate. I never saw him with me.

Every night I had a nightmare. It was a dream of the sea. In it, either Jose or I, I'm not sure whom, floated on a black, rolling sea, gelatinous in substance. The sea began to make a terrifying sound, like a scream, and we would begin to sink beneath its surface. The deeper we sank, the louder the scream. Every night I dreaded this dream and every night I woke, gasping with fear, just as Jose had done when he was a child. I hugged the pillow, yearning for my brother as he had been then: the little boy, warm with sleep beside me, his sweet child's breath on my face.

My psychiatrist, Dr Agnès Saddock, told me that the sea represented our mother's rage.

'*Mer* and *mère*,' she said smugly. 'Only one letter changes.'

After a week, she took me off Lexomil and put me onto a newer, smarter drug. Then she added another pill to eliminate the nightmare. Under the medication my thoughts kept running down blind alleys, as though my memories were on the other side, beyond reach. I preferred my fear to this blindness and stopped taking the drugs.

Dr Saddock said that I would soon be ready to leave, that all I needed was rest and time for the drugs to work. Every morning I was given four pills and in the evening, five. When I left, I had over two hundred pills hidden in a sock.

The day I was discharged, it was hot and sunny. Some of the nurses sat on the lawn and took their shoes off. The patients watched them as if they were foreigners and their laughter an alien language. In the psychiatrist's room there was an electric fan which wobbled on its stand.

'So you're feeling better?'

'Yes, thank you.'

Dr Saddock's toenails were painted dark red. Her shiny black hair was pinned up with a matching red clasp. She looked lovely in her white, fitted coat, her smooth, tanned legs crossed at the ankle. I felt sure that her flawlessness was an additional torment for her more fragile patients.

'The sensory distortion has gone?' she asked, her red mouth closing neatly over her teeth.

'Yes.'

'The nausea?'

'Gone.'

'And what about the medication? Any side effects you'd like to talk about?'

I shook my head.

'I'm going to refer you to a practitioner in town. I think you'll like her. She's a Lacanian, like me.'

I smiled sweetly. How nice, I thought. A Lacanian. Just what I need.

'I think she'll be able to help you with your issues about twinship. She's worked a lot on identity and language.'

'Does she speak Portuguese?' I asked rudely.

The psychiatrist looked at me. At that moment I suppose she realized I had eluded her, but it was too late. She signed my last prescription and handed it to me, her eyes cold.

'Good luck,' she said.

'Good luck to you, doctor.'

In my daily sessions with Dr Saddock we had talked a great deal about my brother's suicide. She decided that he was probably schizophrenic. His muteness had at first suggested autism to her, but then further interrogation about our childhood had revealed his silence to have been a strategy for coping with persecution. His recent locution, accomplished far from the scene of his suffering and accompanied by a flurry of intellectual activity, had most probably heralded the onset of his first symptoms, paranoid schizophrenics being heavily reliant on language for the configuration, if not the expression, of their psychotic fantasies. His religious fervour was, of course, a classic symptom. She inferred that as his twin I could be genetically prone to the same condition but that I had, in her opinion, probably escaped with more minor neurotic disturbances. She suggested, however, that I had in my grief over my brother's death come dangerously close to psychosis and that I should keep on taking the drugs.

As I walked out of the compound with Pierre at my side, I threw the sock full of pills into a dustbin. Had Jose lived, he would almost certainly have ended up here, at Sainte Anne. I had seen what anti-psychotic drugs could do. Those who were on them sat about all day or lay in their beds, their eyes dead, while their family members sat with them, kneading their hands and peering into their faces as though desperately searching for the person who had so frightened them and whom they now wanted back.

Pierre hailed a taxi and we climbed in. After the hospital the city seemed luminous.

'Where do you want to go?' he asked me.

'I don't mind. You decide.'

We went to the Bois de Boulogne and took a boat out on the lake. I sat facing Pierre while he rowed, Chloë's expensive suit-case at my feet. The tall, dark pines looked like cut-outs against the blue sky. I liked the sound of the oars in the water and the cries of the children playing on the bank. I was disap-pointed when Pierre began to talk.

'I've been thinking. I think you should apply for a Masters,' he said.

'I have to get a degree first,' I said.

'Of course, but then you should do a Masters. I think it would help for you to use your brain in a consistent way.'

His dark eyes seemed apprehensive. I smiled at him in an attempt to reassure him but my smile was not a success. He lifted the oars into the boat. The water ran along them and dripped onto my feet.

'What would you choose?' he asked. 'Would you confine yourself to Freud? I was wondering if you might broaden your subject to include those who were against him. I thought about Deleuze.'

I tried another smile.

'I thought it might be helpful for you to work on the idea of death in general . . .'

I caught him hesitating.

'You mean suicide?' I suggested.

He looked eager.

'What do you think?'

I thought he was a little mad. What was his idea, that I would cure myself of my grief by getting to grips with the concept of suicide in Western culture?

'It's an interesting idea,' I said.

He went back to rowing the boat.

I watched a small child pedalling furiously on his tricycle along the water's edge. The boy seemed entirely absorbed, entirely free and at the same time in control. I thought: *We didn't play enough as children.* I was always too busy protecting him. In my mind he was always in danger. Playing seemed out of the question. Perhaps this was part of what the sheikh had meant by my omnipotent love. I looked at the little boy again. He had abandoned his upturned tricycle and was now beating it with a stick.

'You could use Schopenhauer,' Pierre was saying.

I looked at him. It irritated me that he should be talking about Schopenhauer. I wanted him to keep quiet and row the boat.

'Why do children play?' I asked him.

Pierre followed my gaze. The boy stopped beating his tricycle, picked it up and climbed back on.

'To express their aggression. Or more accurately to master their anxiety in the face of their aggressive impulses. It's a way of keeping their fantasies under control. What do you think?'

This tagging on of a question as a concession to dialogue was one of Pierre's techniques. I had once found it charming. I dipped my fingers in the water.

'I think I drove my brother mad,' I said.

'Aisha,' Pierre said gently. 'Guilt is a natural part of mourning.'

I withdrew my fingers from the water.

'Shall we go for a drink?' I asked.

We went to La Rotonde in Passy and sat outside and I watched the lovely Parisian women on parade. I was happy to be sitting next to Pierre. It was more restful than facing him. He went on planning my thesis while I sipped my Orangina. He was talking about Schopenhauer again, saying that the key to his thinking lay in what he had said about suicide,

'Or rather what he didn't say,' Pierre added with a chuckle.

My head ached and I was tired. I thought of Fausto's house in the hills and yearned to be there, lying next to Jose, listening to the wind in the grass.

I watched Pierre's mouth moving. He was still talking about suicide. It sounded like gibberish to me but I could not be sure because my mind kept sliding off his words. I was thinking of Coelhoso and of how the warm weather would have arrived. Our mother would be out planting potatoes, cabbages, onions, carrots, beans, chickpeas. In that moment, I realized that I had to get out of the city. But first I had to get away from Pierre.

Chloë's suitcase was under the table. I reached down and gripped the handle.

'I have to go,' I said, standing up.

Pierre hurriedly reached for the bill.

'No. You stay,' I told him, laying my hand on his. 'Enjoy the sunshine. I'm going to Odile's. I need to lie down for a while. I've got a headache.'

'Don't you want to lie down at my place?'

I did not tell him that I never wanted to see his place again, that all his books and his erudition suffocated me.

'Maybe later,' I said.

But I did not go round later. I caught the train and went back to Block A.

❧

The trees of Blanville were in blossom again. I was about to climb the stairs when a dark-haired woman in a denim miniskirt stepped out of the lift. I stood aside, smiling tri-umphantly.

'It works!' I said to her, stepping into the lift.

The woman scowled at me and I had time to recognize poor Stephanie's mother before the doors closed.

I took the lift to the seventh floor, where Rachida's friend Fatima lived. When she came to the door she did not recognize me.

'Aisha,' I prompted. 'Jose's sister. Rachida had me to stay.'

'Aisha! It's you!' Fatima cried, touching her headscarf. 'The haircut. It's . . . very modern . . . Please come in. My husband is not home. Come and have tea with me.'

I drank her tea and ate her cakes. They were like the ones she had brought me when I had arrived at the sheikh's all those months before. I listened to news of the estate. Z and Hamed were still in Fleury Mérogis with two years of their sentence left to serve and Raoul and Dab had been sent to some new remand centre in the Massif Central where they were being made to work on the land. Three brothers now ran things and Blanville was awash with drugs again. Apparently, even bour-geois kids flocked from Paris to score. Meanwhile Ortoli and his men sat in their vans and watched.

'It's a circus,' Fatima said. 'But that is how they like it.'

The community was still waiting for a new sheikh. A month after he had gone, a replacement had appeared from nowhere, an old man from Algiers who preached the separation of poli-tics and religion and the doctrine of faith as a private matter, not to be brought into public life. The congregation quickly detected the hand of the Ministry of Interior and saw him off.

'The mosque has been closed ever since,' Fatima said. 'Every now and then my husband goes to Sheikh Omar's mosque in Paris.'

She poured me more tea.

'Did Rachida leave an address?'

Fatima looked uncertain.

'I would like to write to her,' I said.

'I don't think Rachida can read.'

'She can.'

'Really?' she asked, stalling. 'I didn't know that.'

'Fatima, please. They're the only link to Jose I have left.'

I looked down at my lap, mostly through shame at having used his name to get what I wanted. I heard the rustle of Fatima's jellaba as she stood up and left the room. She returned with a slip of paper. I recognized the sheikh's immaculate writing. Fatima watched me copy out the address.

'Will you send them our love and tell them that we miss them?'

'Of course I will.'

She hugged me, murmuring a blessing in Arabic.

Back at the hotel I told Odile that the doctor had recommended a holiday.

'What a good idea!' Odile said, clapping her hands. 'That's what you need. A rest and some sunshine. Where are you going?'

'I thought about Morocco,' I said.

Her smile faded.

'Morocco? Where? By the sea? I think Tunisia's better. Tunisia's meant to be very nice.'

'Morocco's cheaper. I can get a special price for Morocco.'

She gave me a pained look. 'Oh, Aisha, I've been so worried about you. Are you . . . better?'

'Yes, I am. I'm a little hungry, though.'

Odile's face lit up.

'That's a *good* sickness,' she said, clasping my hand and leading me to the kitchen.

WHEN I GOT ON THAT PLANE to Marrakech I didn't know where I was going or what I was looking for. All I knew was that, as a wearied twenty-two-year-old fresh out of psychiatric care, I had to escape this feeling of discomfort. I didn't know the nature of that discomfort: whether it was moral, psychological or spiritual. All I knew was that the only time I had felt free of it since my brother's death was in the presence of the sheikh and his family. My decision to get on that plane was a somnambulant quest for a paregoric, nothing more.

During the flight to Marrakech no one witnessed my fear. The window seat beside me was empty. As the plane tore us from the earth, I pressed my head into the seat and closed my eyes. For three hours, I prayed. Clearly, I was still a peasant.

A stewardess held out a menu. I shook my head violently, unable to let go of the armrest.

'Nothing to eat? Would you like something to drink?'

I shook my head again.

She did not insist but moved on up the aisle.

The plane dropped suddenly and I heard my own cry.

Hail Mary, full of grace . . .

They showed us a film to distract us from our fear. But it was no distraction; it only made us more vigilant.

When we landed I threw up into a paper bag. All the passengers left the plane and I was still sitting in my seat, waiting for the strength to stand. The stewardess came and took me by the arm and led me off. I raised my face to the hot breeze. We walked down the steps.

'There,' she purred as we stepped onto the tarmac. 'You're in Africa.'

I looked at her, taking in her overstretched smile.

'Africa,' I murmured.

Through the heat haze I saw a row of palm trees. The sun was blinding. I shielded my eyes with my hand and looked at the snow-capped mountains in the distance.

The stewardess carried my luggage. I walked beside her towards the terminal building. There was a sweet smell in the air: jasmine.

She put me in the queue for passport control and handed me my suitcase.

'Better?' she asked.

'Thank you,' I said.

'No problem,' she sang. Then she drifted away.

A young, handsome Moroccan woman in a tight uniform chewed gum while she studied my passport.

'Business or pleasure?' she asked in French.

'Pleasure,' I told her.

'How long will you be staying?'

I hesitated. I had not considered how long I would stay.

'One month,' I said.

The young woman tapped the immigration form with her index finger.

'An address,' she said. 'I need an address in Morocco.'

I wrote down the address I had been given for Sheikh Laraoui's daughter.

She chewed at me, four times, stamped my passport and then urged me aside with a nod of her head.

The arrivals hall was like a cartoon version of medieval Islamic splendour: tiles, stucco and ornamental fountains. I went to the luggage carousel and picked up Chloë's suitcase and the carefully packed Klee picture.

Outside the terminal building I stood on the pavement and looked for a bus going into town. A group of men crowded round me. One of them bent down and picked up my luggage.

'Taxi,' the man urged. 'It's sixty dirhams to the medina.'

'I only have euros.'

A fat man with a perspiring face stepped forward.

'In there,' he ordered, pointing at the terminal building. 'There is a machine for money. I will wait here. My name is Omar.'

I pulled my suitcase from the other man's grip and returned to the cool interior.

When I came outside again, Omar was standing alone. He wiped his bald head with a handkerchief and took my luggage from me. The other drivers were in a group, hovering at a respectful distance further along the pavement.

I followed Omar to his cab, a low-slung beige Mercedes. The seats were covered with golden teddy-bear fur. I climbed onto the pitted back seat. His car was a furnace and it stank of sweat and diesel. A multitude of trinkets hung from the rear-view mirror: the hand of Fatima, a tasselled bookmark, some Arabic script in moulded plastic and some worry beads. On the dashboard stood a photo in a gold plastic frame of a fat little girl with wet lips and round, black eyes. In the rear-view mirror he saw me looking at her and said, 'My princess.'

'Very sweet.'

'She is three.' He held up three fingers and I nodded and smiled. 'To Jamaa al-Fna?' he asked.

I handed him the piece of paper with the sheikh's address. Omar shook his head.

'Oh dear. This is not the centre. This is the suburbs. That will be one hundred dirhams.'

'Fine.'

He turned the key in the ignition. Music blared from the radio. A man sang plaintively, sometimes in Arabic, sometimes in French.

The drive from the airport was a game of chicken for Omar. He had decided that oncoming traffic should give way to him. He used his horn instead of his brakes. Occasionally, he glanced at me in his mirror to see the effect of his mastery. I could not help smiling. How strange, after my terror in the plane, that I should feel no fear at the hands of this maniac.

I opened my window and caught the smell of mule dung and

orange blossom. I leaned back, and closed my eyes. I heard the clatter of hooves as we overtook the tourists in their horse-drawn carts, the roar of mopeds and the whine of Omar's music. Omar sounded his horn and we swerved. I kept my eyes closed. Perhaps Jose and I were descended from Portugal's Arab invaders. I felt good here in Omar's stinking cab, surrounded by mule dung and human chaos.

He pulled up outside a pristine apartment block that sat in the middle of a building site littered with other, unfinished buildings. A pneumatic drill shattered away in the distance.

I asked Omar to wait and I took my luggage and walked up the steps to the glass doors of the entrance. There was a list of names but no Laraoui. The address said 'Apartment 25' but there were no numbers beside the names. I rang a bell at random. A woman's voice answered.

'Excuse me. I'm looking for a sheikh,' I said in French. 'His name is Laraoui.'

'Laraoui?' she shrieked.

'That's right. An old man, with a wife and son.'

'No Laraoui in this building.'

'His wife is Rachida.'

'Rachida!'

'That's right.'

'I'm so sorry,' she said and hung up.

I rang again.

'Yes?' the woman said patiently.

'He is staying with his son-in-law who owns a pharmacy.'

There was a pause.

'You mean Rachid Ali, the pharmacist? Of course! It is Rachid and his wife Rabia! Rabia is here!'

'Thank you!' I called back into the intercom. 'She's the sheikh's daughter.'

'I did not know the good man was a sheikh. Come in!' The door clicked open.

I pressed her bell again.

'I'm sorry, what is their name? Which bell do I press?'

'Forgive me!' she shrieked. 'You must press Boussalem! Rachid and Rabia Boussalem.'

I paid Omar, who gave me his business card and drove off in a cloud of dust.

❧

Rabia looked like her mother. She had Rachida's beautiful golden eyes and curved brow, but she was more retiring, more demure. She sat opposite me on the sofa, her bare feet folded beneath her, and apologized for her indoor clothes. She was wearing a pink jellaba and gold bangles on both wrists that jangled like her mother's when she poured the tea.

'I begged them to stay with us,' she explained. 'But my father said that he had to take whatever he was offered. It is a mosque that is being built in the middle of nowhere. I do not like to think of my mother living in such a place, but she says that she does not mind. She was brought up in a village like the one they were sent to.'

'Where is the village?' I asked.

'It is in the mountains. It is called Tamghurt. It takes two days by mule to get to the nearest shop.' She shook her head miserably. 'It is terrible for Khaled. I don't know how he will receive an education up there.'

'Are there no schools?'

She looked towards the window and then back at me.

'There are shacks where ignorant peasants teach the alphabet. The children all leave school by the age of twelve.'

'It sounds like the village where I come from.'

'You are not from France?'

'I'm from Portugal. Where I grew up, schools were not much better than the ones you're describing. But I was lucky. I had a good teacher.'

'You're from Portugal? I thought you were French. You have no accent. But then your name: Aisha . . .'

'Aisha is a common name in Portugal.' I took a sip of sweet

tea and thought of Rachida. I was struck by how much freer the mother seemed than the daughter. 'Your French is very good,' I told her.

'Thank you! I love to speak French!'

She looked away towards the window again.

I asked her where exactly the village was.

'It is in the Atlas, less than an hour by car from here, but then the road stops and you must take a path for two or three days through the mountains.' She sighed. 'We will never see them if they live up there. You have beautiful luggage,' she said.

'It's not very practical.'

'Is it *real* Louis Vuitton?'

'Yes. The woman I used to work for gave it to me.'

Rabia beamed. She must have thought that if I had an employer, we were not so far removed from one another after all.

'She was a kind woman then?' Rabia asked me.

'Yes,' I said. 'Yes, she was.'

Rabia was looking at my clothes, as if they might give her a clearer reading of my position on the social grid.

'So you are searching for my parents. They spoke fondly of you,' she said. 'Particularly my mother.'

'They helped me a lot. I would like to find a way of thanking them.'

She looked at me, wondering no doubt what form these thanks would take.

'You are welcome to stay here for as long as you like,' she said. 'My husband Rachid would be happy to receive anyone who is a friend of my father's. He admires my father a great deal. We have a spare room. We do not have any children,' she added.

She looked towards the window again as if help might come from there at any time.

'Perhaps you would like to visit your parents with me,' I suggested.

She looked as though she had been slapped.

'Thank you,' she said, recovering herself. 'You're very kind. But I can't. My husband needs me here.'

'I see.'

'The men here are not like the men in Europe. They cannot cook!' she added, becoming high-pitched.

'Surely he would be all right for a week or so,' I said.

She blushed and looked at her lap.

'Perhaps you would like to rest after your journey?' she suggested.

In Rabia's spare room there were perforated metal blinds on the windows that threw tiny diamonds of light onto the ceiling. I lay on the double bed and watched the fan turning slowly above me.

Only three days before, I had been a psychiatric patient, monitored around the clock. As I lay on my back, watching the diamonds on Rabia's ceiling, I was filled with a rush of joy: I had got away.

The wind shook the blind and the diamonds on the ceiling quivered. I was alone in Morocco. Tomorrow I would be in the Atlas Mountains.

I was exhausted from the tension of flying, but I couldn't sleep. I took the sheikh's book of poetry from my suitcase and went back and lay on the bed. I read until the light had dropped and the diamonds on the ceiling had disappeared.

> Wash yourself of yourself.
> A white flower grows in the quietness.
> Let your tongue become that flower.

In the light of those words, the sheikh's infatuation with my mute brother made sense. At last I fell asleep with the book in my hands.

◈

Rabia's husband Rachid was clean-shaven, scented and oiled, and dressed from head to toe in beige. While he talked to me over dinner, I made plans to kidnap Rabia and take her to the mountains.

'We must take you for a stroll in the medina,' Rachid said. 'I have a comfortable car. You cannot leave without seeing the old town of Marrakech.'

I declined, appealing to Rabia.

'I'm sorry. I'd like to but I'm very tired.'

Rachid sucked on his sorbet spoon. He was put out that I was addressing his wife. I got him to talk about the sheikh.

He dabbed the sides of his mouth with a napkin and leant back in his chair.

'It has been very difficult finding him a position. I have many contacts and I pulled many strings but, well . . . the circumstances of his departure from France. I know that his expulsion was unjustified. You don't have to convince *me* of that. I know what kind of man my father-in-law is. But the fact is, it is there, in his files. Still, we have found him somewhere at last.'

I glanced at Rabia, who was staring blankly at her melting sorbet.

'It will be a good mosque. It is being built by the local authorities and by private subscription. Much of the money is coming from an Englishman, a millionaire from London who is not a Muslim. I gather he is not even a religious man, but he came on holiday to the Atlas with a group of friends five years ago and fell in love with the place. The Berbers are a very welcoming people. Rabia's parents are both Berber. They are also hard-working and honest people. This wealthy Englishman made friends with his guide, a man named Hadj, who by all accounts has had no education but is pretty clever none the less.' Rachid tapped the side of his nose. 'The Englishman asked Hadj to tell him what the village needed most and Hadj convinced him that what they needed most was a mosque. They have no sanitation, no school and no doctor and what they need is a mosque!'

He leaned back in his chair and laughed, showing me his molars.

Rabia's eyes were brimming with tears. His sarcasm shamed her father. She gathered up the plates and disappeared into the kitchen.

The next morning Rabia opened the door to my room several times before I admitted to being awake. I wanted to be sure that Rachid had left for work. When I heard the front door close I got up and got dressed. I had decided to go into town after all, but with Rabia. I would ask her to help me exchange Chloë's suitcase for things that I might need for the trek in the mountains.

Rabia was nervous as we sat in Omar's taxi on the way into town. She was afraid of being spotted by one of her husband's friends or relatives. I took her hand.

'Surely you're allowed to go into town, Rabia. You're showing your guest the sights.'

'But Rachid wanted to show you!'

'I know, but I have to leave before he returns from work. It's not your fault.'

Rabia squeezed my hand. She was wearing Western clothes that day, a navy-blue pleated skirt and white silk blouse with puffed sleeves and a high collar.

'You look very pretty,' I told her and she smiled at me. 'You look like your mother.'

'She is prettier than me.'

'She is pretty, Rabia. But so are you.'

'I wish I could come with you into the mountains, Aisha.'

'So do I. Perhaps you'll come soon.'

'Rachid will never come. He will never go up there. It is not his element.'

She smiled sadly at me and then looked out of her window.

Omar screeched to a halt in front of a metal barricade barring the entrance to a thronging square. Rabia revived in an instant.

'We are here! Place Jaama al Fna!'

187

We worked our way through the crowd, from one corner of the immense square to the other. Through the cooking smoke of a hundred food stalls, we wove among musicians and snake charmers, child boxers and medicine men, soothsayers and cobblers and hairdressers. Two young men, walking hand in hand, hissed at us as we passed.

'Here,' Rabia said, pulling a black scarf from her handbag. 'Cover your shoulders. You will feel more comfortable.'

We entered the dark *souk* and the temperature dropped. I could smell poorly cured leather and spices. Carrying Chloë's empty suitcase, I followed Rabia quickly along the network of covered alleys, ignoring the calls from stallholders on either side of us.

'Oh gazelles! Just for the pleasure of your eyes. Look!'

Someone grabbed my arm and draped a heavy gold chain over my wrist.

'Look, gazelle! Twenty-two carats!'

I looked down at a small man in a dark brown jellaba. Rabia turned on him, hissing at him in Arabic, and he backed away, holding up his palms.

'It is not far,' she told me.

We passed a series of meat stalls, bedecked with hanging mutton carcasses. Blood collected in pools beneath them, drawing flies. We turned a corner and found ourselves in an alley devoted mainly to luggage. Rabia stopped at a stall. A tired-looking old man raised himself from an aluminium chair at the back of a little shop packed full of camping equipment. He greeted Rabia warmly and cocooned her hand with both of his while she spoke to him in Arabic. He nodded slowly as she explained, looking at me occasionally to get the measure of me.

'I have brought you a bargain,' she said to him in French. 'It's real Louis Vuitton. We would like to swap it for all she needs for her journey in the Atlas.'

The old man took Chloë's suitcase to the back of his shop and inspected it closely, springing the brass locks, examining the lining and the reinforced leather corners. He stowed it beside his chair and then swept the shop with his hand.

'Take what you need,' he said.

Then he sat.

I found a large rucksack, a bedroll and a sleeping bag.

'Will I need a mosquito net?'

He clicked his tongue.

'Too high for mosquitoes,' he said.

'I need boots,' I told Rabia.

'What size?' The old man asked.

'Forty,' I told him.

'Please wait here.'

And he stood and left his stall.

'What else do I need, Rabia?'

Rabia grinned at me.

'I don't know. It is exciting,' she said. 'An adventure.' Suddenly her expression changed. 'I am sorry about your brother, Aisha.'

Her mother's compassion illuminated her face for the first time since we'd met.

'Thank you, Rabia.' Looking at the hub of life all around me, I felt ashamed for not having thought of Jose without her prompting. 'He would have loved it here,' I told her.

The old man returned with a pair of solid-looking leather walking boots.

'They are size forty-one but they are good.' He turned them over to show me the heavy soles. 'You will wear thick socks.' And he handed me the boots and a pair of socks.

'You will need a knife,' he said, digging into the pocket of his jellaba.

His was a pocket knife with a curved wooden handle that looked worn and shiny from use.

'I can't take your knife.'

'Take it,' he said gruffly. 'It is a good one.'

'Thank you.'

He shook his head, almost irritably.

He plucked a metal gourd from above his head and put it in the rucksack with a tin plate, a bowl and a saucepan. He wrapped the boots in plastic and put them in too. Then he tied the bed roll and sleeping bag to straps on the rucksack and handed me the whole bundle.

'Do you have a map?' he asked me.

'No. But I can buy one.'

He wagged his finger at me.

'There are no good maps in Marrakech. I have a good one. It is from Rabat. You will return it to me.'

'Of course.'

He went to the table with the cash register on it and opened the single drawer. He took out several old-fashioned-looking maps and handed me one.

'It is a detailed map from the Ministry of Agriculture. It is accurate.' He turned to Rabia and spoke to her in Arabic. He put his hand on his heart and gave her a slight bow.

'Thank you,' I said again, as Rabia led me away.

He inclined his head a little then turned away.

We walked quickly back along the alleys and I asked Rabia what the old man had said.

'He is a very old friend of my father's. His name is Ahmed. He knows that you are going to see my father and he is pleased. But we must hurry, Aisha. I must get back. Sometimes Rachid comes home for lunch.'

Rachid didn't come home, but my presence unsettled Rabia and she seemed eager to hurry me on my way. She filled my rucksack with three loaves of flat bread, several tins of tuna and sardines, a box of Vache Qui Rit cheese, onions, tomatoes and oranges, a few bars of chocolate, a box of tea and a loaf of sugar. Then she added a torch and purification tablets.

'Leave the water for at least an hour after you have put the tablet in,' she told me. 'Otherwise you will get sick.'

Rabia went to her bathroom cupboard and pulled out a first aid kit.

'This is for your journey,' she said proudly. 'It comes from

Rachid's pharmacy. Tourists like them. There is everything you need in here.' She unzipped the square pouch and held up various items: sterile gauze, a bandage, scissors, burn ointment. 'Even penicillin,' she had said happily. She was like a girl at play. 'Three complete doses in case of infection. Don't give it away, though. They love medicine up there, but you might need it. You must remember that in the mountains you are weaker than they are.'

I gave Rabia Chloë's Klee picture. When she unwrapped it and looked down at the naïve image of the sleeping man, she was unable to hide her disappointment.

'It will remind me of you,' she said, smiling bravely.

'I don't know why,' I said. 'I just liked it.'

She looked up at me.

'I am glad you came here, Aisha. I hope that you find what you're looking for.'

I picked up my rucksack.

'Thank you, Rabia.'

'Thanks are not necessary.'

We kissed goodbye on the steps of her building.

Through the window of Omar's cab I watched her walk up the steps to that stranded building and I thought of poor Fatima returning to her Bluebeard.

Omar raced along the Avenue Mohammed V, overtaking on the inside lane. It was a forty-minute drive to Agour, where the path into the mountains began, and he was in a good mood at the thought of the fare. He sang along to the radio.

The road out of town was lined with tall eucalyptus trees. We overtook a moped straining beneath a man, a woman and a little girl. In the middle of a bald field, a camel stood beside a single thorny tree. Jose would have loved the camel.

Omar was heading towards a roadblock. He slowed as a policeman in khaki uniform flagged him down.

The policeman touched his cap and addressed him in French.

'Where are you taking this woman?'

191

'To Agour.'

The policeman scanned the inside of the car and then turned to me.

'French?' he inquired. 'Italian?'

'Portuguese,' I answered.

'You are going walking?'

'Yes,' I answered.

'Not alone?'

'She will get a guide in Agour,' Omar cut in.

'Only an official guide please, *mademoiselle*. Ask to see his card. It will have the stamp of the Ministry of Tourism. Unofficial guides will cheat you. There are many thieves in Agour.'

'I will look after her,' Omar said.

The policeman glanced irritably at him then gave me a slight bow.

'Have an agreeable stay in Morocco, *mademoiselle*.' He touched the brim of his cap again and waved us on.

'Why did he stop us?' I asked Omar as we pulled away.

'No reason,' Omar sang. 'The police like tourists.'

In the distance the mountains were turning pink in the setting sun. Omar saw me looking at them and announced smugly, 'Yes, *mademoiselle*, you will like it here.'

❀

Omar had a cousin in Agour. His name was Salim.

'Salim will be your guide,' Omar announced as we drove along the only asphalt road in town.

'I don't want a guide, thank you, Omar.'

'But first,' he added, 'we will celebrate. Salim's wife will prepare a couscous. We will spend the night at Salim's house. He has plenty of room. And in the morning you will set out on your walk.'

'I don't want a guide, Omar.'

Omar smiled and shook his head.

'I don't need a guide.' I told him firmly. 'I have a map.'

'We will see,' he said. 'First we will eat.'

He parked the car beneath a cluster of eucalyptus trees and then, carrying my rucksack, he led me across a scraggy field littered with refuse and grazing goats, towards a group of low white houses. Children, appearing from nowhere, gathered around us, clamouring in French for pens or sweets. The older ones asked for coins.

'There!' said Omar, pointing to a stony path that sloped steeply down towards a wood. 'That is the path into the mountains.'

I could hear rushing water.

'A river?'

'Small river,' Omar said.

When we reached the houses we passed several men wandering through the network of muddy alleys but no women. The men all turned their heads to look at me. Some came up to Omar and greeted him in order to get a closer look at me.

A little hand touched my watch. I looked down and saw a girl of six or seven smiling up at me. I smiled back and she stuck out her tongue. Omar's hand shot out and smacked her cheek. She ran away, crying loudly.

'Don't do that again, please,' I told him.

'Children must be punished for rudeness.' I was about to object when Omar threw up his hands in delight. 'Salim! My cousin!'

Salim was a tall, handsome youth. His wavy hair glistened with oil. He wore a Brazilian football shirt and green wristbands. He came at me with the most insincere of smiles and shook my hand. I stepped into his courtyard, knowing that I was walking into a trap.

Salim was young but he had already produced three daughters. They gathered around me in the small yard, touching and stroking me. He introduced his wife Myriam, who smiled shyly at me, then retreated behind the laundry that she was hanging out to dry.

'We will go and buy food for the journey,' Salim explained. 'We will need a little money. Not much. The market is cheap.'

'I have food, thank you, and I wish to make the journey alone.'

Salim glanced uneasily at Omar, who said, 'I have tried to explain to her that she cannot walk in these mountains without a guide.'

'It is dangerous,' Salim said to me, speaking as he might to a child. 'In April there is still a lot of snow. You will get lost.'

'Thank you for your concern, but I will not get lost. I have a map. I was brought up in the mountains. I do not need a guide.'

'Not *these* mountains,' Omar said. 'Even *I* would not go up there alone.'

'I am grateful for your help, but I must insist. I am visiting a close friend and I do not want company.'

Omar faced me with new interest while Salim asked, 'A friend? From where? Who is this friend?'

I hesitated.

'He is a sheikh,' I told them. 'He has recently arrived here from Paris. He is living with his family in the village of Tamghurt.'

'This is Sheikh Laraoui!' Salim cried. 'I know him!' He rested his hand piously on his heart. 'He is a holy man. And I know Tamghurt well. I have family there. It would be an honour for me to take you.'

'No!' I snapped. 'Thank you.'

The men stared at me, shocked by my vehemence.

'I am grateful for your hospitality,' I said. 'For tonight. And of course I'll pay you for it, but I'm leaving at dawn, without a guide.'

I reached down and picked up the smallest daughter.

'What's your name?' I asked her, putting an end to the conversation. The little girl grinned enchantingly and hid her face in her hands.

'Ayesha!' the tallest girl said. 'Name Ayesha.'

I touched my own chest.

'That is my name too.' I pointed to the little girl in my arms: 'Ayesha.' Then I pointed to myself: 'Ayesha.'

Her two elder sisters began to chant my name and clap in a quick, syncopated rhythm.

'Ayesha, Ayesha,' they sang in clear, high voices. Their mother watched them from behind the laundry, poised to stop them at the first sign of my displeasure.

Meanwhile their father shouted at Omar in Arabic. I guessed at his complaint: *Look what you've brought me. Only one night. It's more trouble than it's worth . . .*

I paid Omar the fare from Marrakech and Salim the money for the night. Salim offered fifty of the hundred dirhams to his wife, then changed his mind and gave her a twenty-dirham note, which she stuffed into her bra. The two men, satisfied to be in possession of at least some money, went off together without a backward glance. Myriam disappeared into the dark bungalow and I was left alone with the three little girls, who took my hand and led me to my room.

The room was about ten square metres, with a low, bamboo-lined ceiling. The walls were limewashed and the concrete floor was covered with thick rugs. The girls led me to the cushions that lined the far wall and sat me down. They took my rucksack from my shoulders and gestured for me to lie down. I lay down on the cushions. Little Ayesha stroked my hair, while her sisters began to clap softly in their quick, off-beat rhythm. I closed my eyes and listened to their song.

❖

When I woke it was almost dark. I saw that the girls had taken off my boots and set them in the corner of the room with my rucksack. I found a candle on the windowsill and lit it. I could hear the girls chatting across the yard and smell boiled vegetables.

I sat in the light of the candle and unfolded Ahmed's map.

The heading read: *Ministère de l'agriculture et de la réforme agraire – Rabat*. It was a detailed map of the High Atlas. The peaks were all well over three thousand metres high. I found the sheikh's village. It was in a valley, at an altitude of 2,200 metres. There would be snow at that height and I realized that I was poorly equipped for the cold. I had no waterproof clothing and no gloves. Still, the route seemed to be littered with villages. I could pay for lodging. I folded the map and imagined Jose looking over me, amused by my inexperience.

I heard men shouting at the gate. I looked through my window into the courtyard. Salim and Omar were back, swaying arm in arm. I heard Myriam chastising them. Then she sent them packing. The metal gate banged shut behind them. I felt cold. I lay on the cushions and wrapped myself in a blanket. I looked through the window at the night sky, thick with stars. It was hard to imagine that only a few months before I had been lying in Jose's flat with the notion of starving myself to death. I wondered, with shame, what the sheikh had thought of my behaviour. Suicidal gesturing, Pierre would have called it.

My thoughts were interrupted by little Ayesha standing in the doorway. I beckoned to her and she came and tugged me by the hand. I got up and followed her across the courtyard and into one of the two rooms that made up the little bungalow. Myriam and the two elder girls were sitting cross-legged on the floor. Myriam smiled at me and nodded encouragingly. I noticed that she had outlined her eyes with black kohl.

'Come,' the eldest girl said in French and she patted a cushion beside her. In the centre of the room was a steaming tajine dish set on an upturned washbasin. Myriam tore the flat bread and handed each of us a piece to scoop up the food with. It was not couscous but lamb tajine. They ate noisily, mopping up the sauce, pausing occasionally to smile at me.

While Myriam cleared up, the girls sang for me, their chins raised. They used the washbasin and a plastic bucket for percussion. Myriam returned and sat down beside me on the cushions, her hennaed feet folded beneath her, and joined in the singing. When they had finished, I went to my room to look for presents for them. I returned with my sponge-bag and handed out the few creams and lotions that I had. I gave all the make-up to Myriam, who nodded and smiled her approval. Then she pulled out the hairbrush and began to brush my hair.

The men returned after we had gone to bed. I was woken by the noise of the gate slamming. One of them kicked over a metal bucket in the courtyard. I reached for my clock. It was one a.m. I had no wish to meet them, so I set the alarm for five. Soon I could hear snoring.

I opened my eyes just before the alarm sounded and felt wide awake. I dressed and put on my rucksack. I put a one-hundred-dirham note under the candle, thinking that this would more than pay for the blanket that I was taking as a cloak. Carrying my boots, I tiptoed out into the courtyard. The night was black and cold. Dogs all over the village were howling at each other.

I opened the gate and walked a little way in my socks. Then I sat down on a rock and put on my boots. There was a smell of refuse and I realized that I was sitting beside some kind of rubbish dump. There appeared to be no moon. I stood and held the blanket around me as I walked down the hill towards the stream.

The boots were comfortable; my feet felt held and weighted. I walked down Agour's main street, enjoying the sound of the soles striking the tarmac, emulating my brother's long, sure stride.

✤

The air was a little warmer as I came up out of the valley and looked back at the glow of dawn over the ridge above Agour. I had followed the path across the rushing stream, over boulders and up through a steep walnut grove. Now I could see movement in the town far below. Salim and Omar would probably be sleeping off their hangovers, but Myriam would be up. They would soon find me gone. Myriam's blanket was rolled up and strapped to the top of my rucksack. I walked quickly along the level path that had been cut into the flank of the mountain.

An hour later I was startled by the sound of footsteps running behind me. I spun round. A wiry old man with a staff called out 'Salaam!' as he passed and then disappeared around the bend. I walked on.

The sun was climbing and I was hungry, so I looked for somewhere to stop. I considered building a fire to make tea but could see nowhere suitable. The path dropped steeply before me. Running beside it was an irrigation channel. I could hear children's voices and see the terraces of the first village on Ahmed's map. I followed the path until it levelled out in a walnut grove. A stone wall bordered the path and several children ran along the wall beside me, calling for sweets.

'Bonbons! Bonbons!'

I showed them empty hands.

'Un dirham!' one of them called.

I quickened my pace and one by one they began to fall back.

The path wove steeply down through the village. The houses, built of red earth and stone, clung to the hillside in terraces. There was a bang like a gun going off, and I looked up in the direction of the noise. A woman in a bright pink headscarf was smiling down at me from her roof. She was shaking out a heavy rug. I smiled back at her and walked on. The path descended to a wide, grassy riverbed. Women were bent over, gathering weeds from the shallow water. They stood and waved to me as I passed. I waved back at them from the muddy bank.

I found a large boulder in a spot sheltered from the cold breeze and sat down. I decided not to bother with a fire and instead drank water from my gourd. Using Ahmed's knife, I spread Vache Qui Rit and sliced tomato onto some bread and ate hungrily. When I had finished, I looked at the map and found the first village: Illissi. Driven by their curiosity, women and children were moving through the shallows towards me. I decided to move on.

The path started to climb steeply and I found that I was slower after the food. In the next village I filled my gourd at a well and added one of Rabia's tablets. I was thirsty and out of breath when I sat down on the low wall bordering the irrigation channel. I patted my neck with the icy water but remembered Rabia's advice and didn't drink. I started again up the path. There were few trees now and the flanks of the mountain were mostly rock and scree. Here and there, small goats with eerily human voices bleated at me.

The sun was high when I decided to find a place to stop and drink from my gourd. Up ahead, a large red boulder bordered the path where it began to curl around the spur of the mountain. When I reached the rock I was panting. I took my rucksack from my shoulders and sat down on its smooth surface. Sweat dripped from my hairline. I gulped down the cold water.

I thought of the sheikh, who a few months before would have travelled along this same path with his family. With his breathlessness, he would surely have ridden on a mule. Perhaps Rachida and Khaled had made the journey on foot. I thought of the wisdom of that letter of his, of how he had warned me against myself. He had urged me to open my eyes and live. Only now did his exhortation make sense. Surely that was what I was doing now?

I took another swig from the gourd and screwed on the lid. I wrapped the black scarf that Rabia had given me around my head and walked on. This walking was all I wanted: my feet treading the hard earth, the sound of dislodged stones falling as I passed, the rhythm of my breath.

I reached the village of Aadi at dusk. I smelled wood smoke before I turned the bend and saw the cluster of houses settled in a bluish mist below me. My legs felt weak and unsteady on the downward slope. Stones fell on the path before me and I looked up. Coming straight down the steep, rocky slope was a teenage girl driving her goats before her with a stick. She dropped down in front of me onto the path.

'Aadi?' I asked her.

'Aadi,' she repeated and walked on.

I caught up with her and we walked side by side. She clicked her tongue at her goats when they strayed from the path, and they obeyed her immediately.

'Is there somewhere in the village I can stay for the night?' I asked, pointing towards the village and resting my cheek on my praying hands to mime sleep.

'You can stay in my house,' she said in French. 'Come.'

She quickened her pace. As we entered the village, she shrieked something in her own language and two boys appeared from one of the alleys as though they had been summoned. The tallest of the two had a roughly shaven scalp that was covered in pink sores. Averting his eyes from me, he took her stick from her and drove the goats on through the village, his little companion running behind him.

The girl urged me to keep up and I followed her down some stone steps to a large door covered in colourful and ornate patterns. As we drew near I saw that they were flattened sardine tins that had been nailed onto the wood. The girl opened the door and called out again in her shrill voice. We were standing on a small balcony. Ahead were steps down to a garden and on either side of us was a room. A woman appeared in the doorway to my right and stood watching me, her arms folded. The young girl tugged at my rucksack.

'Take off your shoes,' she said. 'My mother will bring you tea.'

I put down my rucksack and began to untie my boots.

The girl's mother had markings tattooed in black on her chin. She said something to her daughter, then stood aside and spread her hand to show me the room.

'This is where you will sleep,' the girl said. 'We will bring tea.'

I stepped into the room and let my legs fold under me.

Almost as soon as I felt the rugs beneath me, I fell asleep. I woke minutes or hours later to the strange call of those goats. A man's face appeared behind the ornate bars on the window and then vanished. I crawled over to the window. It gave onto a narrow alley. The man, wearing a grey jellaba with the hood up, hurried away without looking back. Beyond him I looked at the terraces on the far side of the steep valley, lit by the setting sun.

The girl stepped into the room, her mother following with the tea tray.

'Thank you,' I said. 'Please tell me. How much is it for food and a bed for the night?'

'Ten dirhams,' the girl said, setting the tray down in front of me. The mother smiled at me and followed her dour daughter out of the room.

I drank the sweet tea and read some of the sheikh's poems. My mind skated off the words. Did I stand between my brother and life? Was that why he destroyed himself?

The young girl came back and announced that I was to follow her. She led me down some cement steps to a garden with a small vegetable plot at one end. Scrawny chickens scattered before us. We passed beneath the steps and through a door into a dark room that smelled of damp. Her mother was stirring an omelette over a gas stove with a single ring. It was made with vegetables from the garden and I ate ravenously, happy with the lack of conversation. I provided oranges, which we washed down with sweet tea.

Lying in my sleeping bag afterwards, I closed my eyes. The rugs beneath me floated as if on water. I pictured the miraculous village clinging in perilous tiers to the mountainside and I adrift within it, like the sleeping man in the Klee painting.

❧

I left the village of Aadi at six the next morning, after a breakfast of tea, bread and apricot jam. The girl's mother accepted the ten dirhams, gave me some almonds and some dried apricots for my journey and sent me off with a blessing in Berber.

The sun was rising behind me as I began the steep climb up to the ridge called Tizi-n-Ifri. Beyond that was Adrar Idris, the highest peak in the region, and beyond that, the sheikh's valley. My pack felt heavier than it had the day before and within minutes I was out of breath. I stopped and leaned over, panting, my hands resting on my knees. The goats stopped their grazing among the barren rocks to watch me.

I walked on, trying, in spite of the steep angle, to place the soles of my boots flat on the ground as Jose had taught me. The cold air burned my lungs. I drove my hands into my pockets and wished for gloves. I could hear my pulse banging in my ears. At each plateau, I stopped to rest. I climbed for two hours, my mind free of thought.

Soon the path was so steep that I would slide backwards unless I could find a stone to rest the toe of my boot on. I began to sing in an attempt to keep up a steady pace. I sang the Portuguese children's song that Katarina had taught us. It was a song about a butterfly, *borboleta,* and we would sing it when we rode Castagna, our stepfather's mule. Sylvino used to punch the mule in the face when she refused to move, but his anger only made her more stubborn. When Jose and I rode her she was obedient. Her ears would twitch at the sound of our song.

I stopped at a large rock where I sat and ate my lunch, the food balanced on my knee. I ate bread and sardines from the tin followed by half a bar of chocolate. I drank a little water and walked on.

An hour later I was climbing on all fours and my hands were freezing. I looked back and saw two men walking towards me on the path. They were moving quickly on foot, driving a mule before them. I kept climbing but soon I had to stand aside because I could hear their voices behind me. I leaned against a boulder and waited. The men did not seem to be feeling the cold. They were dressed lightly in tattered Western clothes and on their feet were worn leather shoes. I guessed they were father and son. They greeted me in Arabic, bowing their heads, and passed quickly on. I stood and watched them and their heavily laden mule disappear over the crest of the hill.

White clouds began to gather and block out the sun, and the wind turned bitter cold. I took out Myriam's blanket, folded it in half lengthways and wrapped it around my upper body. I tried to fix the blanket around my waist but my belt was not long enough, so I tucked the blanket into my jeans as best I could.

When I reached the top of the hill I looked out over a plateau which sloped gently upwards. Here was the snow. At first it only dusted the stones, but soon it covered the land, rubbing out its contours. The father and son and their mule were black spots moving steadily towards the next ridge. I was grateful for their footprints because the path had vanished. I hurried on towards them, my hands wrapped in the blanket. I was hungry and thirsty, but didn't dare stop in case I lost sight of them. My anxiety made me lose faith in my abilities with the map and I ran blindly after the two strangers.

I had to struggle not to lose balance in the wind. The father and son were moving too quickly. Soon they disappeared over the ridge. I began to feel afraid. I tried to run faster but my rucksack was weighing me down. I wished Ahmed had not burdened me with so much stuff, all of it useless to me. I didn't have what I needed: gloves, a hat and waterproof clothes. The wind pushed against me, whipping snow from the ground into my face.

I reached the next ridge and below me stretched a wide valley with a frozen lake overlooked by a cluster of stone huts. Rising up behind them was Idris, a forbidding, square mountain shrouded in black cloud. I spotted the father and son moving towards the lake. I shouted out to them, but my voice was carried off by the wind.

I began to walk down the slope towards the huts. The light seemed to darken a shade every time I blinked. The wind had dropped and it was snowing hard. Soon all I could see were snowflakes, lit by an oblique grey light and floating all around me. The men, the huts and the lake had disappeared.

There was something calming about the snow. I thought of Jose and his Paris snow scene, of how it had soothed him when I had given it to him in his cave. He loved snow. It had been in the air the week he had killed himself. I remembered the smell of it that week, something like wet cardboard. On my first night at the sheikh's, it had begun to fall. I imagined my brother there with me on that frozen mountain. With him beside me I would not have been scared. I would have been able to admire its majesty.

When I reached the valley it had stopped snowing. The ground had flattened out and every few steps my boots sank deep into the snow. I stopped to rest. Before me was the lake. Black reeds rose up through the ice and rattled in the wind. I looked out across the lake to the huts, but there was no light and no sign of the two travellers. I guessed that they were strong and would be able to make the walk into the next valley before dark. I would have to do the same or find shelter in the hut. I looked for footprints but the wind constantly swept the surface of the lake.

The climb up to the huts was steeper than it had looked. When I reached them my lungs were burning. I took off my rucksack and dropped it on the ground and walked among the stone buildings. There were seven of them and they were all deserted. I went from hut to hut, trying the doors, but they were all locked or barred. I stood and listened to the wind howling through the gaps in the stone walls. There was no sign of life.

I trudged back to my rucksack and took out Ahmed's map and held it as best I could between my numb fingers. I found the lake and the huts, marked with the word *Azib,* and saw that the footpath ran along the far side of the lake, then perpendicular to it and zigzagged up the slope on the far side of the valley. I looked out over the white landscape for the two men but I could only see as far as the lake. My legs were weak and shaking from the last descent. I had to make up my mind: either to walk on or to find shelter and rest.

I was wondering what my brother would have done when I heard the sound of something flapping in the wind. I turned and looked at the hut behind me. Up on the roof some plastic sheeting had torn loose. I walked round the side of the hut. Against the wall was a metal barrel for collecting rainwater. I folded the map and put it in my pocket and climbed onto the barrel and stood on the frozen surface of the water. It was a short climb to the roof and there were gaps in the masonry for my toes. My legs trembled as I climbed. I pulled myself onto the roof and I felt a rush of optimism. The flapping plastic sheet covered a hole in the roof wide enough, I could see, to climb through. I crawled along the slate tiles and looked down through the hole into the dark interior. It was a long drop to the mud floor and there were no rugs or cushions, just a scythe hanging from a hook in the wall. I realized then that I might be able to sleep in there, but that I wouldn't be able to get out again. I would imprison myself.

I sat on the roof, hugging myself against the wind. Then I crawled back along the tiles and climbed down and went back to my rucksack. I emptied out several objects – the plate, bowl, sponge bag – and dropped them where I stood, in the snow. I put on more clothes beneath the blanket and wrapped a sweater around my head, all the time talking to myself. *Come on, you stupid girl. Keep moving.* I wrapped plastic bags around my boots, tying them on with the laces. Then I put socks on my hands. *That's right, you idiot. Now move if you want to stay alive.*

My muscles were cold again and my legs shook with each step as I walked back down the hill to the lake. I concentrated on the business of placing one foot in front of the other. I walked around the lake and then turned towards the mountain. My left leg became stiff in the climb and my hips started to ache, slowing me down. I heard bleating and I looked up and saw a white ram. Snow swirled in the night sky behind its head. The animal was a good size. I thought if I could catch it and kill it with Ahmed's knife, then I could cut it open and crawl inside its warm body and go to sleep. The ram looked down at me, then turned and disappeared. The wind had dropped and I did not feel so cold. I ate some chocolate and drank from the gourd. Then I walked on.

Soon I regretted having given up the hut. My legs were trembling violently with each step and I was afraid that they might buckle at any moment. If I had only thought a little, I could have found rocks and branches and dropped them through the hole in the roof and built some kind of structure for my exit. I stopped and looked around me. What I saw defeated me. It was dark and the wind had dropped and the snow was still falling gently all around me. There were no features to the landscape: no ridge, no rock, no tree, no lake – *a page with nothing on it.*

I imagined Jose reading that poem on the morning of his death. I thought of him sitting on the train to Saint-Cloud with his can of petrol in his backpack. Had he looked out of the window and watched the world with detachment, with hostility, or with the affection of someone who was about to leave it? I saw him walking, in his steady gait, to that spot of immaculate lawn. What had been in his mind as he poured petrol over himself? Had he thought of me? I looked up at the snow spiralling towards me and heard my own sob. If I had come to this desolate place on some wild quest to know my brother's thoughts, then I had failed. I was alone in the wild, as he had been, but I would never know him. This was all I had learned. We were not alike: he had not only survived in the wilderness, he had thrived on it.

I was lost and scared. I no longer knew in which direction the sheikh's village lay. I could not go on walking blindly into the night. I turned and started back down the slope towards the huts. Several times in the descent I stumbled. Then I drifted off to sleep where I fell.

A new kind of warmth enveloped me. It was as if I was enfolded and weightless, an animal curled up in the snow. My eyes were narrow slits. My mind was free of thought.

I was not woken by the two men. When they found me I was awake and ready to stand, my mind sharp. Something else had woken me: some idea, rising up from the unconscious and bursting on the surface of my mind. I had been looking down into what I thought was a black lake, searching for something precious that lay at the bottom. As I looked I felt dizzy, as though the world had turned and I was looking up and not down and the lake was the night sky, free of snow and clouds but littered with stars.

The two men dropped to their knees on either side of me. The older man gave quick, soft commands to the younger one, who dug the snow out around my body and covered me with a heavy blanket. Then the father spoke to me and I smiled at him and said 'Thank you' in French and English and Portuguese. Then he lifted me into his arms and carried me back down the mountain. I let my head rest on his shoulder and I could feel his breath on my face and smell his digestion and I closed my eyes and imagined that he was my own father Fausto, come to rescue me.

He carried me across the lake and past the huts to a stone refuge that must have been built after Ahmed's map had been drawn. When the two men had passed me on the mountain, they had assumed that I was heading there. When I had not appeared three hours later, they had gone out to find me. This I learned with no common language between us. I also gathered that they were both called Mohammed and they were father and son, as I'd guessed.

They had built a fire in the refuge and they sat me beside it and took off my boots. The father rubbed my frozen feet between his rough palms with quick, expert movements and for a long time. When he had finished he leaned back and gave an order to his son and while he stoked the fire, the young Mohammed fetched some sheepskin slippers from the mule pack and put them on my feet.

The room was soon warm and we could no longer see our breath in the air. I sat in my sleeping bag, watching the flames, while the men boiled water and made tea.

The father didn't seem unkind, but the young Mohammed appeared cowed. He was overshadowed by his father's stature and carried out his orders without a word. At his father's request, he took an object wrapped in newspaper from his saddle-bag and carefully unwrapped it on his lap as if it were something valuable. It was a half-frozen piece of mutton, which he dropped into a pot with a fistful of snow and cooked slowly over the fire. He added potatoes and carrots and onions and made the most delicious stew I had ever tasted. I ate ravenously, grateful for the lack of conversation. The food seemed to thaw the son a little and I heard his voice for the first time. He spoke to his father in staccato bursts between mouthfuls. His face was like his father's, only rounder and softer. When he had wiped his plate clean with his bread, he made a pot of sweet mint tea. I produced the rest of my chocolate, which the two men nibbled slowly as I sat there floating happily on the edge of sleep.

I was woken later that night by old Mohammed. He lightly touched my shoulder and gestured for me to lie down on the thick blanket which he had folded into a mattress for me. I glanced at the sleeping body of his son a few paces away and obeyed, crawling over to the blanket in my sleeping bag. Mohammed the elder then wrapped himself in his blanket and lay down beside his son on the hard floor.

For a while I lay there listening to their breathing and watching the embers of the fire. The father talked in his sleep. Sometimes he shouted and I guessed that he was giving orders to his mule, which was now tied up in the adjoining room. I considered the elegance and tact of these two strangers, who had rescued me without display and had then done me the courtesy of showing not the slightest interest in what I might be doing up there, alone on that mountain. I ran Jose's medallion back and forth on its chain and marvelled at the luck of being alive.

The next morning I woke to see the young Mohammed take a small axe from the saddle-bag and step out of the door and into the immaculate landscape. Framed by the doorway, the valley looked wide and grand in the dazzling sunshine. A lone bird sang close by, its three notes striking the emptiness over and over again. The father came into view and began to snap twigs from a scraggy tree. I lay listening, my sleeping bag pulled up to my nose. When he came inside with an armful of twigs, I sat up and said *Bonjour*. He nodded graciously at me and said something in Berber and then set about rebuilding the fire.

When the young Mohammed returned with more firewood, I crawled out of my sleeping bag and put on my boots. My body ached all over. The men lit the fire and boiled water for tea, and we ate breakfast with my provisions, toasting the hard bread and eating it with Vache Qui Rit. After breakfast they began to load up their mule and I felt dread at the moment when I would be left alone again.

We took the path that I had seen on Ahmed's map. As we set off across the valley, Mohammed offered his mule for me to ride on but I declined, knowing that it would be harder for me when we parted. White clouds raced across the sky, casting shadows over the ice lake. When we reached the far side I saw the men's footprints from their search for me the night before. After ten minutes of climbing my hips ached and I was limping again. The young Mohammed took my hand and drew me up the slope behind him. With his help I could have walked for another day.

When we reached the crest of the hill, the next slope rose up steeply before us. Old Mohammed turned to me and bowed slightly. This was where we would separate. I watched him open his saddle-bag and I tried to smile, but I felt bereft when he handed me a jar of honey as a parting gift. I took off my rucksack and gave them the last few slices of Vache Qui Rit.

The old man pointed out the path. I could see it clearly now, an indentation in the snow weaving up the next mountain. Old Mohammed squinted into the sun and gestured to me that they would be turning east into another valley, and that theirs was a village in the valley beyond that. I understood that their journey would take them two more days. I looked at the deep lines around his eyes and across the bridge of his nose and thought that if he had lived my father would have been about the same age.

As we parted, they put their hands on their hearts. I thanked them, delaying the moment when they would leave me alone again, and as I spoke, they shifted uncomfortably on the spot. Young Mohammed kept his eyes on the ground and did not look at me once. As soon as I had stopped talking they turned and walked off. I watched them until they had disappeared over the ridge.

Being alone was not as bad as I had anticipated. My spirits were lifted by the sound of my tread on the squeaking snow and by the glare of the sunshine on the pristine landscape. As long as I didn't have to spend another night on that mountain, I was happy. My hips still ached and I was limping, but I walked slowly and steadily and was only a little short of breath when I reached the next ridge. By midday I was crossing a wide plateau strewn with vast boulders that looked as though they had been left there by gods or aliens. As I walked among them I felt like a trespasser.

Three hours later I reached the edge of a precipice and looked down into the last valley. The magnificent view made me think of Satan's brag: *All this shall be yours*. I remembered wondering as a child why Christ had not simply answered: *But it is all mine*. The suggestion was that the world belonged to Satan and that Christ was a guest in it. I sat down on my rucksack and let my feet hang over the edge. I drank water from the gourd and contemplated the sheikh's valley far below. The descent was steep and south-facing and the snow soon gave way to green. The narrow path wound down the rocky slope, a mosaic of russet and sage green, then disappeared where the lush terraces began. Below the cultivated land was a dark forest and below that a sliver of water gleaming in the sunlight.

As I surveyed the sheikh's village I was struck, by the absurdity of this journey. I'd come all this way with no clear idea of what I was looking for, except perhaps for escape. I wondered how I'd explain my presence at the sheikh's door. With luck I wouldn't have to: Rachida would sweep me up with her welcome.

I remembered the sheikh sitting on Jose's red chair, his long shoes poking out from beneath his white robe, lost in thought as he waited out my hatred and my scorn. I remembered the feeling of his hand grasping the back of my neck as he lifted my head to the water glass. A vestige of some dark tradition from my past made me believe, then, that I'd come to repay a debt. I looked down into that radiant valley. Then I stood up, shouldered my rucksack and began the descent.

❦

On my first night in Tamghurt I lay awake wishing I'd never come. For all my grand ideas of debt and redemption, my meeting with the sheikh had been a disappointment. I told myself that I'd been stupid to expect anything other than the circumspect welcome I'd received from him. He hadn't even been surprised to see me at his door.

He had stood in the dark hall of his house, shorter and frailer than I'd remembered him, leaning on a stick, unable to look me in the eye. He seemed to be waiting out Rachida's effusions of wonder and delight as if they were an embarrassment.

'Khaled will be so happy,' she said, taking my rucksack from my shoulders and laying it on the floor. Then she opened the front door and called sternly in Berber to the group of children who had escorted me to her house. 'I have sent them to fetch him,' she told me, closing the door. Then she took my hands in hers. 'I cannot believe you came all this way. I cannot believe you walked from Agour. Isn't it wonderful?' she said, turning to her husband.

I saved him from the need to reply:

'You have a stick now.'

He answered defensively:

'It is necessary on these paths.'

For a long moment no one spoke. Rachida let go of my hands. I sensed her discomfort. Absurdly, I bent down and began rifling through my rucksack.

'Here,' I said, taking out the small leather-bound volume. 'I brought your poems back.'

The sheikh looked down at the book in my hand and said:

'It was a gift to your brother. I do not want it returned to me.'

I blushed, then said cheerily:

'I'll keep it then.'

'Yes,' he had said, more gently. 'It is better if you keep it.'

That first day in Tamghurt was spent in a daze of tiredness and disappointment. That day I was blind to the beauty of the tear-shaped valley; to the mountains, like velvet, fading from purple to lilac to mauve; to the lush green terraces; to the eagles wheeling overhead. I was immune to the scent of flowering broom filling the air and to the wonder of that village, clawed by generations from the mountainside and teeming with life.

After the sheikh had refused his book of poems, Rachida sent us up to the roof terrace.

'Go with my husband,' she had said. 'I am sure you have much to tell him. I will hear it later.'

After she'd gone the sheikh waited for me to take off my boots and led me up a flight of outside steps to the roof. A large rug was spread on the cement floor and shaded by a bower of jasmine. The sheikh gestured for me to sit, then sat down cross-legged opposite me.

'We're both limping,' I said.

He looked at my bruised and blistered feet.

'You walked from Agour?'

'Yes.'

I could not help feeling proud.

'Alone?'

'I met people on the way,' I said. 'I was a little lost when I got to Idris. A father and son helped me.'

'It is a long walk.'

'Yes.'

'It was dangerous to do it alone, especially at this time of year,' he said. 'Even people who were born here do not cross that mountain alone until the snow melts.'

I blushed a second time.

After this chastisement we endured each other's attempts at conversation until Khaled bounded up the steps and released us.

When I saw him I couldn't help myself:

'You've grown!' I cried.

Khaled beamed. He looked at his father and pointed at me.

'What's *she* doing here?'

'Khaled! Your manners!' his mother said, stepping onto the terrace behind him.

'I've come for a rematch,' I said to him.

'No PlayStation,' Khaled answered gloomily in his new, deep voice. 'There's no electricity.'

Rachida sat down beside me and began to pour tea into four glasses, her bangles jangling on her wrists.

'Come and sit, Khaled,' she said. 'Where have you been?' she added, handing him a glass.

'Nowhere,' he answered sulkily. 'There's nothing to do here.'

I realized that the teenage posturing was for me.

'How boring,' I said. 'Maybe I shouldn't stay.'

'*You* might find it interesting,' he answered hastily. 'Because you're a foreigner.'

'Will you show me around?'

His face lit up.

'Where do we start?' I asked him.

'The mosque,' he answered. 'There are thirty men working on it today because they're doing the roof and it dries quickly, so they need a lot of people. I've been helping . . . a little.'

'She will see the mosque tomorrow,' Rachida said. 'I am taking her to the *hammam* . . .'

'Tomorrow will be too late!' Khaled moaned. 'They'll have already done the roof!'

'Aisha walked alone from Agour, Khaled. She needs a *hammam*. Today is ladies' day.'

Khaled's mouth dropped open.

'You walked from Agour? By yourself?'

Khaled's admiration would not help me win the sheikh's, so I changed the subject.

'I met a friend of yours in Marrakech,' I told the old man.

'Indeed.'

'Ahmed. He gave me his knife. And he lent me a map.'

The sheikh nodded but showed no enthusiasm.

'Ahmed is a good man,' he said.

'Were you scared?' Khaled asked.

'A little,' I answered, smiling at him.

'You seem to have a tendency to put yourself in danger,' the sheikh said. 'You must expect fear by now.'

I couldn't think of an answer to this, so I turned to Rachida:

'It's hard to believe that five days ago I was in Paris.'

'How did you find us?' she asked.

'I went to see Rabia in Marrakech. I got her address from Fatima.'

Rachida shook her head in wonder.

The sheikh rose painfully to his feet.

'Please excuse me,' he said, gesturing for his stick, which Khaled handed him without looking up. It was time for the afternoon prayer. I stood up and held out my hand to help him.

'You are welcome here, Aisha,' he said, gripping my hand with grim determination.

'Thank you, Sheikh Laraoui.'

I wanted to say something about not staying for long, but he quickly turned away. I watched him limp to the steps and wondered at my stupidity at having come all this way for a cantankerous old man.

❦

The sun had disappeared behind the mountain as Rachida and I walked to the *hammam*. There was a smell of firewood in the air and the village was filled with kitchen sounds.

'Do not mistake my husband,' she told me. 'He is happy to see you. He is tired and sicker than he pretends to be.'

She explained that since they had come to the mountains he was often short of breath, especially at night. She would find herself lying awake like the mother of a newborn, listening to his breathing. Sometimes he had periods of apnoea so long that she would wake him to get him to breathe again.

The *hammam* was in a small building made of breeze blocks, set on a muddy slope and surrounded by chickens picking their way through scattered waste. Beneath the building was a large terracotta wood-burning stove, which heated the room above. When Rachida and I arrived, we were alone. We undressed in a little antechamber and Rachida folded our clothes carefully and put them in a basket. Then she took my hand and led me into the hot, dark room.

'Lie down,' she said, so I lay down and she poured water onto the hottest part of the floor to make steam. 'There,' she said. 'Now you will sweat.' And she knelt beside my naked body and began to massage me all over. She started at my head, pressing her fingertips into my scalp, then my face, moving down to my neck and shoulders and arms. She worked vigorously, perspiration dripping from her face onto mine. She rubbed my chest, working around my breasts and pressing hard on the sternum, then she took first one leg, then the other, and bending it at the knee, turned it outwards from my hip so that it cracked in its socket. She rubbed my aching thighs and calves and feet. She poured another cupful of water onto the floor and made more steam so that my body was slippery under her hands, then she told me to turn over and she began to work on my back. I lay with my cheek pressed to the smooth, hot floor, sweat dripping from my face and drool from my mouth.

'Word has got round,' Rachida whispered. 'They have come to look at you.'

Through the steam I saw that the women had left a respectful space around Rachida and me, but otherwise sat and lay on the hot floor, their sweating bodies pressed up together. I didn't care how many they were, nor that they could see me lying face down, stark naked, legs splayed. I had given myself up to the miracle of Rachida's hands.

'Now the glove,' she said, turning me over. 'For soft skin.'

And she set to work, rubbing my body with a rough cloth until my skin smarted.

'Close your eyes,' she whispered.

I let her arrange my limbs, hands and feet so that they were limp. Then she poured warm water from a pitcher all over me, rinsing away the dead skin. She hummed softly as she poured and the water felt like fingers being dragged gently over my skin.

Rachida didn't let me massage her.

'Next time,' she said, giving her body a summary scrub with the glove. While she exchanged a few words with the other women, I sat slumped in the corner. Then she helped me home and made a bed of cushions for me in her weaving room on the top floor of the house. She covered me with a blanket that smelled of goat. Then she leaned over me, enveloping me in the scent of her argan-oil soap, kissed her fingers and pressed them to my forehead and left the room.

Rachida's tenderness had always made me weak. When she had gone, I lay beneath the heavy goat-hair blanket and cried. The reunion was not what I'd dreamed of. The sheikh hadn't welcomed me like some lost disciple. He wouldn't impart some deep wisdom to me or give me the sense that I had been right to come all this way to see him. I'd misread the letter he had written from his cell in Vincennes. It hadn't been an invitation but a dignified farewell. He had loved my brother, not me. My journey had been vain and whimsical.

In the days that followed I learnt how wrong I was about the sheikh's reaction. My appearance at his door had disturbed him profoundly. Ever since his arrival in Tamghurt he had been praying for some sign as to how he should spend the rest of his life. He later told me that he had been feeling redundant as the sheikh of Tamghurt. He missed the lost souls of Blanville, and sensed that these people didn't really need his spiritual guidance. Most of them, he said, lived closer to God in their daily lives than he did. They might be a little slack when it came to *salat,* but as far as he was concerned, two willing prayers were of more value than five reluctant ones. When I had limped up to his door after that impetuous walk over Idris, I'd spooked him. He'd been frightened, more than anything, by what he'd prayed for. Was this what he had been requesting: a visit from this proud, wilful girl in search of a father?

❦

Rachida gave up her weaving room for me. It had a view out to the wide end of the valley. The casement window gave onto her garden and I would wake to the tart, grassy smell of the tomato plants, warmed by the sun. That room was like a chapel or a nun's cell. The window had coloured glass in it, which threw red, blue and green rhomboids onto the whitewashed walls. Rachida pinned up some of her old-fashioned colour-tinted postcards of Paris. They floated above me like small icons of my past: the Sacré Coeur, the Eiffel Tower, Notre Dame, the Arc de Triomphe.

I had brought little with me to add to her decorations, apart from a plastic bag containing Jose's possessions, which I arranged on the windowsill: the Paris snowscape, the Roman oyster shell, the sewing kit from Pan Am and the illegible photograph of our dead father.

That room would become mine in a way that no room ever had before. I'd certainly felt no sense of ownership of the room that I had shared with my brother then slept in alone, filled as it had been with Katarina's tight, oppressive crochet; nor of the stuffy little room with the skylight in my stepfather's DIY palace, which in hot weather smelled of toxic wood varnish. The room that Chloë had made for me under the eaves hooted my betrayal every time I stepped into it. And the room at Odile's, with its fecund wallpaper and plasticized curtains, conceived for adulterous couples, never felt like my own.

My room in Tamghurt was always cool, even on the hottest afternoons. The rising sun turned the walls pink before the cockerels began their pantomime. At night I would sleep with the window open and tilt my head back to look at the stars and listen to the owl in the walnut grove below the sheikh's garden, and sometimes to Ali's groans next door as he delighted in the body of his sweet, shy wife.

I spent so many hours in that room, sitting or lying on my bed beneath the window, dreaming, thinking and reading. It must have been during those hours – with my brother's things on the windowsill behind me and our father's image fading more and more each day – that Jose's spirit or my guilt or whatever it was that had driven me there was set to rest.

❦

On my first morning I was woken by a cockerel. For a moment I thought I was back in Coelhoso. How strange to have come all this way and to find myself in a small village in the mountains with mules and chickens and urchin children. *We've come full circle,* I thought. Then I drifted back to sleep.

I was woken a second time by a new sound: a swelling cry,

too poignant for an animal, beginning low and rising like a distress signal, coming from all around me and dragging me into consciousness. It was the *adhan*, the call to prayer, sung as it should be sung, haunting and exultant.

I got out of bed and opened the window. The sweet smell of flowers hovered above the smell of wood smoke. In the garden below, the laundry flapped in the wind. There was the sheikh's spotless white jellaba hanging beside the coloured aprons and towels.

'Aisha!' I looked up. It was Rachida, waving at me from the roof terrace. She beckoned to me, unwilling to shout over the *muezzin*.

I dressed and went to find her but she was no longer on the roof. I sat down on the parapet and looked out at the mist sitting in the valley. The *muezzin* stopped singing.

'It is a beautiful day!'

I turned to see Rachida carrying a tray.

'Yes, it is.'

I turned back and looked out at the view. The curling terraces were like an ornate amphitheatre and the mist-filled valley was a ghostly stage.

'My husband says that the first settlers must not have been warriors,' Rachida said, laying the tray between us on the low wall. 'Look. As you can see, we are in a circle here, open to attack from all sides.'

'A pretty inaccessible circle,' I said.

Rachida clicked her tongue.

'People are superstitious about Idris. It is not so dangerous. There are places to sleep and the tracks are well marked. The village where I grew up was more remote than this.' She paused, smoothing the creases from her skirt. 'When I was a child my little brother and I would have to cross three valleys to reach the nearest shop.' She smiled. 'We used to run most of the way. My brother was fast and so was I. He wanted to run for Morocco in the Olympic Games. I was his trainer.'

'Where is your brother now?'

'He died when he was twelve, of meningitis.'

'Oh Rachida, I'm sorry.'

She looked down at the tray, then looked up at me and smiled.

'I am happy to be in the mountains again. They remind me of him.'

'What was his name?' I asked.

'Nessim.'

She poured the tea. Then she looked at me, her face brightening with an idea.

'We could go for a picnic,' she said. 'We could go up to the lake. There are big fish that live there.' She held her hands a metre apart. 'They are good to eat. The water is bright green.'

I pictured her as a girl, running all over mountains like these with her little brother at her heels.

'I'd like that,' I said.

'Good. Now eat,' she ordered. On the tray she had laid out a bowl of yoghurt with almonds, the honey from old Mohammed and a plate of her gazelle horns. 'The flour is good here,' she said, holding out the plate. 'It is made with chestnuts.'

I took a cake.

'Our mother used to bake with chestnut flour,' I said.

She watched me eat.

'That is the first time you have mentioned your mother.'

'She's a difficult woman.'

'Our mother was also a difficult woman,' she said. 'She complained all her life. I believe that my father died young to escape her. It is lucky that the daughters of bad mothers are not always bad mothers themselves,' she said. Then she held up her tea glass. '*Bismillah*. To our mothers. Who brought us here.'

Sitting there with Rachida, on that parapet in the Atlas, I surprised myself by raising my glass.

'To our mothers,' I said.

Rachida stayed with me while I ate my breakfast. Her gaze

made me feel like a cosseted child, but this time I didn't back away from her tenderness.

'How long will you stay?' she asked me.

'Not long,' I told her. 'Perhaps a week or two.'

'Why so short? You have come so far! Is it because I have upset you? I was harsh when the sheikh was taken away.'

'You were worried about your husband.'

She shook her head.

'That is no excuse. Will you forgive me?'

'There's nothing to forgive.'

'Then please stay. Stay for as long as you like. My only fear is that you will find life here boring. It is hard for the women. We do nothing but work all day.'

'What about the men? What do they do?'

'Most of them leave the village to find work. They go to Agour for the tourists or they work on the roads.'

'What about Khaled? What will he do?'

Rachida sighed.

'My husband wants him to go to boarding school in Casablanca. He still hopes that Khaled will choose the spiritual life, but I do not think it is likely. He has too much of France in him. Whatever he chooses, he will not be able to get a good education here in the mountains . . .' Then she stopped herself. 'You must let him show you the mosque. He is so happy that you are here.'

Khaled took me to see the mosque after breakfast. With an uncharacteristic show of affection he took my hand and led me up the hill. Occasionally he would stop to quiz me on the details of my journey, particularly the part at Idris.

'You could have died.'

'Rubbish.'

'If those men hadn't come, you would have died.'

'What nonsense. I had warm clothes and food.'

But I hadn't convinced him and when we reached the mosque, he rushed up to the first person he saw to tell them the story of my brush with death.

'This is Ibrahim,' Khaled said. 'He sometimes sings the *adhan* for my father. He has the best voice in the valley,' he added.

I remembered the haunting beauty of the voice that had woken me that morning and I smiled at him. Ibrahim smiled back, revealing a row of black and grey teeth. Apart from his rotting teeth he was remarkably beautiful, with fine, intelligent eyes. He stood clutching a wheelbarrow full of gravel and listened patiently until Khaled had finished his story of my perilous journey. Then he gave his answer to Khaled in Berber, smiling sweetly at me as Khaled translated.

'Ibrahim says that Adrar Idris is wicked. He says that it has eaten many people, especially foreigners.'

Ibrahim seemed kind to Khaled, ruffling his hair affectionately before going back to work. While he raked the gravel over the dry cement at the front of the mosque, he sang in his angelic voice.

The sheikh's new mosque was on a plateau overlooking the village. It was covered with pink cement rendering and there was blue glass above the door, but otherwise it was a simple building with a slender minaret. The muezzin would have a loud-hailer and would not have to climb up for the call to prayer, for there were no stairs: the minaret was just for show.

Khaled introduced me to Hadj, the man who was overseeing the building work. Hadj was slight, with high cheeks and quick, black eyes that eluded mine and never rested. He did not shake my hand but bowed piously at me.

On the walk home I asked Khaled about him.

'No one likes him,' he said. 'He's jealous of my dad. Before my dad came, he was the boss of this village.'

'So the sheikh's the boss of the village?' I asked with amusement.

Khaled shrugged.

'I suppose so. People come to him with their problems. If there's an argument or if someone does something bad, my dad decides what they should do. There aren't any policemen up here.'

'How refreshing,' I said.

'Do you like Ibrahim?' he asked. Then, without waiting for an answer, he added, 'It was Ibrahim who taught me to make a catapult and shoot birds.'

When we got home I looked for the sheikh but there was no sign of him. Rachida led me up to my room to see the improvements she had made. She had moved her loom downstairs and put the postcards of Paris on the walls. She stood in the doorway and watched my face.

'It's lovely, Rachida. Thank you.'

'It is simple,' she said. 'Not like Blanville.'

I smiled.

'It's perfect.'

She laughed.

'I do not know what it is perfect for,' she said. 'Turning in circles, perhaps. Very small circles. The pictures are to make you feel at home. I am sorry that I have no pictures of Portugal.'

'I don't need pictures of Portugal,' I said, moving to the window to look out. 'It is quite like this. Not as beautiful, but almost.' As I looked out at the mountains, the idea came to me that I might try to stay here.

'Aisha! You are scratching.'

She marched over to the window to inspect me, lifting up my shirt to reveal a rash of spots around my midriff. She leant forward to inspect them.

'Fleas. Your skin is too soft. It is because you are new. For Khaled it was the same. Don't worry. They will soon stop bothering you.'

'I'm not worried.'

Rachida took my face in her hands.

'I am the one who must thank you for coming here.' Then she let go of me and said, 'Now, shall we go up to the lake?'

'Yes. Will the sheikh come with us? Or is it too far?'

'The sheikh has gone to Agour to pick up some books.'

Before I could hide my disappointment, Rachida was consoling me.

'He will only be gone one night. He took Hadj's mule. He will be back tomorrow.'

❦

Rachida, Khaled, Ibrahim and I walked up to the lake with a picnic. Rachida kept up a steady pace on the steep path and I was soon out of breath. She stopped and waited for me, resting her hand on her hip and shielding her eyes from the sun.

I stood panting beside her and looked down at the village, cut into the mountainside and wavering in a haze of heat.

'You're not even out of breath,' I said.

'Even though I have not been in these mountains for many years, my body remembers them.'

I heard a cry from one of the boys.

'Monkeys,' Rachida said. 'There are monkeys in the trees. You must look out because they will throw things at you.'

We caught up with the boys and I gazed up into the trees but could see no sign of the monkeys. Ibrahim stood behind me and taking my hand pointed it in the right direction.

'There! Just there. Mother and baby,' he said in his faltering French. He smelt of sweat and a sweet perfume, like bubble gum. I caught sight of a small dark shape moving further up the tree. Ibrahim let go of me and showed me his tattered smile.

The lake was a deep green, like jade, its surface hatched by the cold wind. All around it were flat, blanched rocks. Wild thyme grew in the crevices. Khaled pointed out the fish that glided beneath the surface. He had fashioned a line and a hook and although he tried bread, cheese and even sardines, the ancient fish ignored all bait. Ibrahim looked on benevolently, occasionally readjusting the bait on the hook or making suggestions about where to stand in his soft, kind voice. Soon

Khaled lost patience and they began to skim stones instead.

Rachida and I lay down out of the wind on the warm, smooth rocks.

'Do you swim here?' I asked.

'It is too dangerous. A man drowned once. There is a hole in the bottom of the lake.' Rachida made a spinning motion with her finger. 'What is it called?'

'A whirlpool?'

'Yes, a whirlpool. The man was very big and strong but he was sucked down to the bottom of the lake and never seen again.'

I smiled.

'It is not funny, Aisha. You must not think of swimming here. The story I told you is true. Sometimes those big fish are sucked down and we find them in the *seguia* all the way down in the village. The water goes underground.'

I closed my eyes and turned my face to the sun.

'What's a *seguia*?' I asked her.

'It is the place in the village where the clean water is held.'

A single cloud passed over the sun and the temperature dropped at once.

'You could not swim here anyway, Aisha,' Rachida said. 'Even if it were not dangerous. You will learn that there is no privacy in these mountains. You may think that you are alone but there are eyes everywhere. Sharp eyes that see great distances. You can never be alone.'

'Would it offend people if I swam?'

'I am talking about your nakedness.'

'I see.'

She sighed on my behalf. Then, shielding her eyes from the sun, she addressed her next question to the sky.

'Do you think it would be hard for you to stay here, Aisha?'

I looked at her.

'I don't know,' I said, with forced lightness. 'Perhaps I'll try it and see.'

'You should find yourself a husband.'

'God, Rachida, I can't think of anything I want less than a husband! I'm just finding out what it feels like to be alone.' Superstition stopped me from going any further.

'You will not be alone here,' she said. 'You do not believe me but you will see. There are always eyes looking at an unmarried woman. She is never alone, even when she thinks that she is. The men believe that they have a right to spy on her. It is only when she has a husband that they feel bound to stop.'

I thought of poor, innocent Cassilda sauntering along that hot path, asking for trouble.

'Where I come from, it's no different,' I told her.

We lay side by side in silence, our faces to the sun. I dozed, then woke, and as Rachida had predicted, soon became aware of eyes watching me. Khaled was playing on the far bank. I turned my head to see Ibrahim, squatting alone on a rock a little way off. He quickly looked away, then picked up a stone and skimmed it expertly over the water.

❧

Before supper Rachida sent me off with Khaled to collect some mint down by the river. On our way, I asked him how he was liking life in the village.

He shrugged.

'There's nothing to do here. But at least I don't have school.'

'Doesn't your father teach you?'

He shook his head.

'They're trying to get the money to send me to boarding school. Rabia's husband has offered to pay but that would mean I'd have to be a pharmacist like him.'

'Why?'

'So I can take over his stinking pharmacy.'

'And you don't want to.'

'I told you,' he said indignantly. 'I want to be an engineer. I want to build aeroplanes.'

'Of course you do. I'm sorry.'

He hung his head.

'My father wants me to be a sheikh.'

'I'm sure your father wants you to be what you want to be.'

'No, he doesn't.'

We were at the edge of a fast-flowing stream. I watched Khaled reach down, grab a fistful of mint from the muddy shallows and pull it up by the roots. He did not strike me as a holy man in the making.

'I'll do it, Khaled. You relax.'

He handed me the mint and went and sat down on a thick branch of driftwood.

'Ibrahim loves you,' he said.

I straightened up.

'Oh dear,' I said.

'Why? Don't you like him? Don't you think he's handsome?'

'He's very handsome, but no, I don't like him.'

'He's not intelligent enough for you,' Khaled said sadly.

'I don't want a boyfriend, Khaled.'

'Why not? Do you love somebody else?'

I sat down beside him on the twisted branch.

'Yes,' I said. 'I love somebody else and I'm saving myself for him.'

'Who is he?' he asked eagerly. 'Is he old, young? Is he handsome? Is he *rich*?'

'He's not young and he is not handsome but he is very, very wise.'

'Where is he? Why aren't you with him?'

'Enough questions, Khaled. It makes me sad to talk about him.'

Khaled stared at me.

'Do you miss Jose?'

I held the mint to my nostrils and inhaled the scent. I looked at those bright, searching eyes and I loved him for his candour.

'Yes, Khaled. I miss him.'

'I didn't know him all that long but I miss him too. He used to play chess with me.'

I smiled.

'He was a better chess player than me,' I said.

'He was. He was good at computer games too, but they gave him a headache.'

I thought of Dr Saddock's ruthless diagnosis, delivered in her purring contralto: *Chronic headaches are of course symptomatic. Everything you've told me points to a fairly straightforward schizophrenic profile.* Then she had smiled sweetly and added: *as much as such a condition can be called straightforward.*

I had wanted to take the wobbly fan from her desk and hit her with it. I had imagined the grille of the fan making a waffle pattern in blood on her pretty face.

Khaled and I watched a pair of dragonflies mating, hooked together in tandem flight.

'Do you think they got the idea of a helicopter from a dragonfly?' Khaled asked.

'I'm sure they did. And one day they'll know how to decode the dragonfly's DNA, feed it into a computer and make aircraft exactly the same.'

Khaled seemed to be pondering this idea. Then he announced: 'You're lucky you *had* a brother. Fatima was twelve and Rabia was already ten when I was born. I've never had anyone to play with.'

I looked at him.

'I know. I am lucky.'

❧

The sheikh didn't come back that night. Rachida didn't appear to be worried and went off to bed without a thought for her old, sick husband wandering alone in the mountains.

'Hadj's mule is a good mule,' she announced as though this fact put an end to all anxiety.

I now admire that loving detachment of hers, won after many years from a habit of respect, trust and devotion.

Whenever I feel my own habit of tyrannical love taking hold of me again, I remember the sheikh warning me with a proverb borrowed from my own religion:

'Do not be the dog who returns to its vomit, Aisha.'

That night I lay awake in my new room listening to the owl in the walnut grove. It was so close that I could hear the breath in its call. I sat up and looked out at the garden and at the trunks of the silver birches glowing in the moonlight.

Since Rachida's warning I had been feeling watched. After our return from the lake, in search of a place to shit, I had climbed the same path that had brought me down to the village the day before. I found myself climbing further and further up the steep slope to a plateau above the mosque, where there were no obstacles for my pursuers to hide behind and where I could see for miles. There I squatted like a crazed hermit. I thought of my brother and of his feral childhood. For the first time I considered the loneliness of that life. I imagined him as a thirteen-year-old boy, watching me from the plateau as I walked back along the path towards the village that had cast him out. How could I have let him build a life solely around me? I had helped them cast him out.

I lay down and closed my eyes. Once again I saw the roof of Jose's cave. Had he put those eyes there for company? Were they there to curb his loneliness?

I opened my eyes and looked at the postcards floating above me. The room was flooded with moonlight. My fear this time was not of my brother's ghost but of its absence. The old habit of prayer seemed ineffectual against this new feeling, but I prayed anyway. I prayed to invoke meaning – not in the shape of God, who had gone from my world when I was a little girl – but to ward off madness. I prayed for sanity and for the sheikh's safe return.

It may have been these prayers that set my unconscious on its search, but I woke up the next morning knowing what I would do. I dressed quickly and went to tell Rachida. I found her knee-deep in the river, her strong, supple body bent over as she cut the thick reeds to make baskets. I shouted at her over the sound of rushing water. She straightened up and waved at me, but I couldn't wait to tell her my idea, so I waded into the stream to meet her.

'Rachida!' I shouted. 'I know how I can pay you!'

Her face darkened.

'No, no. Listen! I have an idea! I can teach Khaled!'

My feet grew numb in my boots as I stood in the ice-cold river shouting over the sound of rushing water. I would help Khaled keep pace with the French system. We would use the manuals published by the Ministry of Education for home schooling. I knew how the system worked because Odile had used it to take her *baccalauréat*.

We waded back to the bank and Rachida dropped her armful of reeds on the ground and sat down on a boulder.

'A correspondence course,' she repeated, looking out over the water.

'They send you the teaching manuals for all the various subjects and you send off the child's homework to be marked every few weeks. There's a post office in Agour?'

'Of course.'

'Well, Khaled could take his homework to the post office every month and send it off to France and at the same time pick up his corrected work. It's a system designed for children who can't go to school. Diplomats' children, or children in hospital, or gipsy children.'

Rachida threw back her head and laughed.

'Diplomats' children!' she cried, clapping her hands. Then she suddenly became formal. 'If the sheikh agrees, I would be happy for you to teach our son.'

❦

The sheikh returned at sunset. However good Hadj's mule might have been, the old man's body was battered when he arrived at the door with the usual posse of children. As

Rachida helped him onto the ground his legs gave way beneath him. Frightened by the sight of the sheikh's indignity and knowing that grown-ups tend to lash out at such times, the children ran off, leaving Rachida and Khaled to help him inside.

They settled him on some cushions in the kitchen while I hovered awkwardly. When he spoke to me, his voice was weak and I had to sit close to hear him.

'I have brought you some books, Aisha,' he whispered. 'So that you will not be bored while you are with us. Khaled, go and fetch the parcels from the mule pack.'

I could see from Rachida's glowing face that this was the welcome she'd been waiting for. I watched Khaled unwrap the books and spread them on the ground. Rachida took off her apron and came and sat down.

'Where did you find them?' she asked her husband.

'In Marrakech,' he whispered.

'Marrakech! You went to Marrakech!'

Rachida glanced at me to make sure that I understood the significance of such a journey.

'When I got to Agour I went to pick up my order. I was about to begin the ride back when I saw a group of people waiting for a taxi. They told me that they would make room for me and so I decided to go with them into the city and see my old friend Ahmed. I left the mule with Brahim at the post office and then . . .' The sheikh paused, savouring his wife's delight. 'I went shopping with Ahmed.'

I looked down at the books that the sheikh had chosen for me. There were thirteen of them: *The Theology of Aristotle*, Virgil's *Aeneid*, *Around the World in Eighty Days*, *Germinal*, *Eugénie Grandet*, *Three Sisters*, *Crime and Punishment*, *A Tale of Two Cities*, *Robinson Crusoe*, stories by Edgar Allan Poe, Racine's *Phèdre*, Molière's *Le Misanthrope*, *Le Chanson de Roland* and a shabby Bible in French.

'There is something for you, Rachida,' the sheikh said. 'Khaled. The small box.'

Khaled handed his mother a box wrapped in white tissue paper. Inside was a plain gold bangle.

'I'm afraid it was Ahmed who chose it,' the sheikh whispered. 'There were so many. I had no idea where to begin.'

Rachida pulled the bracelet over her hand and turned it on her wrist. Suddenly she was shy as a girl.

'He chose well,' she said.

The sheikh savoured the sight of her for a moment then turned to his son.

'I have no gift for you this time.'

If Khaled was disappointed, I couldn't see it.

'Sheikh,' Rachida interrupted, 'Aisha has something she wants to give Khaled. Go on, Aisha. Tell the sheikh your idea.'

I was still lost for words about the books. I looked up at the old man.

'Thank you,' I said.

He shook his head.

'It is a selfish gift,' he said. 'To ensure that you do not get bored and leave us.'

'Aisha would like to stay,' Rachida interrupted. 'She has an idea.'

'I thought I could teach Khaled. So that he can continue in the French system.'

Khaled jumped to his feet and began dancing round the room. I kept my eyes on the sheikh.

'Khaled is a lucky boy,' he said quietly. Then as if the matter had long been decided, he added, 'Perhaps if you have time, you might consider helping some of the other children in the village.'

Over supper the sheikh chatted away in his hoarse whisper as though he had forgotten all about his failing body. He recounted his day in Marrakech, telling us how Ahmed had taken him to a French bookshop in the medina that was owned by an old friend of his. The man, who owed Ahmed a favour, had said that they could help themselves to as many books as they could carry.

'His calculation must have been that two old men could not carry much, and I believe his face fell a little when we staggered to the cash register with our arms full.'

Rachida clapped her hands in delight.

'How did you choose from all those books?' she asked.

'We chose the ones we thought might be suitable entertainment for a young woman.'

'I would love to know what you found that you thought was unsuitable,' I said.

'That is Ahmed's and my secret,' the sheikh answered with a smile.

I believe that my friendship with the sheikh really began that evening, as the four of us sat in the small, dank kitchen in the light of a single paraffin lamp. My awe and mistrust fell away that night and I saw him as he was: a kind, quick-witted old man, looking death right in the eye.

The friendship that grew between us after that must have seemed a strange thing to the people in the village. I know that it puzzled some and offended others. For the last months of his life, we spent most of our time together. Every free moment, in fact, when I was not teaching and he was not preaching or praying, was spent learning as much as we could from each other. I sometimes think that it must have been hard for Rachida to see her husband confide so easily in a young woman who hardly knew him. But Rachida was wise. She knew that the time had come for him to talk and that she could not be the listener.

Soon I realized that everything I thought or said or did seemed to be springing from my regard for him. Through this sudden and all-encompassing friendship I started to overcome my terror at finding myself in the world without Jose. As for the sheikh, I'm still not sure what he found in our friendship. Perhaps it was some measure of forgiveness for what he saw as his own part in my brother's death.

❦

The sheikh always spoke freely to me about his illness and seemed relieved not to have to pretend to me that he was not dying. Rachida's good-natured but stubborn denial of this fact was a strain for him.

One evening that summer the sheikh and I were sitting on the cement bench that Ibrahim had made for him overlooking the footbridge. The red sun threw its last glow onto the craggy cliffs that rose up on the other side of the river.

'It is an odd thing, Aisha,' he said to me. 'You are the only person who does not elude the question of my death, and yet you are the only one who does not make me feel moribund.'

'Moribund,' I repeated. 'I must remember to use that word.'

'It is a good word,' he said.

We sat listening to the rushing water. At last he said:

'I am glad to be here and not in Blanville. In Blanville I would be in hospital.'

'You don't like hospitals.'

'I think it is doctors that I don't like.'

Then he recounted his one and only meeting with a cardiologist.

'He pronounced the diagnosis with the kind of professional satisfaction that is a poor substitute for compassion,' the sheikh said. 'Very poor indeed.'

'What was the diagnosis?'

'Inflammation of the pericardium. He said it with pleasure. As though I had won a prize.'

I smiled.

'What does it mean?'

'The pericardium is the envelope which protects the heart.' The sheikh paused. 'I asked him if it would kill me and he answered: *Not necessarily*. While managing to convey the fact that he thought my question a stupid one. Of course, I told him, we may die at any moment from any number of causes. *Exactly*, the man said. At that point I had had enough so I stood up to leave. As I held out my hand he said – and he had been waiting for the moment when his words would have the greatest effect: *Of course we can operate.* I remained standing and asked, out of curiosity, what the operation would involve. *We will simply scrape off the fibrous tissue that is imprisoning the heart.*' The sheikh beamed at me. 'Simple!'

'And you declined.'

'I did. The man could not believe that I was refusing his gift. He had the power of life and death and I was not allowing him to use it.'

The sheikh looked back at the river and said:

'He asked me why I was rejecting the possibility of being cured and I told him that it was precisely because it was only a possibility. He told me that if they did not operate, my life would become very tedious. Very tedious indeed. Of course he was right.'

I thought of all the symptoms the sheikh struggled with every day and it occurred to me that he was paying dearly for that small victory. I thought of the breathlessness, the acute pains in his chest that made him wince, the swollen abdomen and legs, the chronic fatigue, the lack of appetite, the racing, stammering heart. I wondered if he would call his victory pride.

'It is superstition,' the sheikh said, answering my unvoiced question. 'I did not wish to have my heart tampered with.'

I watched him rise from the bench. He was entirely reliant on his stick by then and was hunched over as he walked. I thought of him sitting on Jose's chair only eight months before, upright and dapper in his long, polished shoes.

'I shall see you at supper,' he said, resting his hand on my head.

'See you at supper.'

When he had gone I sat and watched the children playing on the footbridge. Every year, before the snowmelt, the villagers would build that bridge and every year, when the water drained and the riverbed dried up, they would dismantle it. The building of the bridge was a happy occasion. I saw it twice: once shortly after my arrival in the village and once a month before I left. The villagers worked side by side: men and women, old and young, crazy and sane. People worked happily because the building of the bridge heralded the end of winter and the coming of spring. They made it from chestnut and willow, some of it new and some saved and stored from the previous year. One year the river had risen so high that it had washed the bridge away and men from the villages all along the valley had been called in to build another. I imagined them all standing chest-deep in the icy water, handing the heavy branches to each other across the flood. The bridge, suspended between the banks at the narrowest point, swayed as you crossed it. The children liked to run back and forth, rocking the bridge. I once came down the path to see the sheikh standing mid-way over the torrent, gripping the handrail with white knuckles as he waited for the children to show him some mercy. When at last I held out my hand to help him onto the bank he caught sight of my expression.

'Are you not ashamed to mock an old man?'

Slowly I shook my head and he had laughed his thin, wheezing laugh.

❧

I was never allowed to forget that the day I had arrived in the village was the day they had finished building the mosque. This coincidence was not lost on the people, most of them mothers, who believed that I had been sent by Allah to set up the school. To some, most of them men like Hadj, it was a sign of a different nature: I had been sent to try their faith and must be resisted at all cost. And so the village was divided, between those who were for me and those who were against me, between those who were happy for me to teach their children in the mosque and those who saw it as a sacrilege.

It was Hadj who led the campaign to close the little school. He never addressed me directly because I was a woman and below his scorn. He fought against me by attacking the sheikh.

'Thank you,' he said, thoughtfully. 'I did not know that. Another story that we have in common.'

'What's so heretical about it?' I asked.

'Over the thirteen centuries since the story was first told, there has been much speculation as to what the stag actually said to Prince Ibrahim. For the Sufis the question is not an important one. For them the message behind the tale is simple: your spiritual guide can come to you in any form. It does not have to be a sheikh, a professor or a king. It can be anyone or anything. For the Sufis, experience will always be more important than knowledge. Hadj is a man of order and hierarchy. He does not approve of such ideas and that is why he does not like the story.'

I remembered the sheikh's letter: for him Jose had been the stag.

ৎ৵

In the week following my arrival, celebrations were held for the completion of the mosque. People came from all along the valley, even from the neighbouring valleys of Afra and Ouirgane. Mike the Englishman was the guest of honour. The women made food and the ones with the best voices prepared to sing for their benefactor. Hadj even went into Agour on his mule and purchased beer for Mike in a tourist shop at great expense. He didn't realize that the Moroccan beer he had chosen was without alcohol and tasted of soap. Some of the villagers giggled as they watched Mike sipping the beer politely. Mike had white hair and a white beard. He wore a leather hat with a wide brim and a faded denim suit. To me he looked more like my idea of an American than an Englishman. The villagers filed past him and paid their respects, the women kissing their fingertips and the men sweeping his palm and placing their hands on their hearts. Mike stood beside Hadj, smiling awkwardly.

Hadj was not a good conversationalist and a dull expression

soon settled in Mike's watery blue eyes. I felt sorry for Hadj and went over to try and help him entertain the Englishman. That was my first mistake. As soon as I approached, Mike turned his back on Hadj to greet me, taking off his hat in a grand display of gallantry. He became quite animated when I asked him what had first brought him to the Atlas, and he set about telling me how his quest for meaning had begun when he had made his first million.

'You see, I think there are two types of people in this world,' he said, his alcoholic's eyes already laughing at his own wit. 'There are Mammonites and there are tediophobes.'

'What are they?'

'People who love money and people who hate boredom.'

I smiled.

'And which are you?' I asked.

'A tediophobe of course. Why would I be here otherwise?'

Rachida and the sheikh came to join us. I took the aluminium chair from Rachida and opened it for the sheikh, who thanked me and sat down, laying his cane across his knee.

'We were just talking about the love of money and the fear of boredom, Sheikh Laraoui,' Mike told him. 'Which one drives you?'

The sheikh smiled.

'At my great age I would say that I fear money and love boredom.'

Rachida, who was standing behind her husband, adjusted the scarf around his neck.

'You're not old, sheikh,' Mike said jauntily. 'We must be about the same age.'

'Perhaps, but I am old. You, Mike, are still young. That is a gift,' he added kindly. 'It is a gift to remain youthful as you have.'

But the conversation had taken too serious a turn for Mike and he began to look bored. He bowed politely at Rachida and me and moved off in search of more of the unsatisfactory beer.

When he had gone Hadj said:

'Your blessing today was well chosen, Sheikh.'

'I am glad that you approved.'

There was a pause. I could feel Hadj's eyes on me.

'Your son Khaled will benefit greatly from this young woman's lessons.'

'As I hope will all the other children,' the sheikh replied.

'You must be pleased that she has come. Have you known each other long?' he asked, this time addressing me.

The sheikh answered for me.

'Not long.'

'And for how long will you be staying in the village?'

Again, I let the sheikh answer.

'Aisha has not decided. We hope that it will be for a long time.'

'She will live with you in your new house?'

'I will not be moving to a new house after all. I have told the authorities that it is not necessary to rehouse me. The expense could be better allocated, towards the school for example.'

'So you will not move? You have no toilet, no running water.'

'I will wait for these luxuries along with the rest of the village.'

The sheikh's answers offered Hadj few opportunities for engagement and I could feel his irritation growing. He turned to me for a renewed offensive.

'I understand that you had a brother who died. I am sorry for your loss.'

I thanked him politely then stepped closer to Rachida, but he was not discouraged.

'I am told that the boy was remarkable in many ways. He was a good Muslim?'

'He was a Christian,' the sheikh answered calmly.

'You are not a Muslim then, Aisha?' Hadj's voice now sang.

I kept my eyes on the festivities. The women were gathering for their song.

'She is not,' the sheikh said.

Hadj smiled at me.

241

'Then she must not enter the mosque.'

'That, Hadj, is my decision,' the sheikh said.

Turning his vicious smile on me again, Hadj said:

'The villagers will not like it.'

'We shall see. They may be grateful to her.'

This time Hadj spoke between clenched teeth.

'It is not right that a Christian woman should enter the mosque.'

'That is a useful law in a place full of tourists, but it is not practical here. Some of the oldest and most holy mosques in Syria open their doors to People of the Book.'

'We are not in Syria,' Hadj snapped.

'I must insist that this is my decision,' the sheikh said calmly. 'Until we have the money to build a school, the mosque is the only place in the village big enough . . .'

Hadj threw up his hands.

'What good will it do to teach these children to read? There are no jobs for them when they come of age. We will make a village full of malcontents.'

'The world is big, Hadj,' the sheikh said.

'So you would have them all leave? What will become of the village?'

'And you would trap them here?'

'They are not trapped!' Hadj hissed. 'There is a good life here!'

People standing close by turned to look at us. Hadj's face was flushed.

'I prefer to offer them the choice,' the sheikh told him gently.

Rachida turned to Hadj and gave him her glorious smile.

'Look!' she said. 'It is time for the singing!'

I turned my back on Hadj and looked at the women, who had gathered in their finery and were standing in a long row. Five of the men were sitting on the ground at their feet in order to accompany their voices with drums and finger cymbals. As the villagers went quiet and the singing began, Hadj moved off. Rachida took hold of my hand and squeezed it and smiled at me. I smiled back at her. Nothing could spoil this sight. The women were stamping on the ground and moving their hands and hips and making their bangles quiver in a delicate timpani. Their voices were clear and loud. At the end of their song all thirty of them let out their triumphant, high-pitched ululation. I could not stop smiling. The sound was so thrilling, so uplifting, I wanted to be one of them. For the first time in my life I was happy to have been born female.

☙❧

The sheikh and I had plenty of opportunities to talk about my brother but we chose not to. We would sometime approach the subject, pulling back out of superstition. I think we were afraid that talking about him would once again place him between us.

One evening we were on the roof terrace, sitting in the deck chairs I had bought in the market at Agour. It must have been the night sky with its burden of stars that led him to the subject of the Absolute.

'Do you remember the poem in that collection I lent your brother? It was called 'Be Melting Snow . . .'

'I remember it.'

'I believe it was your brother's favourite.'

Of course I remembered it. I knew it by heart.

'You will remember the poet's advice: "Be a page with nothing on it . . ."'

'Yes.'

'When I was in that cell, waiting to discover my fate, I could not have been further from a page with nothing on it.' He sighed. 'I was more like a saucepan being banged with a spoon.'

I didn't answer. I didn't want to talk about Jose.

Instead I asked him to tell me about his expulsion and how it had come about. I was shocked when I discovered the ease with which the Republic dispensed with her undesirables. Apparently there was no trial because the sheikh was being charged with no crime. It was a hearing, held in a shabby room with a big table and three rows of plastic chairs in a building on the rue de Jouy. The judge was a woman in her mid-thirties. The sheikh described her as someone who repeatedly took off and put on a pair of dark glasses.

'It was quite distracting,' he said. 'It occurred to me that she might be suffering from a migraine headache.'

The woman sat behind a table and listened to a man in a dark suit, a representative of the Prefecture whose case was very simple: the sheikh's identity card had expired and the investigators had not recommended a renewal. The man from the Prefecture made no mention of any crime or subversion and did not say a word about Islamic fundamentalism.

The lawyer, Ducray, had done his best to argue for a renewal of the sheikh's papers, stating that he had been a model member of the Arab community for nearly thirty years but it was a lost cause. The case, as he explained afterwards, was purely administrative. During the hearing, which lasted ten minutes, the judge did not look at the sheikh once. She simply took off her sunglasses, signed the document in front of her and upheld the request for expulsion.

'When I thanked Maître Ducray for his efforts he told me that since the attacks on New York, only citizens of the European Union were seeing their papers renewed. Everyone else was being refused as a matter of course.'

The sheikh looked up at the stars.

'What about Ortoli?' I asked. 'Did you see him again?'

'I did. He put me on the plane.'

'Bastard,' I muttered.

The sheikh gave a slow nod as if he thought this an appropriate description.

'He broke his promise to me,' he said.

'That's no surprise.'

'He told me that I would be allowed to fly with my family. They were sent on a different plane. We were reunited at the airport in Marrakech.'

We sat in silence, watching the stars. Ortoli and his knavery seemed like a remote fiction.

'He also lied. When we left the centre,' the sheikh mused, 'he had assured me that there would be no handcuffs. When we got to the airport we were met by two gendarmes who immediately put me in handcuffs. This lie of his made me terrified that I was going to be expelled alone, without my family. I asked him where my wife and son were. He told me that they were already on the plane. I said that I wanted to see them and he told me that I would see them on board. I remember looking into his face and knowing that he was lying. The feeling of hatred I felt for that man was overwhelming.'

We watched the stars in silence. No planes scrambled the constellations.

'You see how important it is to be wary of hatred. Ortoli was the instrument of my present happiness. And the instrument of everything we have achieved here.'

I thought of my little classroom at the mosque. I thought of the children's magical paintings, their cut-out numbers and the Latin and Arabic alphabets all over the walls.

'He was a strange man,' the sheikh mused. 'He was like a destructive child. When I was sitting on the bus which was taking me to the plane I looked out of the window. Ortoli was standing on the tarmac, watching me. He watched me for as long as he could, until the bus turned the corner. His hands were in his pockets, but I knew that what he really wanted to do was to wave.'

❦

That summer they began building the road from Agour. The sheikh told me not to be alarmed, that it would be years before they finished it. Mike was financing the last part, from Idris to our village, and I was assured that there would be no funds for bitumen. It would only be a dirt road, the sheikh said, discouraging to idle tourists. From the schoolroom window I could see the men working on the far side of the valley, shattering rock and clearing stones. By the end of August they had gouged a thick red wound from the flank of the mountain. To me their progress was terrifying.

After only four months, I had come to resent the overweening eco-tourists, who would occasionally come tramping through Tamghurt, showering their coins over the children. I would watch sullenly as they stamped through in their expensive walking boots, their packs clinking with climbing paraphernalia, staring at the women, amongst whom I could now hide undetected. I wore a scarf around my head and long skirts made by Rachida and a fair amount of her silver jewellery, of which she had been gradually divesting herself – because, as she said, gold was for the old and silver for the young.

One day in August one of the trekkers had come through the village equipped with the usual kit: backpack, bedroll, compass and gourd. To my amazement he stopped at the *seguia* and greeted the women in fluent Berber, as if they were old friends. His name was Jean Coujols and he had been coming to this part of the High Atlas every summer for the past ten years. I discovered that the mothers of Tamghurt saw him not only as a respected guest but as a potential match for their daughters, and my antipathy towards him grew when it became clear to me that he would never marry a Berber girl. He was just playing. I would see him in the evenings on my way back from school, smoking Casa Sports with our neighbour Ali on his doorstep, mending his radio for him in that irritating canvas hat of his.

Almost every evening he would have dinner at Salim's, three houses along from ours. Salim was the man whose youngest daughter Zara had been taking chaste but hopeful walks with Jean Coujols every summer since her fourteenth year. Now Zara was nineteen, almost over the hill as far as marriage was concerned and no closer to a proposal. To allay his guilt, Jean brought Salim gifts: alarm clocks, high-beam torches, Swiss

Army knives. He cluttered the man's house with useless junk while he filled his daughter's head with useless fantasies about life beyond the mountains.

Jean taught Middle Eastern studies at the Institute of Political Science in Paris. I believe that he and I disliked each other on sight – both of us cherishing our status as the only foreigner – and as far as I could see, his decision to pursue me that summer was just another manifestation of his perverse nature. He must have been in his late fifties and seemed to me to be pathologically well preserved. He cultivated a quiet manner but I guessed at a nasty temper. Needless to say, in spite of all this, the peasant in me was captivated by his urbane magnetism.

He said he had started coming to this village five years ago. 'God knows, I've seen something of the world,' he added, offering a disingenuous smile. 'And this is the only place on earth where I feel at home.' He explained that whenever he came to Tamghurt, he would always grow his beard and 'shed all the trappings'.

I was peeved by Jean's arrival and the sheikh saw it.

'Jean knows a great deal about these mountains. You should let him show them to you. You could share the knowledge with the children.'

'Are you matchmaking?'

'I would not dare.'

We were in the schoolroom after class. He was watching me stack the chairs.

'He knows the region's palaeolithic sites,' the sheikh said.

I turned round.

'All right. I'll be nice to him.' But instantly I changed my mind. 'I don't like the way he treats Zara.'

The sheikh sighed.

'One must not interfere in matters of the heart.'

'It's not a matter of the heart. It's a matter of exploitation!'

'You're too vehement, Aisha. You should save your anger.'

'What for?'

'Anger should be used sparingly, as a tool to overcome fear

for example. If you overuse your anger, it will control you.'

'I think I'm just hungry.'

The sheikh smiled.

That evening I met Jean on the way down to the river.

'I'm going to get some mint. Would you like to join me?' I asked him. I caught a look of mistrust. 'It's all right. The sheikh says I'm to be nice to you.'

He smiled, putting his hands into his pockets.

'He's quite right.'

We walked a little way and the old demon nudged me.

'I'm just curious about Zara,' I said, stopping on the path and turning to face him. 'You know she's been keeping herself for you?'

His face grew dark and I saw that mean streak again.

'It isn't fair on her,' I said.

'I never made her any promises.'

'I'm sure you didn't. But Salim expects it.'

'Expects what? What do you want me to do? I can't marry her. I can't take her to Paris, can I?'

'Why on earth not?'

He sighed and ran his fingers through his thick grey hair. I watched a thought scud across his pale eyes. Suddenly it was obvious.

'You've got a wife! You're married.'

For an instant I saw a look of violent hatred in those eyes. I had poisoned his idyll. He composed himself.

'Don't be ridiculous,' he said. 'Of course I'm not married.'

But I knew I had guessed right. He turned and left me there on the path.

I didn't join the group which walked him up to the Idris pass in the dawn of his last morning. Zara and two of her friends went and so did Salim and Ali, while I hid in the schoolroom pretending to prepare for the day. I guessed that Jean Coujols would have to seek his pastoral idyll somewhere else.

❦

One morning in October I looked out of the schoolroom window at the new road and saw a lone figure moving along it. I could tell from the gait and the pack that it was another trekker, and I sighed and turned to face the class.

The children were working quietly at their tables, filling in the capital cities on a map of Europe. Since the sheikh and I had started up this school I had lost only two pupils to the fields, a boy of twelve and a girl of ten. In only six months the little classroom had filled with bright, hopeful children whose lives were now tied to mine. Khaled was two years from his baccalaureate but some of the others were more than ten years away. I would push these thoughts from my mind, telling myself that I was simply setting the children on a path and that I would not be there for ever.

After the cold war with Hadj had ended, the more ambitious mothers had begun showing up at the door of the mosque, pushing their reluctant children towards me. I now had fifteen pupils between the ages of seven and twelve, some of whom came from neighbouring villages. I made it known that I would not take anyone older than twelve. Some of the parents had tried to pass off their gawky adolescent boys as twelve-year-olds and I had been forced to call in the sheikh to lay down the law and send the poor boys back to their goats.

From seven to ten every morning, Monday to Friday, I would teach the children reading and writing, then from ten to noon, mathematics. In the afternoons, while I taught Khaled, they were free. Friday afternoons were for the Koran.

There were seven boys and eight girls. One of the girls, Leila, I knew to be very bright. She, like Khaled, was a natural with numbers and I would look at her beautiful face shining with her own achievement as she held out her exercise book and I would fear for her, just as I feared for any of the girls who had the desire and the will to learn. I would lie awake at night, plotting on their behalf, planning the day when they would stand up to their fathers, their uncles or their brothers and leave the village to go to university in Rabat or

Casablanca or Paris. At such moments, it did not seem very likely that I would be going anywhere for a long time.

Hadj had at first tried to get me banned from the mosque and when that had failed, from teaching altogether. A representative from the Ministry of Education had come from Marrakech to inspect the state of affairs Hadj had described: a wanton young Christian woman spreading Western values and discontent.

The inspector, Mouloud Hassan, was a Berber who had been brought up in a village in this region. He was a timid man with a little moustache who sat and listened respectfully to what I had to say. He asked to see the children's exercise books as well as the teaching manuals I had ordered from Paris. He made a repetitive humming noise while I spoke, to indicate that he was listening. Then he had asked to see the sheikh and they had spent the afternoon talking. In the end Hassan offered to request financial aid from the Ministry if the sheikh agreed to make sure that the children had as many hours in Arabic and Berber as they did in French and English. The sheikh, who was now too sick to teach, set about finding an Arabic teacher and Hassan began working on the Ministry for funding.

Soon after the inspector's visit, Hadj had left the village. As it turned out, the people of Tamghurt were not much interested in theology, nor had they been convinced by Hadj's show of holiness. As Rachida said, little escaped these people who could see great distances and had learned to read all the minutiae of the natural world. Hadj now had a well-paid job running Mike's hotel in the new ski resort three valleys to the east. He had his own car and had given up his pseudo-religious cream robes for Western clothing.

As I stood in my schoolroom that morning looking out at the Agour road, I told myself that when I saw the first car moving along it would be the time for me to leave.

'That's enough for today. Leila, collect the work. Everyone else stack the chairs.'

I returned to the sheikh's for lunch to find that he had slipped on a path and hit his head. Rachida said that he was all right, that he was just a little bruised and shaken.

'Can I see him?'

'Later. He's asleep.'

I watched Rachida rushing around the kitchen.

'What's happening? Do we have guests?'

'Didn't Khaled tell you?'

'No.'

'Hassan has found an Arabic teacher, a scholar from Meknes. Ali has gone to fetch him from Agour with a spare mule. They will be back for supper.'

After lunch Khaled asked if we could have our lesson outside. It was a beautiful day with a light breeze and so I agreed. We went down to the *seguia* and sat in the shade of a cedar tree. We were studying Charlemagne in history and *Le Chanson de Roland* in literature, and I asked Khaled to read aloud the account of Roland's magnificent victory on the pass at Roncevaux. I started to daydream, gazing at the first snow on the peaks.

'Aisha!' Khaled said. 'You're not listening.'

'I am,' I said, turning to him. 'It's a good story, isn't it?'

Khaled shrugged, shutting the book.

'It's OK.'

'It's pure fiction. It was an heroic defeat. The Arabs won that battle.'

'No!' he gasped.

I smiled at him.

'It was the only battle with Charlemagne's army that the Arabs did win. You'd better get used to inaccuracy,' I added. 'It's hidden everywhere. What's amusing is trying to dig it out.'

Khaled opened the book again and scrutinized the text.

'What would happen if I said that in my exam? If I said the whole poem was a lie? And that it was racist?'

'Those are two separate points and you'd have to back up

both arguments very strongly with material quoted from the text. If you did that you might be all right.'

'No, he wouldn't.'

I looked up. A tall, lean young man with hair like straw standing out all over his head was looking down at us. Khaled looked up at him, then at me, assuming that I knew him. The young man had spoken French with an accent that I guessed was American. He had a fish tattoo on his forearm and I imagined him gritting his teeth for this act of self-adornment and felt a wave of disgust. I turned my back.

'Did you do the work on the Abbasids?' I asked Khaled.

Khaled opened his satchel and took out his essay. He was bristling with the thrill of having to ignore the glamorous stranger, who vanished while I was scanning his work. Khaled squirmed.

'Where's he gone? Do you know him?'

I shook my head.

There was a crack; a branch snapped above our heads and fell into the water. We looked up and saw the American climbing the cedar. We watched him climb and climb, his long limbs extending as far as they could, up and up. The sheikh had told me that the tree was over a thousand years old, and the sight of an American tourist climbing it seemed like defilement. When he was a tiny figure way up in the highest branches he gave a shout.

I had my hand over my mouth when he dived. It was a dive that defied common sense: a clean leap upwards, his body, now impossibly frail to me, clearing the branches, folding in two and then plummeting. My gut contracted as his head hit the water. I was six again, watching my brother dive from the rock behind the lead mine.

When his grinning face broke through the surface of the water, I shrieked at him:

'How dare you! How dare you!'

Then I stood up, turned my back on him and ran home.

That evening the teacher from Meknes had supper with us.

His name was Hussein and he was young, with an enquiring face and easy smile. Khaled, who had been expecting someone old and stern, was delighted. He was happy and loquacious that evening, chatting away in Arabic and making his mother glow with pride. The sheikh was still too frail after his fall to leave his bed.

After supper, while Khaled played chess with Hussein, I helped Rachida clear up. She asked me if I missed Jean Coujols.

'Why would I miss him?'

Rachida looked coyly at me.

'I didn't like Jean, Rachida. He was pompous.'

'Jean is kind,' she said. 'And he likes you.'

'What makes you think that he's kind?'

'I saw how he was with Khaled. He was kind and patient.'

'He knew Khaled was my pupil. He wanted him on his side.'

'You are too difficult, Aisha,' Rachida said.

'Too difficult for what?'

'For most men.'

Rachida handed me a paraffin lamp to take to bed.

'Rachida?'

'Yes, Aisha.'

'Can I go and see the sheikh?'

'He is sleeping, Aisha. You can see him in the morning, when he wakes up.'

She saw my disappointment and added:

'He does not like people to see him so weak.'

'Isn't pride a sin for Muslims?'

'Yes,' she answered sadly. 'It is the worst sin.'

That night I sat in my room and thought of the American diving out of the cedar. I remembered the elation, then the shrinking in my stomach.

I looked around my room. On the windowsill were Jose's possessions, collecting dust. Khaled had built a single shelf for the books the sheikh had bought me. We had read them all. I decided to go into Marrakech the next day to buy more. I would ask the sheikh if I could take Khaled with me as it was a Saturday. He could have his hair cut, maybe even see a film.

I found that I could not sleep. When I closed my eyes I saw scenes from Coelhoso: our mother's face disfigured by rage, Katarina standing guard outside her bedroom in the old, dark house and Jose sitting with his back to me on that green painted chair. If the sheikh died, I would be alone again with all that.

❧

The next morning I sat at the sheikh's bedside. I was shocked by the change in him. His neck and chest were emaciated and his face was swollen and bruised-looking. I took his hand.

'You should marry,' he whispered. 'Have children.'

Letting go of his hand, I said, 'Not you too.'

'Perhaps not immediately. But make sure you do it.'

It occurred to me that he was only riling me to shift my mood.

'I was reading your Bible last night,' he said.

'Well, stop. What would Hadj think?'

The sheikh tried to smile but his eyes were full of fear from the struggle to pull air into his lungs. I took his hand again.

'You didn't sleep,' I said.

'I could not breathe,' he whispered. 'When I lay down it was worse and so I sat up all night.'

He gave me an imploring look that unsettled me. I had never seen him vulnerable before.

'Last night I imagined Jose at the moment of his death,' he whispered.

Here we were at last. I held still, listening to the thin voice.

'I once read that burn victims often die of suffocation. The skin can no longer breathe and the lungs fill with smoke. Last night I thought that if this were true then his death was like a drowning. They say that drowning is a kind of bliss. Once the struggle is over.' The sheikh was looking at me with wide, pleading eyes. 'But who *knows* this? Who can *know*?'

I let go of his hand. I didn't want to hear this. I wanted nothing to do with his guilt or his fear.

He stared at me. Was it death that did that to your eyes, I wondered. Put such terror into them?

'*We are the night ocean filled with sparkles of light . . .*' he whispered. '*We are the space between the fish and the moon.*'

He closed his eyes.

I said, 'The psychiatrist in Paris said he was mad. She said he was probably hearing voices when he did it.'

The sheikh opened his eyes.

'Hearing voices does not make you mad. I heard voices when I was young. I thought it was a sign that I was a mystic . . .'

I turned on him.

'He wasn't a mystic! He killed himself because he felt too much. Do you understand? He always felt too much.'

'Perhaps we are saying the same thing,' the sheikh whispered. 'Perhaps the excess of feeling you describe is the mystic's nature to some and the madman's to others. Surely Jesus Christ was mad. His suggestion to turn the other cheek must have seemed like madness to most people.'

I sighed, suddenly worn out by my old habit of rage.

'Our problem is vanity,' I said quietly. 'Jose's death had nothing to do with me and it had nothing to do with you.'

The sheikh closed his eyes again and whispered:

'Wise words.'

After a minute or so, I said:

'I'd like to take Khaled into Marrakech to buy some more books. He deserves an outing.'

But the sheikh had fallen asleep.

I took his hand and sat beside him for a while and listened to the shrill whistle of a bird of prey echoing against the cliffs. It was a lammergeier, a bearded vulture. The sheikh had told me that Pliny had described how it would drop the bones of its carrion from high in the air and then fly down to pick out the marrow. He said that Aeschylus was supposed to have been killed by a bone dropped by a lammergeier, which mistook his bald head for a rock.

The sheikh's lungs made a terrible rattle as he slept. I gently set down his hand. Then I stood up and left the room.

❧

That afternoon I left for Marrakech with Khaled. We shared Ali's mule. Khaled was so excited that he ran back and forth to me most of the way, adding a considerable distance to his journey. We spent the night in the house at Aadi where I had stayed on my outward journey. The little girl, whose name was Safi, was as dour as ever. Safi's mother, however, was delighted to see me. She announced that she was making a couscous, the prince's dish, and went to scavenge some meat from the neighbours.

Since I had come to Tamghurt I had been only once to Agour, with Rachida for market day. On that journey we had stayed in a house that belonged to a cousin of our neighbour Ali. I did not feel that I could stay there without Rachida, so I went to Safi's house with the idea of paying my way. When her mother refused my money and then proceeded to get herself into debt with the neighbours, I decided that on our way back, we would try and reach the Idris refuge in one day.

For breakfast the next morning Safi's mother made us fried eggs, yet another luxury. Unfortunately, Khaled did not like fried eggs, so I ate his.

We picked up a group taxi in Agour and sat between two fat, silent sisters. One of them had to get out several times to be sick by the side of the road. Each time Khaled struggled not to laugh while I struggled not to add my four eggs to her ventral offerings.

We reached Marrakech at about four o'clock that afternoon. I was overjoyed to be in a town again. We went to the Café de France and sat on the terrace and watched the passersby. I had my first coffee in months and Khaled had a Coke.

'Should we go and see Rabia's husband? His pharmacy's near here.'

Khaled looked uncertain, then seeing my expression, shook his head decisively.

'OK then,' I said, 'I asked and you said no.'

That day I was no longer his teacher. We were both children.

After we had bought our books we went to a barber's shop called the Coiffeur des Princes in one of the side streets off Jamaa al-Fna. The man gave Khaled an army cut with electric clippers, leaving two bald chevrons on either temple. Khaled was delighted.

An Indian musical was playing at the big cinema near by. Khaled went and stood in the queue with the crowds.

'Are you sure you want to see this? It'll be in Hindi.'

'They'll have subtitles.'

'I know, but are you sure? It's a musical.'

But Khaled was craning his neck to see past the crowds to the ticket booth. I went to see what time the film ended, then went to join Khaled in the queue.

'OK. I'll see you here at eight-thirty.'

Khaled smiled.

'What about food?' I asked him. 'Aren't you hungry?'

'I'll get popcorn,' he said happily.

So I waved goodbye and left him with a fifty-dirham note.

I walked through the smoke on the great square and sat down at one of the food stands. I ordered bread and lamb sausages and began to daydream. Among the books I had chosen for Khaled were Jose's favourites and I wondered what that smart, practical boy would make of heroes like Julien Sorel.

The American must have been watching me eat for some time. When I looked up he smiled at me from his seat on the other side of the food stand. There was too much noise in the square to hear what he was saying. I put my hand to my ear. He picked up his plate and came round to my side and sat down next to me.

He was staring at my profile, so I turned and stared at him.

His mouth was finely drawn and curled up at the edges. The thick, blond hair grew straight up from his forehead in a cow's lick. The eyes were brown and looked a little sad, even with the amused curve of his mouth. There was a tiny hole in the skin of his forehead the size of a ball-bearing.

'What are you doing here?' he asked in French.

'Eating.'

'I mean in Morocco.'

I turned away, waving at the cook and drawing in the air for the bill.

The American plunged his hand into the pocket of his shorts, pulled out a ten-dirham note and slapped it into the cook's hand.

'What are *you* doing here?' I asked.

He shrugged.

'Let's have a coffee,' he said.

I think it was the tiny hole in his forehead that made me accept.

It is strange how the power shifts in love, how it comes and goes. I was all-powerful that afternoon: the girl from the old continent, bolder and wiser than he was. How things change.

We went to the Café de France and sat on the terrace. The world rolled by. While we spun webs of language around each other, drawing each other in, time seemed to stop. We told each other stories: stories designed to make you fall in love . . .

'I hit the road when my father died. I guess I didn't know what else to do.'

'When I lost my twin I didn't know who I was any more.'

'Don't you love being somewhere where nobody knows you?'

'I have to put myself in danger all the time.'

'Me too.'

'Otherwise I don't feel alive.'

'You walked all that way? By yourself? Were you scared?'

'Terrified.'

'What's the most afraid you've been?'

'I don't know – there are different kinds of fear. What's the bravest *you've* been?'

'Watching my father die.'

'Why did you jump out of that tree?'

'To get your attention.'

After our words, our bodies. As night fell we fell silent, letting the chemicals rush over us, sweep away all doubt. I drank in every detail: his long hands, the thick veins on his arms, the coloured skin of the tattoo, the tiny creases on his lips. This was the recognition I'd read about in romantic novels. Here was the feeling that I'd been waiting for this person, this very person, all my life.

I leapt to my feet.

'What time is it?'

He had no watch. We asked a man at the next table. It was nine-twenty. I turned and ran.

Khaled was not there. I ran up and down the street calling his name. Soon I was imagining Rachida's tears.

I found him in an amusement arcade two doors down from the cinema. He looked up at me, smiled and went back to his game.

'Khaled. I'm so sorry.'

'I don't mind.'

Apparently he had not felt time either.

Now I had lost the American. His name was Christopher Molloy, son of Russell and Natasha Molloy. He was twenty-five. He came from San Francisco. His father, who was dead, had been what he called a self-loathing Texan and his mother was French, from Lyon. Christopher had come to look at Moroccan rare birds and learn Arabic. The idea had first come to him after the attacks on New York. Like a million other right-thinking Americans he'd wanted to try and make sense of this culture that everyone was so scared of. I'd smiled when he had said that. *Don't tease me*, he had said, giving me his best smile.

Christopher. I clutched my brother's medallion around my neck and I told myself that if I was right about him, he would come to Tamghurt to find me.

Khaled and I spent that night at Rabia's. Mercifully, Rachid was away at a conference in Casablanca. After Khaled had gone to bed, Rabia and I sat up and talked. I listened to her and responded in all the right ways, but my mind raked over the afternoon in some strange yet familiar withdrawal.

'How is my father?' she asked me.

'He fell and hit his head. Now he's very weak. I think you should come.'

'Rachid won't let me.'

'He's dying, Rabia.'

She stared at me and then looked away. Then she leaned forward and whispered, 'I wish I had listened to him. He knew Rachid was not right for me. He and my mother both knew. They had someone else in mind. Someone I had never met. I was French, so I did not like the idea of an arranged marriage. I was so *stupid*! They knew me better than I knew myself.'

'Who was the other man?'

Rabia smiled coyly.

'It was Ahmed's son.'

I tried to remember Rabia's behaviour that morning in the *souk*. Had she been looking out for him?

'I should have listened to them. Ahmed's son is a good man. He is not rich, but he has a steady business, selling spices. I would have lived in Essaouira, by the sea. It would have been better than living here.' She looked around the room. It was true that it felt as unloved and anonymous as a hotel room.

I looked at Rabia's lovely, manicured hands and her beautiful, melancholy face and remembered the sheikh saying that she had no gift for happiness. I vowed at that moment to make sure he never thought that of me.

That night I fell asleep with the picture of Christopher Molloy diving out of that tree to get my attention.

Rabia woke me the next morning with a cup of tea. She was

dressed soberly in a dark jellaba and she had oiled her hair and scraped it into a tight bun. She sat down on the edge of the bed.

'I have decided to come with you.'

I took her hand.

'I want you to help me write a note,' she said.

After several long drafts, she kept it short. She wrote that her father was dying, that she would be back when she was no longer needed and that she was his loving wife Rabia.

In the taxi to Agour, Khaled was beside himself with excitement at the drama of it.

'What's he going to say? Will he come and get you?'

'Be quiet, Khaled,' Rabia said.

'Are you scared?' he asked.

'Of course not.'

I looked over Khaled's head at his older sister. She was certainly scared.

In Agour I decided to soften Rabia's journey and pick up a guide with mules. I chose a wiry, taciturn old man called Brahim. He made it clear, brandishing his accreditation, that there would be no haggling since he was an official mountain guide. Thanks to Brahim and his blankets and his tins of ravioli in tomato sauce, our night at the Idris refuge was so comfortable that Rabia declared what fun it was to be sleeping rough. Khaled and I shot each other an amused glance. How would this princess cope with life in Tamghurt?

We arrived at lunchtime the next day. Rachida was thrilled. As far as she was concerned, Rabia had come for good. I offered to give up my room on the top floor but Rachida refused.

'We will put Rabia in Khaled's room. Khaled can sleep with Hussein until we can build another room. I'll talk to Ibrahim about it tomorrow.'

'I want the new room!' Khaled cried. 'He can build it on the roof. Can't he, Mum?'

'We'll see.'

Rachida picked up Rabia's suitcase and disappeared.

That afternoon Rabia sat with the sheikh while I went upstairs to mark homework and prepare for class. Marrakech already felt like another world. The American had been a delusion. I settled down to work, remembering that the sheikh had also said that a gift for happiness began with the mastering of desire.

◉⬥◉

The sheikh's health seemed to improve after Rabia arrived. In the cooler weather his breathing was better, but he could no longer walk any distance. He tended to give instructions on village life from his bed, like some ailing caliph. Every evening I would go and sit with him and give him news of Khaled's progress and of the children at the school. He knew all of them: seemed to know their strengths, however young they were, and also their weaknesses, sometimes even before they declared themselves. Even before I saw little Leila tear up one of her own drawings in a fit of self-loathing, he had already warned me about her temper.

The sheikh and I would discuss the progress of our request for permanent funding from the government. Mike now contributed to the school on a sporadic and informal basis, occasionally sending in mules laden with books and coloured pencils. His most recent gift was a beautiful globe on a stand. It stood as tall as the smallest child and I liked to watch them all gather round and spin it and stop it with their pointing fingers and name the countries: the biggest they could find and the smallest. They would squint at the islands and atolls that spotted the oceans and read out their lovely names: Aitutaki, Manihiki, Raratonga, Bora-Bora, Rangiroa, Hiva Oa, Ua Huku. I made them learn the names of the winds: the Doldrums, the Horse Latitudes, the Roaring Forties. To some, of course, Mike's gift was nothing but a poisoned chalice to fill their hearts with wanderlust and discontent.

Sometimes I would read to the sheikh. Increasingly, he

would ask for the New Testament and I would pick up the battered French Bible he had bought with Ahmed. He would doze as I read to him and I would have to endure my reluctant voice, trawling over the stories that I'd heard over and over again on the hard benches of Santa Barbara's chapel.

When Rabia came I was happy to give up my place at the sheikh's bedside. I didn't care for his new reading habits and I wasn't a good nurse. When he and Rabia were together I pictured him as a young, doting father. Rachida said that he had spoiled his younger daughter. Now it was her turn to spoil him. She sat with him for hours and read to him, in her beautiful French or in Arabic, whatever he asked for: thirteenth-century mystical poetry, the Old and New Testaments, natural history books, encyclopaedias. The sheikh did not seem to miss me. I know he believed that I had found my cure in helping others. I didn't tell him, perhaps because I had not yet told myself, that I was beginning to feel restless.

In early December, when the snows had shut us in and I had stopped scanning the path into the village for his return, Christopher appeared. He stood at the door of the mosque, looking past the children's faces all turned to look at him, and grinned at me as if he had just given me a wonderful present.

'Do your sums quietly, children. I'll be back in a moment.'

Outside I looked at him: same face, same sadness, same bravado. He looked back at my face, scanning it for the slightest alteration.

Little Omar was standing in the doorway looking up at us both.

'Go inside, Omar. I'm coming.'

Omar turned and went back in.

This time we had no words. The chemicals were there again but with emotion now and I was afraid. We didn't touch. I backed away and his hand caught mine.

'When can I see you?'

'I finish at noon.'

He let go of my hand and I went inside.

The next two hours crawled by. I couldn't teach properly, so I got the children to sing to me. By noon, I had learnt two new Berber songs. They're songs that I now sing to my own children.

༒

'You should have come two months ago. We wouldn't have frozen out here. Why did you wait so long?'

'I was scared.'

'Of what?'

'Rejection.'

'What made you come?'

He shrugged.

'Nothing. My feet brought me. I just walked out of my hotel two mornings ago and kept walking until I got here.'

'Where did you sleep?'

'In the refuge at Idris.'

I smiled.

'I'd like to sleep there with you,' I said.

'Let's go,' he said. 'Now.'

We were hiding in a narrow cul-de-sac between two houses. I was shivering. He held me against him and breathed hot air onto my skull.

I stayed quiet, unwilling to say what I knew had to be said: that I wasn't leaving. I would not leave the children. He knew my thoughts and didn't want to hear them because he kept quiet and held me.

He spent one night in the village, sleeping at the new guest-house that Mike had built at the entrance to the village. It was run by a man called Abdul, who didn't have much time for me or indeed for anyone who didn't have dollars or euros in their pockets. Christopher said he would choose a room on the ground floor and leave his door open for me.

I waited in my little room, looking out of the casement window, until the house was quiet. Khaled and Hussein had stayed up late playing chess and I cursed every minute I was

264

not spending with Christopher. When the time came to stand up, I could not leave. I sat in the moonlight, too terrified to move. I wanted this person. I wanted him to stay with me and he was going away.

My heart was pounding as I crept down the stairs and out of the house, not from the fear of being caught but from the fear of my own desire. I was wrapped in a blanket and wore Rachida's sheepskin slippers on my feet.

When I crept into the little room, Christopher was fast asleep on the floor. I knelt beside him in my blanket and watched him. He had travelled from Agour in half the time it had taken me and he was exhausted. When I leant over him and touched his face, he took my hand and sat up and shook off the sleep and began to light candles. He lit all the candles he had in his rucksack.

'You should save some for your journey back,' I whispered.

He kept silent as he melted them, stuck them into the wax and lit them, one by one. I kept talking to hide my fear.

'It's no fun in that refuge with no light.'

He went on lighting the candles until the room was ablaze. Then he blew out the match and turned to me. We looked at each other in the flickering candlelight. Nothing in my life had prepared me for my feelings at that moment.

I opened my mouth to speak again, to dissimulate of course, and he came over to me on his knees and kissed me and then he took off the blanket and began to undress me, slowly, reverently. I felt his desire for me, not like something that had to be matched, but as something that was lifting me and carrying me, miraculously, like a ball on a fountain.

Abandonment is such a strange word. To desert and to yield. Why should the word for my worst fear also be the word for my most treasured experience?

That has been the gift that Christopher has taught me: to yield – to desire, to love, to life.

He left the next morning while I was up at the school. I had told him that I didn't want him to come and say goodbye.

Half-way through the second hour, I put down the book I was reading to the children and ran out of the mosque. I looked across the village to the path leading up to Idris. Nothing. No trace of him. I picked up a rock and threw it as far as I could. Then I went back inside.

❧

The sheikh died in his sleep on the last day of December. Rachida let me go off to school that morning without telling me. When I returned for lunch, the house was already in mourning and Rachida was marooned in her grief, beyond reach. I went to my room and sat beneath the casement window and cried.

After an hour or so I stopped crying, wiped my eyes and blew my nose. Half-way down the stairs I buried my face in my hands and cried again. I went back up to my room and stayed there all afternoon, letting the tears pour. As it turned out, I was not crying for the sheikh. I was not crying for my beloved twin or for Christopher. I was not crying for my mother's bitter, loveless life or for my poor father. I was crying for myself. I wiped my face with my skirt. Although I did not yet know it, I was crying because, like Cassilda weeping with her father's mule, I was awash with hormones.

When I emerged from my room, I went straight to Rachida and took her in my arms. Then I brushed her hair for a long time while she stared at the wall.

After the sun had set Rachida and Rabia washed the sheikh with scented water. I could not bring myself to stand over his naked body, so I sat just outside the room. Neither his wife nor his daughter cried. They moved around his body, performing this last gesture of love in silence. Then they wrapped him in a clean white cloth.

When I went to bed I listened to Rachida's low voice uttering the simple mantra of her faith. Over and over again came the gentle alliteration: *La ilaha illa llah* – 'There is no god but God.'

266

I lay awake until dawn when Ali came with the Arabic teacher, Hussein and two other men to collect the sheikh's body and take it to the ragged garden beside the mosque.

The whole village gathered outside in the cold for the funeral prayers, which tradition required to be thought, not said. Ali stood over the body, his back to us, speaking snatches of the prayers for guidance in his smoker's voice. There was no crying or wailing. We stood together, the whole village, as the winter sun rose over Idris, and looked down at the white bundle on the hard ground, knowing that the sheikh was gone and far beyond the reach of our regret.

When it was time for the men to take his body to the cemetery, I followed the women home.

That night Rachid, who had come for his father-in-law's burial, had tried to take Rabia back but she had refused. Losing her father had woken her from her princess's torpor and she had turned on her husband, her lovely eyes blazing.

'Just leave, Rachid. Can't you see my mother needs me? Can't you think about anyone but yourself?'

That was the last night Rabia ever spent with her husband. I'm sure that the whole village had inwardly cheered as they watched that rich, smug man trotting away the next morning on his hired mule.

For weeks after the sheikh's death, I gave no thought to my life or to my future. I got up early every morning to look after Rachida as she had looked after me. I felt slightly sick all the time and put it down to one of grief's strange manifestations. Winter moved in closer.

At my request, Rabia began to take more and more classes instead of me. I looked after the house and helped Khaled with his work when I could. By the beginning of February Rabia had, in practice, taken over the school. She was made for teaching. Although she was stricter than I was, the children loved her, except for Leila who clung to me every time she saw me, begging me to come back.

'I *hate* Rabia,' she said dramatically. 'I *hate* her!'

When I asked her to tell me why, she would sulk and say, 'I just do.' I think that Rabia saw herself in little Leila and was terrified of spoiling her.

In early March, as the snow was beginning to thaw, I missed my third period and went to Rachida to tell her that I was pregnant. She was sitting at her loom in the light from the kitchen window. She looked up and for the first time in months seemed to take me in. She held out her hand and I went over and knelt down beside her.

Clasping my hand she looked at me for a long time. Then she asked:

'Was there love in this?'

My eyes filled with tears.

'I think so.'

'Where is he?'

I shook my head.

'Did you chase him away?'

I looked down.

'You must go and find him.'

'I can't.'

She patted my hand and went back to her weaving.

'Yes, you can.'

The next day, Rachida had taken off her dull brown jellaba and was wearing her skirt with the roses on it. She had gold earrings on. I smiled and went over to kiss her.

'You look beautiful!'

'With the news of this new child comes the end of my *iddah*,' she said happily. The *iddah* was the time that wives were meant to mourn their husbands: four months and ten days. She opened her hands. 'You see how life is?'

The midwife came from Ouirgane and examined me while Rachida stood over and watched proprietarily, giving curt instructions in Berber.

'Everything is good in there,' she translated. 'The womb is closed like this,' she added, clenching her fist. 'You can make the journey but you must sleep often so that the baby can grow.'

I lay on a blanket on the kitchen floor and she reached down and squeezed my hand. I burst into tears. Since I had acknowledged my pregnancy the slightest thing made me cry.

When I left the village I was four and a half months pregnant and I could feel the child moving inside me.

Khaled was to take me as far as Agour, where I would pick up a taxi to Marrakech. This time I was well equipped. Rachida strapped a horsehair mattress to the mule and I sat high on its back just as my mother had done. Khaled and I spent the night in the refuge at Idris. We sat together in the little hut and stared into the flames of the fire.

'You'll never come back,' he said.

'Of course I will.'

'You'll go to America and you'll forget me.'

'I'm not going to America, Khaled. I don't even know if I'll find him.'

Khaled gave a long sigh.

'You'll find him.'

Poor Khaled. He was torn that night between the desire to punish me for leaving him and the fear of sabotaging my return.

'I'm going to fail my exams without you.'

'No, you are not, Khaled. I'll never forgive you if you do.'

'I can't do it without you.'

'Of course you can. You're better than me at maths and physics. I'm just a prop now. You do the work by yourself anyway.'

He dropped his head.

'I'll never be an engineer.'

'That's enough, Khaled. I'm tired. I'm going to sleep.'

Khaled stayed up and watched the fire. I woke a few hours later and got up and covered him with a blanket. Since he had come to Morocco he had lost his puppy fat and turned into a handsome boy. I looked at the long lashes, the shadow of down around the cherubic mouth. He had still been a child when I had met him. I rested my hand on his cheek. He stirred and rolled over.

In the morning he was in a better mood. We set out after breakfast and reached Agour without incident early that evening. In town I saw Salim, who pretended not to recognize me. His treatment of me on my first night in these mountains had not helped his reputation. I was too tired to go straight on to Marrakech, so Khaled and I spent the night at Mike's palace on the outskirts of town.

The palace was modelled on one of the country houses of the Pasha of Marrakech, but it had been built too quickly and was beginning to look shabby. The ornate stucco was chipped and crumbling in some places and the metalwork bled rust onto the walls. There were three internal gardens, each with mosaic fountains, and some of the tiles were missing. The ornamental pools were cracked and so were many of the pillars forming the cloisters. I began to wonder if Mike might be losing his money.

He was not. As he put it to me that evening, it was structurally impossible for him to lose money: he simply had too much of it.

'Why don't you give it away?' Khaled suggested.

Mike smiled at him.

'That might work.'

'Who would you give it to?' Khaled asked.

'The problem is that when you're rich you find out just how rotten people are. I've never come across a cause that wasn't a little corrupt.'

'What about the school?' Khaled said.

Mike smiled.

'That wouldn't even make a dent in my fortune.'

Khaled shrugged.

'If I had all that money I'd buy all the weapons. Guns, nuclear warheads, missiles. And then I'd destroy them.'

'Interesting idea,' Mike said.

Khaled was thriving on the attention. For the first time I could imagine him with a room full of friends.

'I would love to hear more but I can't stay awake,' I said, standing up and kissing them both goodnight.

Mike's butler Mohammed led me along various candle-lit corridors to my room. I climbed onto the huge, carved mahogany bed and lay down with all my clothes on and went to sleep.

The next morning I came down to find Mike and Khaled having breakfast. Mike was full of plans about setting up a boarding school at Ouirgane.

'A boarding school,' I said. 'How exciting.'

'It was Khaled's idea,' Mike said proudly. 'I'm thinking about taking him on as my financial adviser.'

Khaled blushed.

'Good idea,' I said.

Mike speared a piece of pineapple.

'Khaled can be one of the first pupils,' he said.

'A boy's boarding school? What about the girls?' I asked.

Khaled looked uneasily from me to Mike.

'First things first,' Mike said, ruffling Khaled's hair.

I ignored my misgivings as I left Khaled that morning. I kissed Mike goodbye, then Khaled, holding him for too long and leaving him a little embarrassed. I turned back to see them standing side by side before Mike's magnificent iron gates and for a moment the palace seemed to me like the ogre's lair. Khaled looked so vulnerable beside Mike, who raised his hand and called out his promise to have the boy back to his mother before nightfall.

❧

In Marrakech I booked into a cheap hotel off Jamaa al-Fna called Hôtel Ali. Every night, I lay in that too-soft bed with my hands laid like sensors on my belly, monitoring the gently shifting tide inside me. For the first time in my life, I found myself trusting what life would serve me. I would either find Christopher or I would not. If after a week in this hotel, we had not met, I would go back to Tamghurt.

Every morning, after a night of rich, unfathomable dreams, I got up and went to the Café de France. I sat all day on the terrace in the winter sun. I wore Rachida's thick brown woollen jellaba, only raising the hood when the wind blew. I drank endless cups of mint tea and read *Anna Karenina*. I thank God for that book, which kept me from the madness of waiting. There is no doubt that my predicament must have heightened my susceptibility to the story, but it is and always will be my favourite book. At first I read it piecemeal, looking up at the end of every paragraph to scan the crowds for the father of my child, but soon, as the story took hold, I sat hunched over, my hand on my belly, entirely absorbed. If Christopher had tapped me on the shoulder while Anna was making her last journey, I'm sure that I would have held up my hand and made him wait until I had finished the chapter.

As I read, Christopher went about his business, cutting back and forth across Jamaa al-Fna, unaware of his own child's life embedded in the human fabric of that square. He no longer stopped at the Café de France, because the place reminded him of me. Instead he went to a small café behind the public gardens where he could watch soccer on the screen behind the bar and practise his Arabic. Since he had left America he had discovered that football was the great leveller and the best, the only way to avoid discussing his own nationality. By the time that subject did come up, he had usually won his drinking buddy over. He found that most Moroccans were happy to believe in the idea of a gaping chasm between the American people and their leaders, an idea that was not far from their own experience.

I finished *Anna Karenina* on the fourth day at around five in the afternoon. The sun had burnt one side of my face and my hands were cold. I closed the book, put my hands in my pockets and looked at the passing crowds. At this time of year there were even fewer women on the streets. I leant back in my chair and savoured the memory of Levin's profession of faith in life. At that moment I decided to stay only one more day in Marrakech and return to the village. I had considered going to Paris to have the baby, but the idea of leaving Rachida for the birth seemed cruel. She already loved the child inside me. Why deprive her and deprive the child of the best of grandmothers? I would have the baby in Tamghurt.

He stood behind my chair and put his hands over my eyes.

I gripped his hands and held them.

'What was that sigh for?' he asked.

He came and knelt down at my feet and looked up at me.

For a long moment I was so overwhelmed by the sight of his face, I couldn't answer him.

'I just finished *Anna Karenina*.'

'Ah.'

'Have you read it?'

He shook his head.

'I'll lend it to you.'

'Was it a sigh of happiness or sadness?'

'Happiness.'

'How come?'

'I was about to see you.'

He grinned.

'Slut.'

He lifted my hands to his mouth and kissed them.

'I can't believe you're here. I hope you've come to elope?'

I held on to his hands then and laid them on my stomach and looked at him. There was no telling of it.

He pulled his hands away as if he had burnt them. Then he held them close to my belly again, as if to warm them.

'You're not?'

'I'm four and a half months pregnant.'

'Oh Aisha.'

Suddenly I was a precious object. He lifted his hands to my face and held it gently, then let go and laid them on my stomach.

I smiled at him.

'There. Feel that? It moved.'

He looked up at me and I saw his doubt.

'Were you looking for me?' he asked bravely.

'Of course.'

His eyes filled with tears.

'You want me.'

'I do.'

And in that busy square surrounded by crooks and thieves and snake charmers and child boxers and medicine men and soothsayers and cobblers and hairdressers, he clung to me and cried.

We spent our second night together in the Hôtel Ali because Christopher's landlord did not accept women visitors. The blankets had fleas and Christopher woke up badly bitten. I had become immune to fleas and parasites. I could drink the water straight from the tap while my delicate man still had to buy mineral water. I know how prosaic these details are. All I can say about that night, the first night of our life together as parents, is that my body had never felt beautiful until then.

❦

Christopher and I stayed for a week making love at the Hôtel Ali. We would only venture out to eat or walk in the Jardin Majorelle. It was here, by the lily pond, that I plucked up the courage to ask him if he would come back to Tamghurt with me.

'When?'

I hesitated and he said:

'Sure. We can go when you want. There's nothing keeping me here.'

'What about your Arabic?'

He smiled.

'I'm afraid I haven't made much progress with that. I've learned a fair bit about the breeding habits of the Atlas shore lark, though.'

On the journey back to the village, we slept in the refuge at Idris and it was my turn to cry. After we had made love we lay in the firelight and I sobbed into his chest: hot, indulgent, purifying tears, while he held me, knowing this was all that was required, and gazed into the flames.

Rachida put us into the new room on the roof and waited on us hand and foot. That spring we would wake every morning to the smell of jasmine in the bower outside our door and then shower together beneath the hose that Ibrahim had set up for us on the terrace. By the time we got up the sun had warmed the water in the pipe and we would stand there clinging to each other when it ran ice-cold. I'm sure that is where our daughter got her immunity to the temperatures of the North Pacific.

We lived every day in a haze of mutual awe, like two mystics cut off from the past and the future. Rachida was the high priestess of our love affair, protecting us from the scrutiny of the villagers and shielding us from daily concerns.

'This is your time and you must enjoy every minute of it,' she told us. 'There will be enough time for hard work and obligation when the child comes.'

Until the very last days of my pregnancy, Christopher would take my hand and lead me through those mountains in search of its precious bird life. We sat in a box tree and watched a Levaillant's woodpecker. We saw a pair of golden eagles floating above Adrar Afra. We saw Alpine accentors, rock sparrows and crimson-winged finches.

That time, waiting for the birth of our first child, was our idyll. It was the fountainhead of our relationship. Whenever we are estranged I try to go back to those memories and drink.

AMBER MENDEZ MOLLOY was born in Tamghurt on 15 June 2004. Rachida nudged the midwife out of the way at the point of expulsion. Like a good quarterback, Christopher said.

Amber has red hair. Rachida, whose own father had red hair, clapped her hands in delight when she saw her.

'She is like her great-grandfather!' she exclaimed, sweeping aside the details of kinship and feeding my nipple expertly into the baby's mouth.

Amber's red hair comes from Russ, Christopher's father, but Rachida tends to ignore this fact. Since Rabia has made it clear that she won't remarry and Fatima hasn't been able to conceive, Rachida thinks of Amber as her granddaughter. Although we never discuss Khaled's homosexuality, she knows that her son will never give her grandchildren.

I once told Christopher that I felt guilty about having thrown Khaled into Mike's arms.

'Don't kid yourself,' he said. 'When I met Khaled, he'd already decided who he was.'

I stared at him.

'Better close that mouth,' he said, picking up his coffee cup. 'The wind might change.'

I watched him walk out through the screen door onto the redwood deck. I still get a pang every time he leaves the room.

'What do you want for supper?' I called after him.

He stepped back inside. He had grown a beard since he had started working for the Audubon Society on the lagoon. He thought it made him look older, more respectable.

'Rat's ass with relish. Why do you always stop me on the way out like that?'

'I don't.'

He leant over and kissed me. Then he went out again.

◈

In September, when Amber was three months old, we left Tamghurt and came to America. During the flight Christopher held Amber while I talked to cover my fear. It was the first time that I had told him about my parents. Until that moment I had felt a superstitious reluctance to evoke our conception. I had talked about Jose many times: recounting only the good memories, the stories from our childhood that would only amplify my present happiness. I suppose that my terror on the flight to America was the first sign that our idyll was behind us. It was time to confront the past and the future.

As I told our parents' story, I tried at first to dissimulate all the darkness of it, but Christopher drew it out of me. When I had finished he whispered over our sleeping child:

'You think your mother fell in love with the man who raped her? You really believe that?'

'I can't be sure of anything she says. In the days when she still talked about him, she told us that it was love. It's what we always wanted to believe.'

He kissed the top of Amber's head.

'No rape and pillage in my background, I'm afraid. It's kind of boring.'

He must have accepted the romantic version of our parents' story, because it was his idea to give our daughter Fausto's surname as her middle name. I didn't like the name Molloy at first. It sounded ugly to me. It's supposed to mean bald, after the shaven heads of the first Irish monks. One day we will go to Ireland to visit Christopher's relatives.

The American language is still ugly to me. It always will be. That's one of the reasons why Christopher and I still speak French together. I miss the sound of perfect French. I even miss the sound of Portuguese. If I go to my mother's funeral, I'll hear Portuguese again.

When I arrived in America, I wrote to my mother, telling her about Jose's suicide and my journey to Morocco and my marriage to Christopher. It was, of course, Christopher's idea. The answer came, not from my mother, but from my sister Barbara, who has kept up a steady stream of letters ever since. In our bedroom, under the glass top of my dressing table, I have photographs of her boys Kevin and Elvis. In one of her recent letters, Barbara told me that our mother had refused, in the last months of her life, to acknowledge Jose's death. As far as she was concerned, he was still living in the hills. Apparently she made Katarina take food up to Santa Barbara's chapel for him.

Under the glass, there is also a photo of Rachida that Christopher took on our trip to Tamghurt when Amber was two. She is standing behind my daughter, looking down at her as she sifts her curls through her fingers.

Beside Rachida is a photograph of Christopher's dead father. The picture, taken by one of his colleagues up a tree in the Amazon, has him brandishing a twenty-second snake – so named because twenty seconds after you've been bitten by one, you're dead. Russ got to the snake before it got to him. He's holding the snake up and wearing a big grin like Christopher's. I miss him, even though we never met. He died a slow death from cancer when Christopher was thirteen.

Khaled sent me a photo of himself standing beside a red Ferrari. On the back he wrote: *Not mine!* He went to the University of Rabat and specialized in optometry and his mother's very proud of him. She doesn't ask him and he doesn't tell her that he lives with a kind, handsome forty-year-old man from Belgium. His name is Jan and he owns a *riad*, which he has turned into a luxury hotel. When we took Amber to Marrakech last year, we stayed at Khaled and Jan's.

There's also a photo of Rabia, standing stiff and unsmiling outside the new school building. In the end, the government came through for the boys' boarding school in Ouirgane, and the little school in Tamghurt became a school for girls from six to eighteen. Rabia still teaches the youngest ones and there are three new teachers for the older girls. Five years after Khaled first gave Mike the idea, funds have started coming in for a girls' annexe at Ouirgane.

❧

I look up from my sleeping baby to see Christopher standing in the screen door. He tells me that when Amber wakes up he's going to take her out on the boat. He asks if I need him to pick anything up in town and I ask for some fresh parsley and coriander from the co-op. He walks over to the edge of the deck and sits down on the step, at the foot of my chair.

'You OK?' he asks.

I reach out and stroke his hair.

'You know, you don't have to go to that funeral,' he says, looking out over the lagoon.

'I think I do.'

'You can forgive her without going back, Aisha. You don't have to punish yourself.'

The baby is searching for the breast again. I help him to latch on.

'I've realized it's not about forgiving her,' I tell him.

I focus on the baby's diligent mouth to control my tears. Then I look up at Christopher and try to explain.

'Rachilda once said that having a bad mother doesn't necessarily mean you'll be a bad mother yourself. She was right, but I think that one of my biggest fears was that I would be a bad mother. When Amber was born and I looked down at her in my arms and realized that I loved her, that I wasn't going to reject her, that's when I forgave my mother. I think it's *myself* I have to forgive . . .' I swallow, afraid to cry with the baby in my arms, '. . . for what I did to Jose.'

Christopher knows not to comfort me. He just looks at me, waiting for me to compose myself.

'I have to go back to Coelhoso. I have to forgive myself for what I did to him. For my part in what the village did to him. I drove him out as much as they did.'

Christopher smiles and shakes his head.

'No. You kept him for yourself, Aisha, because you had no one else. You did what was natural.'

I cover my face with my hands. His kindness is always my undoing. I break down. He comes and squats beside me, embracing me and the baby. My tears drip onto the baby's face, collecting in a pool beside his suckling mouth. Christopher wipes them away with his shirt.

'I abandoned him, Christopher. I set him apart from everyone else and then I abandoned him. I'm terrified to go back there,' I sob. 'But I have to.'

'You don't have to, Aisha. But you're right. You do have to forgive yourself.'

I look at him through my tears.

'Will you come with me?'

I watch his face as he makes an internal review of the constraints, the logistics, the practicalities.

'You want me to come back to your village with you?'

'Please.'

'Sure. If that's what you want.'

'I think I have to, Christopher. It's where we're from. It's part of me. I can't go on pretending it isn't.'

Christopher smiles again and smoothes my hair from my face.

'Amber will be delighted at the idea of meeting a real witch.'

I look at him and smile at the idea of showing him Jose's cave, Fausto's ruin, the tree where we learnt to read.

'I'll show you the rock where Jose used to dive from,' I tell him. 'I bet it'll be too high for you.'

'I bet it won't.'

Then he kisses me and stands up. I watch him leave, resisting the temptation to call him back.

It is late September and the turkey buzzards are floating

283

above the hills on the far side of the lagoon. On the sand bars, just out of view, seals will be lying like indolent eunuchs, catching the last warmth of the day and of the season. The sky and water are touched with gold and the dry grass on the hills is caramel, the colour of this baby's hair.

His father will take our fearless daughter out on the Boston whaler. They'll race through the channels towards the open sea, at full throttle, casting about for a gap in the breakers because Christopher likes to take them at speed. The first time we went out on that boat together I was terrified. We left Amber with Natasha and took the afternoon off. The hull is as flat as a tray and a wave taken at the wrong angle at such speed can flip her over in an instant. That time I clung to his back and buried my face in his neck and thought: *I've lost my nerve – I must be a real mother.*

It was Christopher who built this house on the lagoon. It was a tattered boathouse that had belonged to Russ, who had bought it in the 1970s from an oysterman called Donald the Oyster. Russ only had this sanctuary on the water for two years before his cancer was diagnosed. Christopher's most tender memories of his father are out here on the lagoon. Here, with his binoculars trained on the ibis and the egrets and the sandpipers and the cormorants, his brave father, tree surgeon and adventurer, would become an awestruck infant. That was when Christopher knew he wanted to work with birds.

I look down at our boy, fast sleep. He has Jose's forehead.

When I accepted Christopher's invitation to come and share this house on the lagoon, I didn't know that he had built most of it himself. Perhaps if I had, the parallels with my mother's unlucky life might have frightened me. I know that I was first drawn to Christopher, at that moment when he leapt out of the old cedar, because he reminded me of my brother. Sometimes I am even reminded of the crazed romantic who raped and fell in love with my mother. Indeed, often when he holds me, it feels like the fatherly embrace I never had.

I wonder what Sheikh Laraoui would have made of my husband. I think he would have liked him. Christopher doesn't talk unless he has something to say, and like the sheikh, he tends not to judge other people.

I think of what the sheikh said to me a few days before he died. At the time it had seemed like a non sequitur. Now I wonder if he had guessed that my heart was finally ready to let someone in.

'You thought that you and Jose were a couple but you were not. A couple is made by the will of both parties to share a life. A brother and sister cannot be a couple because life has thrown them together.'

A breeze rattles the reeds. I close my eyes to better savour the moment. When I open them again the sun has dropped behind the hills and the water has gone dark. I hear Christopher's pick-up clattering along the edge of the lagoon. I wrap my baby up in his shawl and breathe in the butter smell of his hair. Then I stand up and go inside.

Acknowledgements

I would like to thank my agent, Anthony Goff, my editor, Walter Donohue and Stephen Page for their unfailing support. My thanks also to Felix and Lily Lambert, Joe Holden, Jon Riley, Aurea Carpenter, Kerry Glencorse and Anna Vaux for their valuable advice. I'm also indebted to Cidalia Maltez for taking me to her village, to Percy Kemp for his careful corrections, to Kasper Winding for introducing me to Rumi and to my uncle, Charles Fox of Creeley, CA, for generally inspiring me.